A YOUNG WIFE'S TALE

It all began on the golden July day when the hair-dresser's blew up in Santa Vilga, a Tuscan port where Julia and Mark Forster were on holiday. It was then that Julia first saw the lean and elegant Contessa Renata, and the Contessa first laid eyes on Mark.

Mark is an advertising consultant with ambitions to be a composer of electronic music, an art in which the Contessa professes a keen interest. She could undoubtedly make him into a celebrity, for she owns newspapers, a film studio and a recording company, and is the power behind a number of other thrones. But the Contessa is a hard task-master, exacting a twenty-four hour devotion from her protégés, and so Julia must go home to London alone. What follows is a lively and sympathetic study of a lonely woman whose husband has been called abroad on business. However, this young wife's tale is by no means finished. There is more, much more, to come . . .

A
YOUNG WIFE'S
TALE

By

WILLIAM SANSOM

1974

THE HOGARTH PRESS

LONDON

Published by
The Hogarth Press Ltd
42 William IV Street
London WC2N 4DF

*

Clarke, Irwin & Co Ltd
Toronto

For Nick

ISBN 7012 0396 X

Printed in Great Britain by
Ebenezer Baylis & Son Limited
The Trinity Press, Worcester, and London

I

It all began the day the hairdresser's blew up.

One moment the sunny little Italian street, the small tallness, the balconies, the strollers of the late afternoon — and the next whooosh-boomp and pandemonium, screams, anguish, crowds from nowhere, Christmas trees.

I was in the middle of the street. A minute later and I would have been in it. I was on my way to have my own hair done. It was thick with salt and sand from bathing. Mark and I were on holiday, there was a lot of bathing at Porto Santa Vilga, the port of the bearded lady-saint, on the warm and soothing Tuscan littoral. We had a room in a little house for four weeks, two already gone. It was the first time I had had my hair done; it was matted and awful. I didn't care and I did.

The season was not, of course, Christmas. It was breathless golden July. The Christmas trees were all the hot steaming, black and blonde-haired mammas who now piled out of the hairdresser's with their hair spangled in coloured plastic curlers, red, yellow, blue, green, and their faces and dresses mottled with coloured dyes, blue, brown, orange, black.

A coloured confusion indeed; if anyone wore blood you could hardly have seen it. Now they stood in a little knot in the middle of the street, shouting, crying, gesticulating, a kind of parrots' cage gone mad without the cage. Or could you say the cage was the sun, its golden bars fretting the shadowed pavement, crowning the housetops above? There went my painter's eye again (or my childish eye still arrested in a love of colour or brilliance?) and I remember in that short moment of stasis, the stasis after an explosion, ears and

5

eyes stopped with violent sound, that I still had time to notice how strongly these sudden new colours stood out against what normally I thought to be a high-coloured street; with its pink façades, its green shutters, its stands of massed blue sea and sky postcards, its shops with yellow and red plastic buckets, its bright parked cars, its multi-coloured holiday clothes.

It was like a carnival eruption, a colloquy of clowns. But of course in the same instant one both hesitated and ran forward, frightened but impelled to help. Confused. Compassionate. Cold. Hot. Curious.

Their bosoms heaved, their hands twittered like birds, their cries rang high to the apricot roofs. *'Impossibile!'* *'Mamma mia!'* *'Una bomba!'* One of them still wore a torn-off domed drying helmet and swayed like a crashed motor-cyclist above the others. Most of them were streaked with dye, their mascara ran black down their cheeks.

No one was much hurt. Lotions and dyes had stung a few eyes. Hot but not scalding steam had made most of the panic. It seemed the explosion had popped in the house next door, a caffè whose espresso machine had blown, and blown through the very thinly-partitioned wall, without that much force, but enough to manage quite a mess. Now the caffè people were coming out, too, more slowly, to join the merry throng.

Then, after the first frightened moment, someone began to laugh. One of the coloured women pointed at the other's face and burst out laughing. It was infectious. One after the other they all began to scream with laughter. Nervous, of course, too: for there these warm-weather customers were without their blouses, in slips or bras, out in the street. Caught, as it were, with their trousers down. Not that they minded. Only one or two were appalled, but more by the laughter; it might have been so tragic, their downdrawn faces and tongues remonstrated, as with holy horror in a desecrated church.

Out came the assistant hairdresser. Voluble above the others, a Mr-Strike-up-the-Orchestra-Strike-down-the-Panic: would the ladies kindly join the *signore parruchiere* in a restorative glass across the street? A coffee at the Caffè Santa Vilga, an aperitivo? A cognac for the heart? The *signore parruchiere* presents his condolences and would be overjoyed? The *signore parruchiere*, the crestfallen Mister Wigmaster, was just then squatted head-in-hands in his broken shop, not at all overjoyed.

One could see him through the open door. Occasionally he straightened up and threw out a hopelessness of spread arms at the face of the espresso proprietor, wild with excuses, poking through the hole in the wall.

In a moment the ladies were crowded into the bar of the Caffè Santa Vilga. Not more than a couple of dozen, really, but it felt like a hundred in that cool grey-brown room with its polish and its silver espresso machines. I went in with them, plainly my appointment was to be postponed. This was the posh caffè—hell, let's write it 'café', we know we're in Italy by now. The café, then, that had exploded was a smaller joint with lesser drinks at smaller prices and a football calendar on the wall. But here all was shadowed southern grace, modern and polished, walls a giraffe pattern of brown and grey stone, a bar of marble, a mosaic floor. All the suave greys and browns the colourful Italians love.

'Mother mine, I thought it was the atom bomb!'

Half-red, half-black, more chessboard than woman . . .

'We could have all been killed!'

'By the grace of Our Lady.'

'Or the Bearded One.'

'We could have been *killed*.'

'Look at Maria, green as a gorgonzola!'

'La Bel Paese!'

And the scintillating spangled ladies in their carnival colours began to call each other by the names of all manner of cheeses. This gave rise to hunger, tit-bits were ordered, cups and glasses and spoons rattled higher, voices, like heavy rain after the thunder, settled in to a continual up-pour.

And that was the first time I saw her, the Nose which was to poke itself so forcibly into my life.

She was standing apart with two boatmen. Elegant and expensive, smart as tomorrow in a trouser contraption, she looked like a model photographed with peasants in a fashion magazine. A statue of snobbery. Slumming. Only she wasn't dumb, she wasn't slumming. She had an air of natural authority, she had one of the boatmen by the sleeve, laughing with him.

'Three more,' she called to the barman. 'And kindly keep an eye on that malignant obus,' pointing to the quietly gleaming espresso machine. 'An obus,' she repeated to the boatman in his blue cap, 'and a jagged hole in the wall—too like a cartoon from the 15–18 war.'

'You weren't born then, Contessa.'

'My fascist grand-father was, and hence these lovely baubles,' shaking an armful of gold bracelets at the man. She looked at him closely, olive dark snake's eyes eating him up, a slight smile like hunger on her lips. It was malicious, a kind of cruelty exonerated by a so-honest frankness. *She* hadn't made the money, poured the castor oil. It was grandad, distant gran. Dead old gran.

The boatman smiled nervously, shrugging it into a man-of-the-world laugh. Then Mark came in, saw me, came over and kissed.

At that moment her face turned to look at him, and for the first time I saw the nose. It was very long and very straight. It gave her a bit of the look of an ant-eater. Somehow it did nothing to spoil an otherwise very beautiful face. Very beautiful, I'll give her that. That nose just accentuated the beauty, perhaps called attention to it. A sign-post of a nose, which now paused sniffing at my husband, while the upper eye-lids lowered themselves very, very slightly.

All over in a fractional second. She turned back to her boatmen. Mark hadn't noticed her, he stood with his arm round my shoulder and just looked round at the vivacious Christmas trees packing the bar. 'Well,' he said, 'well.' Mark is six foot and about an inch, grizzled blondish hair, small eyes with a secret twinkle, heavenly long serious jowls. I love these jowls. Doggy, my man. A right tall hound of a husband. And full of beeps. A devout composer of electronic music, he must be full of secret beeps. That 'Well, well' was like a kind of beeping. He doesn't say much. How could he, with all that going on inside him?

I told him what had happened and he giggled and the Contessa had me by the sleeve – she was good at sleeves – and was saying:

'Hello! You're English.'

Palpably. But the obviousness was quite excused by her authority, her beauty. She had an address, that woman. And it was plain she wasn't one to let the grass grow beneath her feet. Of course, she wouldn't have spoken directly to Mark.

'Cornish,' I said, like a bucket of cold water.

She was waterproof.

'I love it,' she said. 'Magical place. You have the highest hedges in Europe, clever girl.'

You see? None of the rugged rocks, the Atlantic rollers, the Finisterra for her. No, the much-travelled Contessa had to trump my ace with her hedges.

'Pasties, piskies,' she went on in the spangled Italian gloom, and she must have noticed my face for she added with a quite unnervingly pleasant smile, 'Cotted cream. Cotted? Cottage?'

'Clotted,' I said delighted. Countess One-up had been upped, and I actively *liked* her at that moment. How human can you be?

9

She was soon asking Mark how he liked Italy and Santa Vilga, where she herself had a house — because, of course, the harbour was so convenient for her yacht.

I won't describe what she wore, for it was absolutely up to the minute, or even later, some minutes ahead, and its immediacy would be lost since by now these fashions have passed. All I'll say is it was all pale, pale of a lilac grey, against which her brown-olive skin glowed strong and her jewellery glinted. Because she was the only un-daubed woman in the place, she stood out clear and cool against those carnival masks of streaked dye, tearful mascara, rainbow curlers. Cool, with cool black hair lacquered into silk, and a restless body that snaked about inside her clothes. And a snake-face with an ant-eater's nose. Snake-face? The small face of a small head, with a neat curved mouth, a way of talking which flickered the tongue; and slanted eyes as old as Eden. Eyes like grey jade, a very beautiful snake: with a very, very long nose, a rigidly poised snake in itself.

My God, they had already discovered a mutual acquaintance! She said, Are you an artist like all the others? Mark nodded his beep. She said, What — our lovely little pink houses, our picturesque peasants, or abstractions of our lovely washing? He laughed her a no-beep and then actually spoke saying his art was music and the thing he liked best about Italy was a new Milanese pocket tape cassetteer and she said heigh-ho, me too, I own it.

Trust my beeper to get acquainted by tape.

The clever Contessa now swung round on me, the wife, as a kind of ante-room to her husband, a sort of secretary to be assuaged. She complimented me on my matted hair and on my lucky escape from the explosive wigmaster's establishment. And was *I* enjoying myself here, what did I like best about Santa Vilga? The Englisha tea made special without tea-bags, I told her. We all used tea-bags in England now.

This light bitchiness she reported with a light laugh to her boatmen friends. Their deep brown eyes, their liquid lips quavered at this incomprehensibility. Then they caught themselves and showered loving white teeth all over the so amusing signorina inglesa. I was the life and soul of the party. The Contessa had been charming, and I fell in hate at first sight.

Because she was so smart and rich? The beautiful rich, though reported to be racked with such inconsolable ennuis, have an infuriating ease about them. Kings of the castle indeed. Or was it because, rich or not, she seemed to be so much in charge of things, and of herself, without the hesitations, reticence, fears of most people, particularly of us from the north? Or was it because as a woman I sensed, from nothing spoken but more from attitudes behind the eye, emanations unknown, that this other woman was a danger? And particularly a danger, since he was to hand, to my man?

My man and I had been married for seven years. We all know the myth of the itch, and we joke about it, but now and again I had my misgivings that there is never smoke without fire. Was Mark quite so safe as a few years before? Did his eye, his mind if not his heart, from time to time wander? How in the hell did I know? Officially, we were in love. I loved him and he loved me, and told me so, though less frequently than earlier. But men never say it enough for women, women the talkers, men the pipe-smokers, that's an old one. However, did I feel so *sure* about him as before? No. Yes and no. Surer from habit, less sure because of the Way of the World.

And I suppose I related him to my own experience—that is, to my own wandering eye. This eye of mine sometimes wandered because of time going by, because there were only so and so many years left to live in some sort of prime state. But with me, of course, it was *different*. I knew my eye wandered innocently. I would never follow my eye. My wanderings were in a different department to his, if his existed. So it came about that through my own innocence I suspected him. Suspected? Too strong. Was on my guard a little.

Mark ordered another round of drinks for the Contessa and her boatfolk. Italianwise, the Contessa drank little, small fruit juices, *she* didn't need alcohol: this made our own brandies gross, boozy in a boorish British way. But now I caught at myself, mustn't let her think I was on the defensive, and so out came the charm back at her, and she was charming back, we were all so charming there in the bar among the painted women and the worthy mariners.

And why should the smart, svelte, suave Contessa have such time on her hands for us? This was answered by one of the boatmen, in his best American. It seemed she was a true Santa Vilgan, mixed with the *people*. Not like the others with their villas or yachts, or all those absentee rich who owned all the land but never appeared. No, the Contessa, the Renata who had billions of lire, a castle here, a villa there, a grand apartment in Milano, was a pal, no airs, only graces: of course, she was busy much of the time, she herself controlled many of her interests, her large business concerns, she personally, but nevertheless she had time to come down and mix with the ordinary folk. Perhaps, the mariner thought, this might be why her factories were so successful, she knew the workers? A profitable kind of slumming then? I thought. And: Oho, then were Mark and I 'the people'? No, I must control myself. Why shouldn't she be like a hundred others who liked the life in ports, and the spurious sea-life? Was he, I asked the man, one of her crew? He? If he was, he would have SPADA on his jersey, his chest. He was a fisherman. He had a crayfish tank. I must come and see. This was almost a prophecy: for very much later, under very changed circumstances, I indeed did.

The victims of the great explosion were dispersing. It was like the end of a party, when you do not notice people leaving but suddenly they have mostly left and the room feels empty.

Two or three remained, and looked the stranger for their isolation—one large and voluble woman, looking oddly undressed in her black silk shift (though a bikini in such bars would look dressed) had a bright blue rinse across the lower half of her face, green smears streaking her orange hair, and some sort of silver powder all over her dark-skinned shoulders: she gesticulated at her companion, a birdlike blonde crowned with a gemlike cornucopia of plastic curlers. How, as women, could they continue so unselfconsciously? But how, as vigorous Italians, could they not have continued with the all-consuming question of Vittorio's lost job and the soldi to pay for Bianca's new curtains? Isolated thus, surreal objects bright in the gloom, their real peculiarity was still their foreignness, just as the Contessa with all her viable sophistication and her Cornish hedges was above all foreign and thus unpredictable.

She was asking Mark what kind of music he composed and Mark told her, in the peculiar jargon of his field, the kind of electronic stuff he was after. Amazingly, she seemed to understand him, even answered in the same language. She seemed very interested. She would like to hear some of Mark's music, had he any with him? A few tapes. Good! And she had a few variables of the new mini-recorder up at the villa—would he like to see them? Favore, and she would value his opinion.

Mark would be delighted. Then he should come up to the villa whenever he wished: and of course, with a loving smile, his signora-wife as well, she would adore the view, you could even see the towers of Baldicelli across the hills!

The signora-wife, that appendage, returned an equally loving smile and even lent her a pencil to scribble down her telephone number. And there was then one of these long, long discussions on how to get there. One saw in one's mind the narrow road winding up through vine-terraces, the hut of the telegraph station where one turned right, the left turn

13

by the shrine of Our Blessed Lady, a way further on an un-
made road—altogether an expedition as impossible as the
Sahara, lost, lost on hot and dusty tracks, and nobody to ask
the way. Shuttered villas about. Animals unattended. Always
the same.

A swift glance at her tiny jewelled watch, the long nose
sniffing it, and: 'Heavens, I must fly! My paper's ringing me
at seven.'

Her paper? Was she then a journalist as well as an elegant
industrialist? Oh dear no, she owned the paper. It was, it
seemed, *one* of her papers.

And the bright square of sun at the door darkened as a
billion lire of trousered slimness passed through and away.

'Phew!' I said.

'*La povera Bianca*—the runners are up, even the hooks
bought!' came from the spangled ladies behind.

Mark looked down, smiled and gave a few consolatory
beeps. The quiet silver espresso machine behind hissed in
the new silence. He raised an ear—it was his kind of language,
and he smiled a remote satisfaction.

When I talk about Mark and his beeping, I do not of course
mean it literally. If you can say literally about a beep. I mean
instead the unheard beeps with which my love was filled. He
talked, in fact, like other men: and like other men contented
himself with taciturn monosyllables for much of his daily
breath; and these came out to me as ambassadors of the
beeps inside. Otherwise, he would speak in quite laudable
sentences. But I knew he was full of beeps—how otherwise,
when his inner art was so? How otherwise, when love too is
so—the loved one's face and personality a perpetual mystery
which one will never, never breach yet perpetually try to?
The beeps I knew to be professionally resident inside him
were therefore symbols of all the rest I could never know and
never understand.

I must be similarly a mystery to Mark. I would like to

make a clean breast of it, divulge to him all my mystery. But this I can't do, no one can. Whatever is said, more is always suspected. Gaze and gaze into a face and you are forever frustrated.

We went outside and sat at a pavement table for another drink. The street had quietened down, but also re-erupted in the busy but less explosive flow of people out to enjoy the evening cool. A mixed moment: beach-bagged bathers returning shook a sandy hand with the silk-dressed who had changed for the night: the sun had left for the sea, and played about with pinnacles and television aerials on the tops of roofs, a lovely gilding but always sad. Ended day.

Mark said what I least expected to hear:

'I expect that's the last we'll see of *her*.'

'Oh?'

'She gave us her number. Sure sign of farewell.'

'I thought you were getting on pretty nicely with her.'

'Ha.'

'But you have something in common? She seemed interested. Did she make sense?'

'As far as it went, yes.'

'If you took her some tapes, surely it might lead to something? Mark? Owning those papers and—'

'A film studio, a theatre agency, a tape factory, a recording factory, a—'

'A woman of substance. How do they do it?'

'Inherited money, I suppose, and well-farmed.'

'She hardly looked the fallow type. Attractive? I mean to men? You?'

'Mmm. You know my ball-and-chain's the only attractive thing around for me.'

'No—seriously?'

'Seriously I've got a gnawing at my vitals. I need now a lot of lasagne.'

'Poor Contessa.'

'Are we eating in or out?'

And that seemed to be that.

But then with my beeper you never knew. He had a habit of pretending he didn't want to do what he wanted to do. Not to appear avid, I supposed; not to let people know, so people wouldn't fuss him about it, devour it before he did it. It happened with small things, like going to a certain film, like visiting a certain shop: he'd express disinterest, be vague and offhand, then in a week he'd be there. On his own. I expect it was inherited from his boyhood, when grown-ups could actually stop him doing what he wanted.

How could I yearn with love for him, yearning that sometimes felt physical, as if I was swelling towards him, and at the same time slily distrust this object of sincere, very sincere adoration? Or possession, or enslavement, or whatever love is?

But distrust is possibly too strong a word: I had no reason at all to think him untrustworthy. He was just, I supposed, complicated, like everyone else: and since I was the one close to him I could see his little moods and turns in a bigger way, they were magnified by inspection. So let us say I did not distrust him, I inspected him.

I inspected the outside, and only deduced what went on within. I saw that six-foot-plus hunk of manly man, with his oblong kind of jowly face, his straight mud-blond hair curled at brow and neck, his small grey eyes puckered with laugh creases, his long teeth and lazy smile, his short upper lip and his predatory nose, a strong beak in its way: over which he seemed to peer, but at nothing. He had that distant look attributed to sailors, engrossed in their horizons. He was a bit bowed, too, by whatever these horizons were, for they involved much deskwork and bending over the little whirling tapes. Deskwork by day in an advertising company, tapework by night in his brown study—it really was brown, wallpaper and curtains.

Then, apart from the arms he used somehow to fling over the back of a chair, as if he were his own coathanger, and apart from those loose-crossed legs with their little socks showing white bits of calf like an abbreviated male can-can dancer, apart from so many other physical facets, like his irritating little sniff through one nostril to denote concentration and like the beautiful pock-marks of long-past boyhood boils on the back of his lovely neck, apart from all this I had a dossier: age, thirty-three, son of a middling prosperous chandler. Plymouth born and London raised. School for the Sons of Gentlemen and University for All, modern studies. After a year in France, entered British rat-race as advertising consultant. Now had to semi-maintain wife. No children. Which could of course run otherwise: age thirty-three, lonely childhood concerned with himself, aptitude for games, masturbation in speechless France, dreams of girls and poetry one day turning into beeps because of record heard on one-day trip to Holland. And so on, I don't nor never will know what.

What, for instance, are the very bright pictures in his memory, the ones we all carry? A memorable tree somewhere, the linseed smell of bat-oil, applause of spectators against a blue sky? The bidet where his first whore washed herself, and he not knowing where to put his rugger-scarf, not on the silk coverlet? Clatter of typewriters, the office clock, bus-drone from the freedom of the street below? A dance on a summer's night — its memories fused with descriptions of other summer nights in novels, too many white dresses in the twilit laurel garden, too many echoes of music through french windows . . . how can I tell what he thus can treasure, and would never recount, not because they are secrets, but because they do not make a recountable story, no point in speaking of them. I own him, but not his experience. His experience is not really his past, it lives on inside him. I haven't got it. How very much is never shared — and what is his exact impression of the

industrious Contessa's thin beige isosceles triangle of an in-
quisitive nose, what of the slender left buttock dimpled by the
impress of a tubular steel chair-back?

Well, these I can ask him. Now. But I do not. If I asked
him about her, I would do so in more general terms. In any
case, I do not want to bring her up again. But thinking thus,
and stopping myself asking, and refusing to think of something else to say as artificial and trustless between people who
should be trusting, I say nothing and poke my finger into a
drip of brandy on the so-elegant plastic table and make there,
in the pool, a round face with eyes and mouth. No nose of
course: my finger hovering and withdrawn.

Meanwhile the street had filled with evening pearl, the
lost light of the gone sun infinitely delicate and glowing with
white and hidden colours. This was the street that in all
small ports runs parallel to the sea, inland by a dozen houses,
shop-filled and busy with buying. Here waited the dark
tobacconist's, with its pale old woman in black fiercely
pleased to have no more stamps; there the hardware shop full
of soft plastic buckets and brooms, bright lemon yellow and
scarlet. The little old dress shop with the bridal figure in
white, dead wasps like confetti about her shoes; the big new
boutique with its bangles and belts, leather this and lizard-
skin that, and coloured fabrics old-fashioned as the hills
looking mountainously new (how many designers' permuta-
tions till the final trump?). And others, the empty stationer's,
with its cheap squared paper and its occasional child buying
a rubber, a ruler: and food shops bulging with cheeses, tins,
latte this and *latte* that, and only the piled vegetable shop
really speaking of the Italy of the tourist brochure.

The hairy legs of Vacational Man passed: spider-furred,
shamelessly bouncy in their coloured shorts—to think these
limbs had co-existed with us all the year round, darkly hidden
in their dark nests of trousers! And their women, freed from
the urban civilities, were now all navel and shank, bottom and

bosom, all revealed even more—somehow, but how?—than present-day urban civilities openly permitted. Fancy-dress, of course: either sex in astounding straw hats, altogether dressed in patterns and colours of outrageous vivacity—but what am I saying, this is now true of the whole year round, the holiday habit has entered our everyday lives in any case, it's all-the-year-round-wear. Except that no, here *everyone* is high-toned: in the city there is still a sober background of the now unconventionally conventional.

And everyone was armed with a straw bag and sunglasses: you wore the sunglasses on top of your head if you had no straw hat. In the end, it was all a kind of uniform. Instead of suits saying 'office', they declaimed 'I'm on holiday.' It was all the great wish to be accepted—and, of course, me too. I'm not going to fall into the trap of 'those tourists'.

Though Mark and I were no package tourists. Strictly independent, we poor fools. Enduring thus a decline of comfort and an increase of cost, in a weird attempt to avoid 'the other English', who were around us like flies in any case, and with whom in any case we finally fraternized with the good old compulsion of water finding its own level.

Meanwhile, romantic Italy proceeded on its plastic, automobilized way. For 'oily' wop read 'axle-greased' wop in this year of gracelessness. Yet gracious Italy persists, almost irritatingly the concrete gives way to a line of yucca-mad bougainvillaea-ed old villas; and above the café-line of little orange plastic chairs rises a façade of pink stucco, battered caryatids, balconies singing with geraniums and Santa Lucia. It is all there still, in gasps. Perhaps more of it than one thinks. Brittle newness attracts and paralyses the eye: the old falls soberly back. Though by now I would feel wrong without those little orange chairs, those coloured posters depicting like school nature-charts different kinds of ice-cream. It's all part of it.

'You're very quiet tonight,' Mark said.

After all that? Musing, one is as busy as talking. I'd forgotten him, though every inch of my nervous system must really have been lulled by his presence: that dear old being-there of cohabitants, unsung but about the best thing in life.

'I was thinking—how composite everyone looked when we got here first, how individual it has become.'

I hadn't been, of course. But automatically the little lie came, presumably to protect at all costs my essential me inside myself. It didn't matter *what* I had been thinking about, it only mattered that I was asked.

'Composite? Individual?'

'Long words? Too early? I mean, Mark, how everybody looked like a—a crowd, a just a lot of people on holiday lot. And now, even after only two weeks, we find that John is having an affair with Matthew's wife, that the Voigt girls are lesbians, that the sinister Raphael with his cadaverous jaws and lizard eyes lives only for the breeding of beagles—'

'Who's a homo, who's a hetero—we're like little doggies sniffing. Incidentally I'm a rather hungry little dog—isn't it time we ate?'

'But more than that—it's a lesson ever to think a crowd's a crowd, or even a man in a suit a man in a suit. Look what's inside Nicolo's suit, if he wore one—a broken marriage, a crippled sister, a disenchantment, a noble struggle to find the best—'

'And an unholy greed for mussels. How that man can eat!'

'Compensatory. Worry puts some people off their food, some on.'

'Wouldn't it be their glands? Mine are pretty bad at the moment—where do you want to go? Do we feast, or is this a night for spinning the money out?'

'Spinning out. The scooter place?'

'I suppose so.'

We went along to a small restaurant with a cool outside

patio behind. It was romantically roofed with grape-vine, studded all over with potted geraniums, and at the edge of a dozen or so white tables there always stood those two scooters, one dusty and travel-stained, one white and new. They belonged to the waiters, who were proud of them, and no doubt believed they added elegance to the view.

By now we knew the thumb-stained menu by heart. It was printed, with a few dishes always added in scrawled ink: these never failed to suggest some sudden loving inspiration in the chef's big warm heart, a devotion to his art and his customers, though there was never anything new about such dishes, nor apparently any connection with the market. Anyway, we always fell for it and chose them, if they were cheap enough.

So probably that night we ate spaghetti with a spattering of mussels and whelk-things, probably laced the carafe of white wine with ice, probably watched with appalled envy somebody else's giant langouste carried through red and rich and bristling with whiskers and succulence. Always on such a big festive plate, always so near and so far.

And in the warm night air full of fish-fry and dish-clatter, we would have talked about the day, or whatever in the satisfied evening holiday air husband and wife talk about. My curse, probably—I must have had it to have put off the beach for the hairdresser's. And I seem to remember talking about all the other things which could in daily life blow up, not only hairdressers: as one rambles on—old bathroom geysers, or those rogue compressed air cylinders which are said at times of midsummer heat to take to the air and play the torpedo along our safe streets: but what I do remember was a sudden remark of Mark's, somewhere at the fruit stage. A cut pear dripping all over his hands, he said out of nowhere: 'Those pocket cassette recorders—they're mighty useful. I could use one. I mean, they're nothing to carry—I could get down all kinds of odd stuff I have to memorize now. You know, the saw-mill, that dredger in the port, or—'

'A sneeze?' I said, thinking of her nose.

He looked at me curiously: 'Sneeze? Couldn't whip it out quick enough for that.'

'I suppose not.'

So my beeper had been thinking about her?

Two days later I was having a morning coffee at the big café in the square, Tonietta's. The sun was high and hot, I was sitting back under the blind, by a low wall of tubbed bushes. Behind the bushes two children played an endless game with pebbles. Their energy and absorbed effort gave an extra sense of peace to my little table, the opposite to what usually is thought the nuisance of children playing: more like the sound of a hammer on a summer's afternoon emphasizing the peace of the hammock.

It was a good time of day. The getting up and breakfasting long over, the shopping done, the long holiday day before me: my Italian newspaper, my little cup of black coffee, my blue and white handout for the illuminations on next Wednesday when Santa Vilga would be carried down to the sea — all lay restful in the shade, and opposite along the street the morning shoppers strolled about their rope-soled business. So much always to be done, even in these holiday places! But leisurely, at a quiet pace in the sun — except for the ceaseless crawling of cars, stinky and bloody as usual. And yet . . . I suppose they too provided something, a kind of shining excitement, a pother of important arrival and passing, a doing, for they did after all have people in them. There was a stopping and a starting, an opening of doors, cries of good morning and don't be late and 'Have you seen Luisa?' Out of one of these, brought to a halt near the café, came the blue linen figure of Geoffrey de.

Geoffrey de — the 'de' was a facetious handling of his French name, which nobody could either remember or bother to pronounce — Geoffrey de was in fact English and the Old Hand who is to be found in every resort throughout the Mediterranean. He is the one who has been there year after year, who knows all about how it was, how it's changed, who everybody is. He even knows the language.

His linen shirt and shorts were old and weathered, as if to proclaim his special capacity. Not for him the gay new wardrobe bought for this year: his speciality was other years. And now he did what the Old Hand always does: waves a hello (*ciao* to him), and hurries inside the café to see the management on some vital errand. There is always an errand: messages from all the people he knows, arrangements about mending an outboard engine, ordering a gallon of some special olive oil from some special farm. He wasn't even a resident. Just came every year for a month or two. That was a one-upper too, that casual 'month or two'. He wasn't rich. Just independent, and knew the ropes.

'And how are the ropes today?' I greet him.

'Ropes?'

'And all the strings you pull?'

He sat down and laughed knowingly. A gold tooth winked in the sun, he had nice dark eyes, greying hair. 'You mean, what's the dirt? Not much. The Bassinis left today for Rome, there's a Scots couple arrived at the Villa Vecchia, they were here two, what is it, three years ago? You'll meet them. And some trouble — I don't know what yet — in that new monstrosity along the coast.'

'You don't know?'

His fingers drummed the table. 'The papers haven't come yet, I see. No, I don't know. Except it's something violent — a fire perhaps, a suicide?'

The arrival of the English papers was a sacred moment of the day. A hard core of elderly residents, the retired military, the remittance beachcombers, was always about waiting for this frantic arrival of the latest homeland news two days late on a sort of three-wheeled semi-motor bicycle. Fat financial

23

bathers would pant up from the beach around the stroke of stock market twelve.

Then there would be a susurrus of reassuring British newsprint, a tinkling of gin glasses, and a kind of extra quiet for a bit. In fact, it was no quieter—the indigenous Italian day continued its bright mechanical brio. But it felt quiet, absorbed.

Suddenly I asked him: 'You've never told me about the great Contessa who lives in the heights above. Who is she, with her yachts and millions?'

'Contessa?'

'With the conk.'

He took out a pipe, a slender wood and steel thing like a little musical instrument. I had been enjoying a black pungency of French tobacco from a table to the left—so foreign! —and now this old Sussex briar-smell would intervene. So be it; his legs were lean and brown, he wore a gold chain round his neck, the atmosphere was not too much invaded.

'Our fair Cyrana? She's fabulous, the power behind many thrones. Owns the thrones too. Her old Dad was very, very rich in the way only an absentee-landlord non-tax-paying eyetie can be.'

'You know her, of course?'

'Not to speak to. To kiss the hand of once or twice. After all, she's hardly of our square little circle down here. Very much Up There, with her steel gates and chauffeurs in black glasses.'

'I thought she mixed with the people so much? When the hairdresser's blew up—'

'Only sorties to the people, perhaps. And why not, they're her bread and butter? But she never mixes with the middle lot like us. Anyway, it's like a lot of the rich, or people with so-called imagination who like the lowest bars, and sailors, fishermen. Romantic in a grisly kind of way. Or realism or something. Fall for it myself sometimes.'

24

Puff came the stench of briar, Italy dissolved in a blue cloud. He was a bit haughty, Geoffrey de. Friendly enough, but speaking always from some remote superior platform. And his eyes were everywhere—you felt you were not the one involved with him: it was like sitting with a head waiter.

'She's got a marvellous place up there,' he pointed vaguely to the hills behind, 'modern as a boot, an elegant white slab of a boot designed by a very expensive Finn. Her yacht in the harbour's like a little palace—why she wants a villa too's beyond me. But then, she *is* beyond me.'

He made an obeisant mew of a mouth; then began drawing at his pipe with fish lips. Old cod, I thought. 'Where's Mark?' he said.

'Down on the beach.'

'Recording the roar of the Mediterranean waves? The squelch of naked heels on ice-cream cartons?'

'Does she have any practical knowledge of those things she makes? I mean, like those tape machines?'

'Who? Oh—Renata? I should think so. She's supposed to be double clever. Brilliant, rather. But most of all brilliant at people, rather than things.

'People? How people?'

'She kind of makes them, too. With all those papers and other media in her control—she makes personalities. Creates people. Builds them into news. Svengalissima, you might say.'

'You might.'

'Anyhow—why so interested?'

'The other day, Mark—'

'Talk of the devil!'

And there she was, standing over us and smiling. I then heard, as one does, what had sounded just before—a mellifluous deep rich motor horn, a chorded thing suggesting some long low powerful car painted some chic colour of subtle mud. I glanced beyond the slim flesh at her waist, and there indeed was the car.

She gave Geoffrey de only the ghost of a royal handshake, shaking and pushing away at the same efficient moment. All her attention was on me. My own was on a ghastly great diamond her fluttering fingers poked at me, together with an envelope.

'Why did you never telephone me?' she effervesced—you couldn't write 'bubbled' of such elegance. 'Am I not persona grata? But you will have been so-o-o busy, the beaches and everything, being on holiday is the hardest work of all, I always think. But really—no, I won't sit down, I have the car there blocking everyone—really I was going to drop this in on your house, the chauffeur and everyone else seems either ill or otherwise indisposed, I don't know *what* they can find to be up to—no, I'm giving this little thing on Saturday night, just a *very* few people, and I would so much like it if you and your husband would come. *Please* do. And tell him to bring those tapes of his. Remember, he *promised*—'

'I'll . . . I'll . . .'

'You're surely not busy on Saturday night?'

Her eyes frowned down at me, the deep knowing olive lids lowering a little over those bluish whites, forcing me to agree. Bitch. She was going to get what she wanted.

And she had me stammering, uncertain: 'I'll—I'll have to ask Mark.'

Eyes opened wide, a sudden gasp: 'Why, that stone you're wearing—but it's *exactly* the colour of your eyes! How clever —and beautiful too. Très chic, chic as the sea, far out, where it's deep.'

A compliment! But she was smiling now as if she meant to eat the stone, her mouth curved like a cat's—by heavens, I checked, she meant it! . . . And they are dangerous things, compliments: the shallowest, the most easily repeated, can set you up. Even if you fight it, it has its effect.

A honking had begun behind. That long car of hers had attracted a tall blue truck with somebody's aperitif written on the side. Round-roofed little grey saloons gathered round them like sheep. Her smile momentarily sneered—that put the people, tourists, peasants in their place. And smiled again at me: 'So you'll come?' She put the envelope squarely on top of my paper. 'There!' she said.

More honking. She shrugged. 'Till Saturday, then. Ciao!'

She walked back to the car, her shoulders very square, her spine very erect, yet all with a slight Italian sway at the hips—though her family would hardly have carried the pannier baskets from which this movement is said to be come.

Naked brown flesh showed dark against the top of her white skirt. I looked for a bulge, alas there was none. Impossible to fault her. I remember vaguely worrying about her expensive white sandals on that rather coarse piece of ground with all its litter of paper, dust, ice-cream spoons, chewing-gum. A heel narrowly missed the end of a bunch of grapes. The truck-driver shouted at her from his cabin. She shot out an arm at him, shoulders flexed in an immense shrug; shrill staccato of undulating Italian echoed back as her shoulders rose and fell, and soon the truck-driver was laughing with her as eventually she got into the car, into the exquisite dirt-colour, while he blew her a wide and operatic kiss.

Outrageous woman, getting away with every damned little thing—appallingly I found I liked the bitch. Magnetism, made up somehow of an immaculate lack of fear, of success before she had succeeded, disarmed me. And that simple compliment, as if I had personally mined the aquamarine on my breast, or since it was artificial, kneaded and boiled it or whatever they do. What, anyway, is there in such a compliment? Why all this, 'What a pretty dress'? You didn't make the thing. Just because you went into a shop and oh so cleverly reached forward a finger and pointed at it. I suppose it's a congratulation on such very good brilliant taste, a mighty creative effort indeed.

27

And envy, loving envy, I was full of it. No good pretending to myself I wanted none of the idle rich, I wanted them with every twenty-nine-year-old muscle of my body. No good telling myself they lived in a big alabaster bubble of boredom: I could well do with a chunk of that myself. Tedium, tedium, lovely hour-long tedium — at home I made lampshades to help with the grotty little junk-shop I ran to help with Mark's royal copy-writing salary. Lampshades, there was a room full of them!

But then she was hardly idle, either. But rich, rich . . . with all the beautiful mobility and security of money.

A sudden puff of blue from Geoffrey de. Deferentially, that malevolent pipe had managed to go out in the Contessa's presence.

'Ho,' he said, 'you seem to be popular in high places.'

'Ho.'

He gave a wise little hiccup. 'Look out,' he said, 'that's all.'

2

ALL?

Was this a backfire from Geoffrey de's offended vanity? That he, the know-all of our little port, had been ignored by this gilded Nose who seemed now to be its crowning personage? And that I, an insignificant young wife-tourist, a newcomer, a here-for-the-month person in the usual holiday uniform of highly-coloured cottons — that I had received the accolade of smiles and more, an invitation to the palace?

But of course I was much less concerned with his reactions than the question of why I had been singled out for this honour. The lesbian thought did cross my mind, but flitted out quick when I remembered that single first glance of hers at Mark. A mere glimpse of a glance, but photographed on my mind most distinctly, and exaggerated on the screen of my protective senses to the size of a giant poster. 'A woman knows.' Good, I'm a woman and plumb full of intuition, tigerish instincts, premonition, deep dark knowledge. Although I should hardly have thought it would need any particular womanly perception to have noticed so definitively possessive a look: a wart-hog would have seen it. But I suppose it would need a female wart-hog to feel the dull fury I did.

But then, thinking is one thing, doing is another. What to *do* about it? Fight shy of the whole thing? Ignore her, don't go on Saturday? . . . Here again I was in trouble, because I wanted to go. I wanted to know how that upper crust lived — I wanted a peep at the palace, and I wouldn't say no to more earthy things, like whatever champagne and foie gras was offered on those silver trays up the hill. And much more than that I wanted that famous first glance to formulate, to explode even: no use having the mind's blown-up photograph with no sequel, nothing but a bad question mark. In fewer words, if she wanted to have a go at Mark it would be a pleasure to show her to whom he belonged.

However, there was some time before I could put to Mark the question of our new escalation to the aristocracy. And this introduces another question – the old one of free will. As far as I was concerned, my free will then told me to go and be damned to her. But time intervenes. Things happen, small things, and the will is not so free any more. Item: to help Geoffrey de carry a large sack of prepared manure to his little roof patio. I quite liked the old know-all, and the sack was not so much heavy as awkward: his car had petered out, I had the time and mercy. But after a cinzano among his potted plants and drying underwear and the walk back in the noonday glare, past cut-out chefs offering pizza and old women sewing and young women lolling and the smell of cooked tomatoes everywhere, I was late for Mark.

There followed the usual quest peculiar to little ports. You say earlier, 'See you about at one or so' as if the place were really little, and then of course there are four or five cafés you might be in, and how long does 'one or so' last for, and who's popped into a shop for a moment? There is a lot of waiting, a lot of peering, in the summer streets. It is then that the 'foreign-ness' of it all overwhelms again, all that had disappeared in the armour of companionship: you are lost, he is gone. And nobody will care, or even understand. Absurd panic, but it can hit you any five minutes of the day. Or not really panic – rather, extra caution.

So there was this, and the walk down a side-street to a small eating place on the quay, and since every side-street in Italy is full of sandals, the daily inspection of the sandals. It all takes time.

And then, when we were at last seated at our little blue-painted tin table by the oily water, half-shadowed not by yachts but by a silent muddy dredger, World Whore I and World Whore II came to join us. These were a painted mother and her painted daughter, called Green and often painted so, whom we knew a bit and who came now to sit at the next table, so that with an extra bright show of affability to cover our reluctance, the tables were edged together, a rickety grating business on the cobbles involving all of us and a waiter and a long wedging of empty cigarette cartons under the table legs.

We must have talked of local matters — which would largely have meant the delight of the slap-up new hotel inhabited by the two world whores at almost no cost, their package tour terms being so what is called advantageous. And advantageous they certainly were. Mark and I had strolled in there once, inspected the swimming pool with its concrete dolphin fountain, its lavatorially glistening mosaics in its lounge de luxe, the cracked new walls and the army of uniformed attendants — and we had laughed. But after two weeks on our own expensive terms, living in a 'charming' room with fin de siècle plumbing and up-to-the-minute creakings everywhere, and eating at inflated small scooter-filled restaurants, the laugh had become a little hollow. Yet — our experience was so very *real*, wasn't it?

The two whores were hardly professional, nor even amateur for all one could judge: they were simply appearances, coloured confections cut out of vibrant magazines and pasted on to human bodies. In fact, overdone. They had not understood the instructions. Where a dab of green eye shadow would have done, the whores applied a heaped teaspoonful; where long ear-rings were advised, they wore immense drooping clusters of metal which jingled like a feast of fairy cutlery; their hair dyes were fluorescent, their assemblages of varied paisley and japanoiserie tops and bottoms beyond description, something like a sales counter of oddments at close of day. Both had big black beauty spots painted on their cheeks. Within this weird array, as of an incensed black night-life dragged out to sun, lived an extraordinary genteelness; one doubted whether either had ever so much as spoken to a strange man. What did they do in life? Whatever it was must have been remarkably enclosed, like running some never-visited bric-à-brac shop: beads, fans, souvenir jugs.

So with these and the big black dredger we sat and must have talked, and the question of the Contessa's curious invitation was forgotten or postponed. Yet one thing I do recollect:

'Isn't it too grue about the Bella Vista?' said the mother through the plum in her mouth.

'Yeth ith-n't it?' daughter brightly agreed through the split plum in hers.

'What is?' beeped Mark.

'Geoffrey was saying,' I said, 'something about it this morning. And d'you know, he didn't know?'

'Oh, everyone knows now! Murder.'

'In our midtht,' echoed the daughter.

Then the mother: 'The manager, they say, the manager *himself* stabbed with a beach pole! To death!'

'A beach pole?' Mark was showing some interest.

'Yeth! A brolly pole! Through hith tummy!' the daughter gave.

'Good God!'

'But how,' I asked, 'was it done? Who did it? When? In broad daylight? Someone rushing at him?'

'Like St George and the dragon?' Mark muttered.

'Oh he wasn't a dragon, he was quite nice. At the Imperia we have chits for the Bella Vista. For our mangiare-s, our lunches at least. We *liked* him, he was most *attentive*. He personally showed Audrey the fish-tank they have there.'

'Yeth,' said Audrey, 'all along one wall!'

'The *most* remarkable fishes.'

'All colourth of the rainbow!'

'That's what some of them are called, dear, rainbow fishes.'

So I persisted: 'But when was he killed? And why?'

The pale blue eyes in their wads of green grew even paler, dimmer. 'Oh, I don't think we know, do we, dear? He was just found.'

'*Found?*'

'Tho they thay.' And with a new rebellious note, protecting Mummy against all comers: 'We don't really *know.*'

'Oh, quite,' Mark said smoothing her, 'no doubt we'll all hear more later. All the same, it shows how life isn't all beer and skittles at glamorous Santa Vilga. Never a dull moment, eh?'

'Who's for cheese?' I managed, blinding through the french windows, board in hand, to help him. Beer and skittles, indeed.

Just then, fortunately, the dredger began to work. Further conversation was impossible. As the buckets clattered and clonked and splathered, we all laughed and mouthed at each other. It was a great relief, no party should be without a good wop dredger.

Do I sound hard on the dear whores? Really, we liked them, as one likes most people in the free-er atmosphere of haunt or resort. Pleasant it is to dip into other lives, as it is pleasant to leave one's own and in turn be dipped into. Probably the two painted ladies found us just as odd as we found them. The ladies were neither pushing nor aggressive; they were content archly to bubble, and in fact it was rather clever of them to appear so gaudy against the wild-coloured background of others.

But their light news of a murdered manager left us with a sense of premonition. This place was not just a poor fishery painted up with new tourist lire, not just a daily pleasuredome. Things happened here, people were murdered here . . . dark cypresses in the sunlight. It seemed impossible, it chilled and exhilarated at the same time. Unseen, it sounded a warning.

We left the two ladies waving to us, chiffon in hand, as to a departing train-load, and slouched back through the streets, past each shop with its accusing sandals, up to our beautiful room and bed.

Pisolino is the liquidly-restful Italian word for siesta. It marks one of the best times of the day. Half the hard work of leisure done, we can thankfully relax. The bright sun has been locked away. Cool sheets, shuttered windows, greyly aqueous light patterns through the slats—there is the sense of a great boiling sun-action outside but inside here we are shaded, the doors are shut against the silent storm of fire, the floor is cool stone, the light is dusky sweet.

Perhaps a rogue sunbeam picks out a prismic corner of glass, a jewelled medal-ribbon in the dark: perhaps sounds echo in from outside, a motor-bike, an airplane's musical hum, but all less interruptive than pacifying.

We make love or we do not make love. It is as lazy as that. No effort either way, it is all languor.

'Asleep?'

'No.'

'We've been asked out.'

'What—*now*?'

'Of course not, on Saturday, to high circles up the hill, to that Contessa's.'

I was watching him. But not a flicker of an eyelid as he lay there on his back, eyes open watching a lonely fly circle a lustre fixture in the middle of the ceiling. Did it look like a musical note to him? 'What Contessa?' he muttered. 'Contessa?'

'The one with the nose.'

'Nose? Don't they all have noses?'

He must have known who I meant? He wasn't that sleepy. His mind was anyway a quick one.

'You know very well who I mean, the one when the hairdresser's blew up and you talked about your music to.'

Over-casually: 'Oh, her. What's she want?'

34

I told him what she wanted, but not whom.

He made a lazy sort of twist to his mouth: 'Um — do we have to bother?'

Still too casual? Or just possibly sleepy, pisolino-ing? Or doing that thing of his, that cautious sort of reluctance which veiled his real wish to act?

He reached over and stroked my arm: 'Aren't we all right as we are, without all that? Aren't we here to relax? Just together?'

Sweet, sweet, I thought. Then: Too sweet?

'You might be talking of some mad social whirl, this is only a little drink on a hill,' I said. 'Don't you want to see how the other half lives? Besides, Mark, she did seem interested in your work, it might lead to something. She has the means. I mean, I suppose she has?'

He seemed to think for a bit. Or at least he lay there silent with his fly.

'Never a circle,' he said. 'A series of ellipses. It would make a strange pattern.' Adding: 'The fly, I mean. The way the fly flies. Well, I suppose she might lend me one.'

'One what?'

'Pocket recorder.'

He was not aiming very high, my Mark. Or was this a double cleverdom? I left it at that. But I was all foreboding. I don't know why it was so strong: the infection of that sunny murder along the coast, perhaps? No. I had felt it before that. And now, perhaps because the feeling was so ridiculously strong, I determined to go up the hill on Saturday. Almost like an exorcism.

All these absurd wellings and subsidings in the tranquil afternoon grey, I must stop them. Why all the fuss? Both Mark and I like the occasional party, or more than the the occasional, we like parties. Social and young, that's us. Meanwhile, there's nothing to worry about in the pisolino room: the big bed, a strange old affair of mahogany and brass more to be looked at than slept in, cossets us. With its weathered wood, its greyish bloom, its extraordinary eagle at the head and the big brass knobs at the bottom, this bed's a room within a room: from it one can study the out-stations, the marble-topped washstand, the frowning wardrobe with its flecked mirror, the chairs, the window with its view, now darkly blinded, of a pleasantly vivacious, disorderly garden. All these are at rest in the quiet. Nothing wrong. Our few books and many clothes and towels and sandals lying about give it an us-ness, too close a feeling to be called 'personality'.

We are the people who live in this room, we go out through the door along the short passage to the lavatory, which has a splendid view into next-door's kitchen. We have the right to the curtained modern shower, erected in a corner of the lavatory, unexpected and impermanent as a mobile library. We are the ones to receive every morning the big cups of milky coffee and the bread, butter and marmalade breakfast brought up by the signora-landlady's twelve-year-old daughter, bright-eyed and exhausted: pale, bloodless, she seems to work a twelve-hour day, though I suppose there are plenty of unseen pauses, personal pisolini. We are the only ones to worry about her, shrug our shoulders at her, agree that she takes the shine out of the marmalade. We over-tip her, she receives the money without passion: plainly it will go to ma.

All this old weathered furniture, I love mahogany with the polish gone, it has a doubly strong sense of the past, like a sea-changed piano. How on earth, in all those summers of southern heat, has such a monster survived? Heavy furniture demands a northern atmosphere. Here, it should have burst its glue, expanded and exploded years ago.

And our young sunweathered selves, what about us traipsing up the hill to the nasal elegancies in store? Would we expand, explode? Pfui and perish the thought . . . quiet . . . sleep . . . love . . . sleep . . . .

36

3

AT THE appointed hour we started out for the Saturday
Countess. Other people would have taken a taxi, we had more
time than money and walked.

When one asks of the townspeople where such a well-
known place is, they point definitively up the hill, assure you
that you can't miss it, then bedevil their certitude by explaining where the road forks—you take the right fork (or is it
the left?, no, the right) at the telegraph station—and then you
turn *left*, oh certainly left, at the shrine, and there is the road
straight on and newly-made, it was for so long a mere track,
but the Contessa etcetera, etcetera.

It was a warm, close evening: no wind, and a vast clear
duck-egg sky, against which the swifts were going wild. Black
dots swooping against the filigree of television aerials—mere
musical notes for Mark, this time printed against the tele-
visual stave ruling?—their silent clamour designated ascent.
And we ascended.

A winding steep street, houses getting smaller at the top of
the town, larger as the town ended and vines began. Now we
could look back and down on apricot roofs unperceived
before. You could see the true lie of the land, which lied in
the other sense of the word when you were down there.
Down there it was close and confusing, streets and bays not
mapped clearly but measured by sunglare and hot sandals.
But now we could pause, Mark and I, and look back at the
'real' port with its dredger and oildrums and boat-yards, and
next door the neater little jetty enclosing the yachts, and
beyond that a rocky bathing place, and further the long
sanded beach just far enough away to make a nice or weary
walk, as you felt.

Motherly Santa Vilga's own blue-tiled dome, though quite

small, managed to brood over the whole place: to one side there rose a square white concrete apartment block to challenge her superiority, to the other a similar block, a factory making guess-what, yes, sandals. Neither of these succeeded, the motherly dome still gathered the apricot roofs round it like a big blue hen. I suppose it had something to do with the winding of the streets. Under one of the roofs lay the bed in which my personal henship received the attentions of the cockerel Mark, beep-a-beep-a-beeeeeep.

We stood hand in hand and looked down and loved it all. Hand-in-hand is nice, an affair of the spirit; it wells with innocence and trust, hand-in-hand. And then we turned and began walking up between the blue-splashed green vines, wondering what a telegraph station could look like.

As one had foreseen, with the end of the town human life had ended too. No lyrical spaghetti-filled peasants to ask the way, only mosquito-filled swifts. 'Why always spaghetti nowadays?' I asked Mark. 'What happened to macaroni? Does pasta have its period charms too?' Hardly the sort of proposition to put to a man looking for a telegraph station. We petered on, and I dumbly remembered the charms of my own period, and thanked heavens it was by now nearly over. Rebirth for another month of no birth. How, by the way, was the pill holding out? Enough?

There it was: a stout wooden shed with a pole and some sort of cross-tree and ropes. A big black ball lay on the ground. It must earlier have been some sort of land-telegraph post, and now acted as a storm signal. A wave or two on the mill-pond sea, and up the black ball would go. Or had that happened years ago? Was it in disuse? How little one knew about what they did, these people of such foreign habit.

Now for the shrine. It was a long way. It is always longer than one thinks. It is also uphill. Gone now is the well-washed, fresh sense of an evening beginning: we are hot, dusty, clammy, it's going to be an awful arrival.

And then, past the shrine, past a lonely black pig, and where the vines stop and a barrier area of scrub begins, we get lost. A human being does at long last emerge, a peasant girl with her black hair and dress white with dust: her eyelids are kohled white with dust. Christ, do I look like that too?

She cannot understand us. Our patois is worse than hers. I find myself saying Contessa-Contessa over and over again like some mad computer, and then less like a computer as finger and thumb elongate my own nose in the air. At this cabbalistic motion, at this aerial triangle, the girl screws up her face and takes fright. She scuttles away. And then stops dead in her tracks. A blessed vision has descended upon her. Thus must many a young saint have moved on the lonely hills. Transfigured, smiling, she turns and shouts back: '*Eh — la villa grande? La villa grande!!*'

It is a beautiful moment. She is so very pleased, a picture of grace. Will she dine out on this for weeks? will she, poor thing, dine at all? Of course she will, there'll be a pasta-packing mamma down the hill. Anyway, she points. And shouts happily. '*Diretto! Diretto!*'

So diretto we went, and at last found the Contessa's newly-tarred road, a black dream of urbanity in the green wasteland. It was, again, very long. But at last the villa came into view, a long low whitish thing alive with curious curves and planes, and we drew our breaths of relief, an hour late, hot, sweaty, dusty and thirsty. Just the thing for an evening of white-gloved elegance.

But then a further foreboding, or in this case, rear-boding overcame me. I had a strong attack of the 'I-have-been-here-before feeling'. Of course I had not. Of course it would have been impossible with a new Finnish building put up the year before. Of course it is never really the place itself but a reminiscent alignment of landscape and architecture and light which produces so treasured a sensation of regret: a landscape, a moment identical to what one once knew somewhere forever forgotten and sweetly lost. With this villa it must have been three pine trees planted just so to one side, and a golden blinding of evening sun on upper windows, and the curve of the road and the gate and a sudden green garden—all set exactly as once I had known somewhere, somewhere . . .

'Journey's end,' Mark said, as if to lyricise my feelings: but of course he meant it otherwise, adding, 'And an accommodating inn at that. Let's get in and beg a bath.'

'Yes' I could only say from the entranced, doomed feeling. He could not have felt the same, his experience was different: in a way, the villa separated us from that very first moment.

Grey French-looking gravel on the path by the front door, and in the flowered shade two large luxurious cars at quietly gleaming rest. (This inn would cost you a month's rent for a night.) A soundless bell, the soundless arrival of a cool-looking young man in white livery, gold epaulettes and all. Would we come this way? The Contessa was by the pool.

By her private sea. By her vast sheet of water shaped like a liver or pancreas or something. Agaves, yuccas, a palm, trumpet flowers of all colours in all the exactly right positions. A cool sight, and cool the Contessa too in her slip of a bathing suit as she rose from a bamboo chaise-longue and came to greet us.

'You've *walked*?' she pealed with sympathetic laughter at this unheard-of pursuit. 'But you must be *dying* of thirst. Come, come—what will you have? Whisky? The daiquiris are cooler . . .'

Bedraggled, we were introduced to several other guests. In that first flurry, it seemed quite a few: but was really only three, two men and a woman. All dressed in light cool clothes, all immensely fresh-looking: you felt that they had spent the previous half hour washing and scenting themselves, only to emerge at this ultimate eau-de-Cologne of a moment. I started bowing, I did not want to shake hands with my own wet hot palms. But of course the men swooped on them and

40

raised them to their lips. Fortunately, unlike the great smacking operation you see in films, they never kiss; it is a hovering gesture, and I don't blame them.

'Most of all, we'd like a wash,' I said outright to the Contessa. 'We got a bit lost.'

'Of course, of course,' and charmingly she took me by the hand, blast her, in fact took Mark too by the hand, and led us up the pink marble path to the house. Hand in hand, three jolly children who had known each other for years.

As we went, a laugh echoed from the pool. It might have followed any chance remark, but sweat and paranoia said otherwise.

Mark was put somewhere downstairs. I was led up to a guest bathroom. There, bottles and bottles of toilet water, scent and powder gleamed in green-shaded light; cool, cool tiles—you felt washed in that place before you had turned a tap. Fresh towels everywhere. Expensive soap intendedly fresh in its paper wrapping—surely she could have got one of her bloody servants to unwrap the *soap*? So, very much the injured poor cousin, I went to work with water and soap. It was infuriating to like it and resent it at the same time.

I came back through the house more slowly. It was of course luxurious and large, gleaming and soft and accented by fine pieces here and there: but no exact character, it could have been an elegant anywhere. Though there was one quality which always and quite stupidly astounds me in houses abroad—people actually *live* in them, there are bookcases with books in them, there is a writing table open to show an unfinished letter. Flowers and ashtrays. Magazines. A white coat draped over a chair. Altogether in some undefined way the opposite to a hotel lounge, which may contain some of the same things, but never in the same way. The visitor used to hotels and cafés and restaurants is astounded: here people *live*, on property private.

There is a feeling of nests about. Nests of cushions where

somebody sits, nests of coats in a passage, a nest of sporting equipage in another corner, the writing nest at the desk, a nest of magazines on a low coffee table peopled by a sofa and three inturned chairs—in this nest people come to confabulate.

Back to the pool, and through the frosted glass of a long daiquiri the other guests came into clearer perspective. It turned out they had really all washed and tidied themselves just before our arrival, they had been bathing and had just changed back: the Contessa apologized for her own bathing suit, made a typically southern business of it being so hot—as if she wasn't used to it—and with much flapping of hands predicted a true heat wave. The wind from the south, Africa. 'Everyone will be bad-tempered for days,' she smiled, 'headaches everywhere.'

And the conversation turned on bad winds. The Austrian *Föhn*, where you were exonerated from crimes of physical assault during the time of the wind; the *mistral* and some story of a man at Les Baux pushing his wife into a barrel and guiltlessly rolling her off the cliff. And so on. Everybody had an ill-wind story.

The one woman was a red-blonde from Venice, tanned and plump and vaguely vivacious. Vaguely, because her interest darted about, not bothering to finish what she was saying, starting on something else. Now she had piled up a very high tide all over the Piazza San Marco for my own uncanonized Mark, a peculiarly-erratic Adriatic wind had helped her in this, and Mark looked mightily pleased and astonished.

A *professore* from Florence leaned forward, and smilingly, with soft brown eyes, described for me the effects of his own chosen wind. He was dressed in a silken blue suit, he was immaculate and looked kind and was far too young to be a professor. Professors should still look old? Why is it so hard to grow out of one's old convictions? There are nimble, glossy, squash-playing professors everywhere.

Attentively he passed me another daiquiri, winked a

charming gold tooth at me, far back in his so agreeable mouth, and confidentially told me of yet another wind he knew. I countered with an October gale in the West Country. While he kept crossing and recrossing his silken legs to emphasize his own various winds.

Of course what we were all doing was a quiet social dance in the sitting position. Nobody gave a fig for winds. But everybody gave a fig for new faces, limbs, personalities, clothes—you could almost hear the quiet cicada burr of fleshy computers sizing each other up. But politely, oh politely in the warm, luxuriant southern evening air, the sky a distant blue and rose, the sea smoothing away somewhere nearer beneath.

From up there, the coastline looked again different. Our eminence enlarged it, you could now only see the edge of the town, with a wide seascape and sequences of bays and promontories stretched far off to a greying distance. The sea was like a vast bowl of greenish milk of almonds, outrageously calm and pure; this was the moment before sunset, when breezes dropped before beginning their nightly offshore stint. A moment of pause, of a beauty that successfully ached.

I told the professor it ached, and he, in the remote manner of an owner, agreed. The other man, a strong wolf-faced fellow with very long teeth, leaned across to tell me the milk of almonds was really full of crabshells and the bones of ships and men. And cans, he added: the new metal outer bones of food.

'Me,' I said, 'I'm already old enough to value illusions. It's still milk of almonds to me.'

The mention of age was a signal for great merriment. It was very funny, my age. Heads thrown back laughing, earnest protestations: 'The signora has no age at all', 'a lady shortly out of school' and so on. Until the big-toothed one nodded with big strong sadness: 'Only later does one truly find disillusionment. It is not something you turn off or on. There comes a time when the choice is no longer there.'

Mark and the Nose and the other woman were talking nineteen to the dozen about something quite else. I hardly listened. I wanted to get my two men straight—and then suddenly saw how they too resembled the deceptive almond-milk sea. All strangers got up for parties, particularly here at such an elegant remove, do just that. They are all surface and shine: how could I know anything about the professor's real life, his journey by bus to the university, the books he read, the students he hated or loved or envied; his wife, if he had one, his local tobacco shop? And my affable wolf-face, who had said he dealt in pictures, but was also nominally a professor (who wasn't in these parts?)—could I see his thumbed black notebook full of prices and dates, the streets and daily faces he knew, his lonely moments by a window? In a word, these two were appearances, not people: desires, regrets did not show.

Gradually we all eased together. It is remarkable how people's sense of alarm is quietened by a few words, a few minutes getting to know a face. Little reason for the defences to go down, but they often do.

Meanwhile it was growing shadowy, the sky showed a sultry-slate colour away from the sun, the sun itself had grown huge and red as in winter and was sinking into an ice-dark sea. Shadows lengthened, velvety purple patches began to play in corners, and then bonk! and it was all over. Night had fallen.

As with this subtropical efficiency, with none of your long sad northern twilights, night fell, so with well-mannered precision the lights round the pool, and in it, went on. Yes, there were lights in the pool, as if some recondite other life were contained there below. And the Nose rose up and announced she was taking my husband in to hear the tapes he had brought with him. (Actually, he had forgotten to bring them as we left the house: he had even said, 'Why bother, after all', the modest one, but I had insisted on going back myself to fetch these spools of personal plastic spaghetti.)

'But please don't disturb yourselves,' she said. 'There are drinks, and in a little while Giovanni will be bringing food. Out here I think—it is so warm, no?'

Yes it was warm, no. And it was nicely arranged, no, feeding me with nice new Italian friends while the real business went on elsewhere inside. 'Without', as the plays have it.

So I smiled very, very graciously.

And we all settled ourselves to the contemplation of light and shadow, night and sea, to our effervescent words and the long iced drinks.

Daiquiris came, daiquiris went, so we all went on forever. God knows what we prattled about—when you think of the thousands of words, the millions you have spoken to people, how many can you remember? How can you even imagine what could have been said, and why, and even how? The tongue and lips seem to be engaged in some sort of nervous tic, flabby muscle things scratching at the air, at the faces opposite, and more than often with no relationship to what goes on in the brain behind. The brain is otherwise concerned. Very much so. Try and remember a memorable young love affair you had—'memorable' means you have only a series of incomplete pictures, a blurred record of some place you were and one or two small episodes in the company of what seemed so vital a love. And the words you spoke? They must have been hundreds, thousands—but where are they now, what possibly could they have been? The mind indeed boggles, a distressing loss indeed.

So that evening with the silk suits and the darkening sea, I can remember few spoken words, but most certainly other words, a kind of silent shouting in the mind behind my liquidly-blabbing mouth. For one thing, of course I shouted to be inside with Mark and that woman. For another, I shouted that this would look shamefully suspicious, both knew I'd heard the tapes many times before, and anyway I was a guest, wasn't I, with a job to do, a sitting job with other poolside guests, a job of inventing the social hour. We were here to enjoy ourselves!

Did I suspect anything? Not really. Not beyond the expert strategy of this grouping, they together, we poolbound: but it was after all quite in the nature of things, quite in the nature too of this expertly-run, well-oiled establishment: after all, there was so much space, pools, rooms, nests; after all people could wander here and there at will, couldn't they? Just as in those old Russian novels when somebody asks somebody else to walk in the garden, and they do, and all is set for the scent of lilacs and love. After all, I thought, I was quite at liberty to go back to that bathroom again. I was not chained.

Only bound by pride. Nothing, really nothing, would have sent me nosing about that Nose. I'd rather my bladder burst.

But it never did. And it managed to accommodate far too many daiquiris. While the elegant eyeties almost disdainfully sipped their drinks, I gulped mine in a hardened British manner. Were they a race of camels, facing the breathless warm air with Arab fortitude? Moreover, they put their glasses down on the smooth polished stone tables about. I clutched mine, an elegant habit, I suppose, which must directly be derived from the so characterful olde Englishe pub. Once or twice, feeling boorish, I did put my glass down, very intentionally; a few minutes later, by magic, it was back in hand again.

Still, these my companions were most polite camels. For instance, they took care to speak English most of the time. This was a further light embarrassment, it was assumed that the visiting signora would not wish to speak Italian, and it was assumed rightly, for her Italian was mostly confined to a passable *prego*, a fluent *uscita*. Yet they, of course, spoke English perfectly.

As usual in Italy, I felt envy: envy of their apparent ease and their almost liquid movement of body, their energy and their smiles, and now of course envy of their depressing facility for a foreign and not too simple tongue. And then the graceful assumption that Mark was a 'great' composer, was it not indeed thrilling to be married to so great a composer? I have noticed it always in foreign countries—an English writer or painter becomes a great writer or painter, elevated far above his home attic and grubbing. Could it be some hangover from the milord days?

Yet sadly the envy was mutual. The wolf-faced picture-dealer was a convinced anglophile. Our island reputation for solidity and riches and justice was as strong as ever. 'Oh, I would love to live in London with its fine parks,' said the picture-dealer, as if nowhere else had a park. 'I was once in a hotel near Victoria station, very nice. And in Manchester, with my brolly. Your long wet northern summer evenings . . .' And suddenly his face broke into a big loving smile, his eyes danced, his arms opened to embrace the whole of life: 'I would love to own a scottie,' he joyfully said, 'yes a little black scottie. That would be so cute!'

In that wide warm southern evening, with the concealed floodlights making a coloured theatre of agaves and aloes and papery-bright bougainvillaea, I saw his sallow figure sniffing with delight the northern rain, striding the Manchester streets with black brolly above and grave-faced black Aberdeen at his heels. A pork pie and a pint of bitter under his belt. Happy as a drenched lark, he was the epitome of human content.

Then another epitome of human content returned to our little circle, Mark and the bellissima Renata. I must say my Mark looked the part, big and blond, a bit towering above our snaky dark elegant hostess who now had a long white skirt swathed over her lower half: she voluble and hands a-flutter, he bending casually attentive, the perfect escort. In the half-dark, I saw him suddenly as a figure removed from me, objectively, and noted with surprise that his pale trousers looked as impeccably southern and silken as everyone else's, though I knew very well where they were bought, on the bargain counter and dirt cheap.

There was an atmosphere, too, of collusion between them, really only the simple separateness of any two people with half an hour's experience of their own; nothing secret, only something not generally shared. And she looked so beautiful, the right duskiness of skin in the lamp light and against her white skirt, the right small flash of jewellery and gold here and there . . . and she was charming . . .

Delighted with Mark's brilliant beepage. 'But he is stupendous,' she flashed her little teeth at me, 'he is so original, exceptional—a real find.'

Find?

'Some of those passages—so, so viscous, do you say? Gummy. Not electronic, but like a living thing, only a *new* living thing . . . yes, I think he is wasted.'

'Wasted?'

'Yes, wasted in what is it—this advertising.'

'Bread and butter, you know.' Mark put in pleasantly.

'*Ché*! And you, you are all jam, marmalade . . .'

So my Mark was all marmalade, and now the white-coated troopers arrived with plates and little delights in aspic and a silver grill red with charcoal.

So with much quiet clatter we poised plates on ourselves and ate, as now champagne corks popped, to a new tune: 'Wasted in England.'

I strove a little: 'But why in England? I thought we were now a centre for most of the modern arts, the most various and youthfully energetic of all capitals?'

'Yes?' she smiled. 'No,' her head shook.

'No, you do not yet take it seriously enough. You have many young talents, much exuberance—strange indeed in the reserved English—but you are not serious, you do not elevate it above a kind of fair of fun. Fun-fair,' she corrected herself, blast her.

My wolf-faced anglophile rose in our defence. Luckily he never introduced the invincible scottie, but plunged headfirst into the Shakespeare lark, swinging young Shakespeare indeed. And—he was very much in the musical know—thumped a fulsome Elgar note.

Mark winced, then stuck out his jaw to hide it. A concealed light hit it, he seemed all beefy Englishness for a moment—but the Renata smiled charmingly at the Elgar, nodding at him as at a child, a long-nosed madonna lullabying him to a stop.

Then with a final, 'No, he's wasted in England,' she swirled round on a canapé of pâté and plunged it seemed all her teeth into it. She was one of those who do not eat but devour.

Mark leant over to me and produced a little grey box from his pocket. 'Look,' he said, 'Renata lent me this!'

Renata? Nothing much in a Christian name these days. Nevertheless there must have been that moment when she trilled to him, 'But you must call me Renata!'—nothing much, except for the look that went with it, the conspiracy of eyes—much can be made of little if you want to.

But he was excited by the little box, and I was pleased for him, it gave me the dear big baby feeling. Now he could go take his little box and go recording all sorts of little sounds, dripping taps, flapping papers, whistling grasses, plopping wavelets—a great big boy with a nice new toy.

Meanwhile we were served with mullets from the charcoal grill, and a huge yellow moon rose lonely against the vast velvet dark; while Renata chattered to Mark about oscillations and synthesizers, crescendos and modules, beneath which there played a melodic backing of soft Italian as the others relapsed into an undertone of their own language.

And I could relax with mullet and moon? Though it is in a way hard to relax with those vast southern skies and their multitude of clean bright stars. They invite, they draw one up into their velvet immensity and the eye roams and it is never-ending, it is altogether too big, it poses uneasy questions of eternity and infinity and how small we all are, and it's quite a relief to jump into the one solid fact up there, the moon.

Or leave it, and come down to earth and sea. On the sea, the moon had marked its exact golden track, a corridor for a night-swim to nowhere. But mysteries elsewhere came and went, the firefly lights of small fishing boats gathered at some fertile point, and once the passing quite close of what must have been a liner, a mass of light gliding across the dark without sound, so that, with neither smoke nor sound of engines, one could only imagine it was rowed, a ghostly giant trireme from a world as ancient as this present one looked.

On terra firma, blacker than the sea, there sailed to and fro the headlights of cars. These too were silenced by distance, their cone-shaped beams looked like the sails of phantom yachts: and so much coming and going—who, where, why? They also only pointed the immensity of the nothingness we are supposed to live in.

So I was doing nicely with the night, when suddenly I returned to our rich little lounging group and caught a strange look on the young professor's face. He had stopped talking and was quietly watching Mark and the Contessa. And, very quietly to himself, smiling. A wise and knowing smile. A smile which to me only said: 'There she goes again.' A smile which emphasized its personal and knowing nature of disappearing instantly as by chance his eye wandered and caught mine. A very found-out smile.

'Have you ever been there?' he said to cover himself, pointing out into the night. 'There to what we call the Belladonna? After the poison, of course.'

Behind a hill some kilometres off a luminous haze of light showed. It outlined the hill with a mysterious crock-of-gold presence. It was, of course, that big hotel, the Bella Vista, and the facetious misnomer was well-known down in the port.

'We call it the Inhabited Flyover,' I said, describing how its curved architecture-conscious roof-shape gave it the monstrous look of a raised road complex studded with the windows and balconies of troglodytes.

He laughed at this, he had to: but then added, 'And now the chieftain of the troglodytes has fallen to a spear.'

'Carlo! Carlo!' the Contessa called to him. She said nothing more, what it was she did not want was not stated, but it was nevertheless an implicit order. She was put out, and to emphasize some distaste she felt she raised her voice on what she was saying to Mark: 'The amplification of *silent* sounds,' she said, 'quiet sounds like the breeze in the stays of a yacht, with all the silence of the sea round . . .' and at the same time she tore off a big white trumpet flower hanging by her chair and threw it in the pool.

'You must come on my boat, my lovely *Spada*,' she said, 'and go to town.'

Curious phrase for a seabound yacht, I momentarily saw it ploughing up the Via Roma, the rigging catching in sun-blinds, people cheering, taxis cursing . . . but what of course really impressed me was the invitation itself, were we now to be boon companions of the beneficent countess, whatever 'boon' could mean?

And what had she against the spearing at the Bella Vista? I watched the trumpet flower, its delicate pallor enhanced by the lights underwater, float slowly across the pool. Why did it float, there was no wind? Draughts, little draughts every-where—little pulls of human intuition, little glances meaning so much. . . .

Of an evening out, a social evening somewhere in the past, what do you remember? Think. A few photographic glimpses, faces, an atmosphere, floral perhaps, or sordid with a res-taurant kitchen in view . . . but of it all, among remote ideas of what was talked about, and perhaps one solid remark or at most two, you will recall objects. Objects which could be anywhere, but which at the time irradiated for your discon-solate eye the tedium of that particular evening—thus no more than a certain vase, a gathering of grey bread-pills by your neighbour's plate, ashtrays.

For me, though I have talked of moon and night atmospheres, though I remember so well the warmth of the air, the molten heaviness of the southern night air not fanning but plastically breathing on the skin—for me two objects really stand out, violent as symbols: that white delicacy, a floral nautilus floating on the electric green water; and the Renata's jewelled sandal, one exquisite sandal, sparking against her white silk skirt. Her brown foot was beautifully arched, a high pony hoof of a foot. The jewelled look, spangles of cut coloured glass, shone with an Indian richness against the dark skin . . . they were otherwise so soft and delicate, they were six times more expensive than anything I could ever touch, and I envied, envied them . . .

What was this envy? I was well conditioned to overlook money, not exactly to despise it, but to relegate it to its proper low rung in the ladder of the good things of life. To say the Best things were Free, that lucre isn't everything, lucre's more trouble than it's worth—the usual defences of the relatively improvident. Actually, I love the stuff. To daydream about a legacy gives me the tingling feeling all over, quite sets me up.

So in a minor way the atmosphere of that sandal gleaming its red glass; so the waterborn trumpet flower, whitely belling its silent song across the pool . . . those, for what they are worth, which is nothing, are what seem to mark that evening in the memory. Not even symbols, simply exercises of the hungry eye. On defences set up by the nerves.

But I do also remember that a certain nerve impelled me at one moment to make up to the vulpine anglophile. I was annoyed by that knowing smile on the professor's lips—how dare he include Mark in his facile conclusions?—and at the same time I wanted to show Mark he was not the only one who could play the flirting game. So, absurdly for these two quite opposed reasons, I wandered off with the unknown, silk-suited, big-toothed Italian — only about five yards away, but to a compromising patch of shadow, and stood with him there looking seawards in some animated fashion. And my God, if he didn't bring up his Aberdeen again! . . . though in a sense the picture of that black-jowled, disapproving, indeed puritanically-faced short-arsed hound suited me well, I had no practical intention of flirting, only wanted the others to think I was.

Even so, speaking of Aberdeens against the Ligurian moonlight, I grew that much closer to the man. A light intimacy, a two-togetherness, arose: it is odd, this communication beyond words, this co-projection of glances and twitches of the face, and whatever extra-sensory waves are put out by people at other people. In that short time I grew to know his face quite well, only by virtue of our isolation together: it ceased to look wolfish — which was in any case a mere matter of sunken cheeks, a square nose, those big incisors — and took on qualities of kindness and consideration. Not that I liked him particularly. But I think I would know him anywhere again.

All this little episode gained me was a swift, sure, satisfied look from our Renata. Mark did not seem to notice. Or, innocent himself, saw no reason to suppose me to be otherwise.

Oh, and also a lift home.

But settled in my wolf-man's quite ample car, the thing would not start. Those breathless whirrings of the starter, the drowned silence after.

So the immaculate white skirt of the Countess strode towards her garage door, 'How tedious for you. We'll see to it in the morning. In the meantime, take one of mine.'

And hey presto she pressed a button and the garage door did its weird balancing act, a light went on automatically, cars were revealed. 'Take the Porsche.'

The rich, as they say, are different.

4

ONE has to employ the mind's eye. The mind's eye of the earliest morning bather going down to the Bella Vista's carefully raked beach.

It must have been quite early, seven or before, because otherwise the staff would already have been alerted to this strange situation. The July dawn is good and early, rosy-grey and purifying with its little breezes and wavelets busy with the beginning of another day.

But this must have occurred after dawn, not the doing of it, but the seeing.

What that early bather, descending from the hotel terrace, saw surprised him only mildly. For he liked the beach at this hour, it was deserted, it had the miraculous feeling, true of the most crowded places, that no man has ever stepped there before.

But in this case, this early morning, there were men. Not indeed stepping, but lying sprawled under umbrellas. Big yellow and blue beach umbrellas usually stacked away for the night, but today already desecrating the pristine view of sand and sea, soft yellow sand and soft turquoise sea, none of your brash beach-umbrella blues and yellows.

'Confound them,' the early bather must have thought, his morning peace spoiled. Then he looked closer, shading his eyes against a sun already risen strong, and saw with surprise that the two figures, each under its own umbrella, were clothed: informally, to be sure, white shirts and dark trousers, red cummerbunds, but unusual for the beach and the sun.

'Drunks,' the bather thought. 'Damn drunks left over from the night before.' Or possibly he thought: New guests arrived, and no beds for them, just like this outrageous hotel, so beautifully situated, so fiercely imbued with the will to suck in every living lira.

Then, as he went down the steps, still considering their black trousers, white shirts, he thought: 'Staff. Staff that have given up their beds to squeeze in more guests. What a lookout.'

But staff so very soundly asleep? As he got closer, he thought surely they should be up and doing by now, and why in the hell put up beach umbrellas in the night? Shelter from the dew? Was there dew in these parts? He had never really looked.

Shuffling in his rope-soles across the morning sand, he got now really close to the first man. And then saw, with ice down his spine, what really had happened. For the man was not lying beside the beach umbrella. The beach umbrella was in him. Lying on his back, the pole went right through his stomach and into the sand beneath. The red cummerbund was blood.

Impaled, pinned down like a big black and white moth, his face waxen with death, with other more lively winged creatures already blackening the blood . . . the bather took one quick glance away at the second man, saw his condition was the same, and ran shouting through the wide silence back to the hotel.

It was a curious kind of bathing on the beach that day. Long after the police had arrived, long after the notebooks and the photographers, long after the bodies had been carried in and the sand nicely raked over—that particular part of the sand was left bare of bathers. They all clustered towards the rocks on either side of the crescent beach centred by the hotel. Overcrowded, they still preferred this to that ominous bald patch. Also, there were few beach umbrellas erected.

The bodies, Geoffrey de said, were those of the manager and of a beach-boy who looked after those umbrellas and slept in a hut beside them. He, poor young chap, was simply embroiled—if that could be the word—because he happened to be there. It was the manager they were after. And this method of exposing the victims, a considerable effort, suggested a strange purpose—publicity. The killers wanted it to be known.

'And that,' Geoffrey de pontificated, pulling at his pipe, 'points to only one thing. This was the rough end of some sort of protection racket. The hotel either refused to pay, or was not paying enough, to whatever kind of cosa nostra "protected" this particular coast. And so it was decided to let the manager have it. And the hotel is equally wounded. Mud sticks, the Belladonna now smells. A number of guests have left already. Few jolly tourists want a beach umbrella rammed through their guts.'

Of course, he had made it his business to go along to the hotel and spend half a day speculating. The Old Hand must never be caught short of information. Mark gave me a huge private wink.

It was the time of the papers at Tonietta's, we were in that same café in the square, surrounded now by English headlines and a curious muffling of voices, as if in an open-air reading room. There were French and Dutch headlines too. A crowded café without voices is disturbing. Even Geoffrey de had lowered his voice when he was speaking, and I found myself doing so too:

'Gosh, a meaty tale indeed. No wonder our divine Contessa started tearing up the garden.'

'What?'

'She hardly thought the subject would make for suitably exquisite conversation. Panned it, in fact.'

Geoffrey half-closed his eyes as wisdom struck:

'I wonder why? They usually go for a good gossip. Perhaps you're right, it's a little squalid for the marble air up there. Or perhaps—the matter is a little too close to her?'

'Close? How?'

'Wheels within wheels. Behind every muscle man there's a master mind, *nicht*?'

His voice was down to a whisper, and I whispered back:

'Really, Geoff, that's going far too far.'

'Who knows?'

Papers rustled, a white cat blew past like a paper bag. £40,000 COSH RAID yelled at me from one headline, £30,000 WAGES RAID lowered the odds from another. *Le Monde* galvanized me with *L'interprétation des manoeuvres monégasques*.

'Tearing up the garden?' Mark said. 'You mean throwing that flower into the pool? But wasn't that more to do with you having a go at the prof?'

'What?'

'Wasn't it just then,' he said, 'that you rounded on him? You may not have thought it, but we heard quite clearly.'

And now I remembered what no doubt I had suppressed, being either ashamed of my behaviour or alarmed at the result. Memories of the moonlit sea, the Aberdeen fancier, the lighted pool had smoothed it over—yet now indeed the jewelled sandal and the floating flower showed their true connection.

It was after noticing that curiously contented smile on the professor's face as he watched Mark and the Contessa. It had naturally irritated me; it seemed too possessive of Mark, who was my possession. And stimulated in the hardy northern fashion by daiquiris and wine, I had leaned over to him, just as he caught my eye and politely removed the smile, and said what must have sounded a trifle too crazy even from a hardy Britisher:

'You seem to have swallowed the canary!'

He took a quick look at his plate, at the innocent mullet bones.

'No, what you were thinking—and looking so all-knowing about. But then omniscience is a professor's job.'

He smiled quite pleasantly: 'Job? I was indeed thinking of a job. I was thinking your husband has got himself a new job. I mean, if he wants it.'

And then he had pointed over to the lights of the Bella Vista to change the conversation.

I must have obliterated from my mind the whole little episode. How often — it's frightening — does one do this? How often do we just cancel the painful?

'Job,' Mark said, 'you suddenly raised your voice and said something about a job. And me, I remember. In fact Renata had just been describing a new film she had on the stocks, and the kind of music it needed, something like mine . . .'

Which was why I had blacked it all out. Or transformed it into sandals and flower. Job, music, Big Chance, working in Italy . . . an instant computation.

'Does she make films?' I now dumbly asked, as now around us the newspapers, digested, began to unrustle and the air was charged with English snorts of horror and disgust at the happenings back at happy home.

Mark went into a kind of dangerous reverie, talking as if to himself, and thus the more interested: 'She was talking about some immense SF project in mind, some phenomenon which turned machines into flesh, not as is usual the other way round, but about, say, animated typewriters full of their own blood, about the love affairs of hoovers, the giant copulations of power stations . . .'

Geoffrey bit clean in two a plastic straw he was sucking: 'God, and she was worried by a mere umbrella pole sticking through a manager?'

'You see,' Mark went on, 'there's this theory that future mankind becomes so involved with its machines that it turns into machines, a rationalization of effort — why have a pedal and a foot if the pedal can *be* a foot? — robots re-animating themselves, as it were. The future future, progress as retrogression.'

I stared at my man-hulk, my normal-looking holiday-clad café-sipping husband, with the usual wonder: what on earth went on in that bone helmet of his? How could he wear an ordinary shirt and think like that?

'You mean' I said, 'you two said all this by the pool? Under the southern stars?'

He looked at me glumly: 'Well, the sort of dramatic conception she has in mind needs special sounds. Doesn't it?'

'Squelch,' I said.

"Blooop,' interposed Geoffrey.

Twaaang, went our tin table as I kicked it by mistake on purpose.

'See?' said Mark. 'Table-talk.'

A young man on a cheap scooter roared by with rousing decibels.

'Work that in wool for your countess,' I shouted, 'and that reminds me, where shall we lunch? With the scooters, or with the dredger? Or are they both on the quiet side for you?'

Mark made his eyes even smaller, part of a placating grin, taking my hand even: 'For God's sake, can't we find a bit of Real Old Italy? Geoffrey—you should know?'

'Il Torre,' he said. 'It's not old, there's nothing old left. But at least there's no machinery about.'

'Would you come too?'

'It's not cheap.'

'Nor are we any more! Untold millions lie ahead. Hard film lire.'

So along we slouched to the other end of the port, the part away from the dredger where a lot of little yachts, and the Nose's big *Spada*, lay quietly tethered. These boats with their bright blue and orange awnings never bobbed as in a salty northern harbour; they just floated, gently oozing to and fro in the warm, polluted water. In them, their owners sat squatted eating in open steering wells, as in bearpits, with the quay-strollers standing and staring down at them. What luxury, one thought enviously; what acute discomfort, worse than *le camping*.

On the *Spada* a baby mewed in a plastic box. Something to do with the crew, the Nose being childless by two husbands.

Bambini everywhere, I thought—a sexy place, Italy, even shaped on the map like a woman's leg, toe and heel and all. Yet a hell of a lot of good a light, so felicitous thought like that was; who looked at maps? The sexed-up truth was down to earth in a few square metres of sun and plaster and dust, boredom, economy; and the more economy—that is the less electric light—the more bambini.

Which brilliant succession of thought—a think-walk close to cafard in a sun too blinding to look right and left—brought us to Il Torre, a terraced restaurant placed among fortifications surrounding the remains of a medieval tower.

'Pirates,' Geoffrey explained from his tilted neck. 'Built against pirates from the sea. And now it welcomes them in, the new kind from the autostrada inland.'

The pirates that day looked rather beautiful. This was an upgrade eating place, floral and freshly painted, with big printed menus in three languages. These were hell on windy days, but now in the continuing sullen heat came in handy as fans. All over the terrace the beautiful pirates were fanning themselves, the menus waving to and fro; a vista of white sails, it was all a bit like a regatta, dinghy class.

Buttocks bulged and breasts and chests heaved among the flapping of menus, faces and dark glasses came and went, the coarse canvas and flowered silks of these the wallet-rich gave a sense of occasion against tiered pots of plants and a stretch of sun-umbrellas on the beach beneath. Geoffrey chose for us in knowing Italian.

The waiter pointed, and Geoffrey gravely nodded his tilted head. The outcome was the usual endless hors d'oeuvres, a splodge of tomato-sodden pastas, a mixed fry-up of the easiest local fish swollen with brassy batter.

Yet the edge was taken off by the thoughtful habit of the Italians, reputedly a non-drinking nation, of plonking down a big bulbous carafe of wine immediately, almost of its own accord, and allowing us to get on with this and those paper-wrapped sticks of bread for the many, many minutes before the understaffed food arrived.

This suited the liquid-loving northern contingent, who demanded a further carafe all too soon. At some time during this, I asked Geoffrey more about the high Contessa. 'What makes her tick?' I asked. 'What is she really after?'

He mused a bit. 'Not quite power,' he said, 'but something like it. Making her mark on people, I would say. A pretty ordinary human desire, but blown up very big indeed with her.

'I expect you're wondering about her mark on Mark? Sex? No. Not sex. Though of course that could be some sort of short cut . . .'

'What on earth are you talking about?' Mark removed his attention from the light sounds of swishing menus. 'Sex? Me? Nonsense. Those soundtracks, that was all.'

Geoffrey shook his head, an oddly oblique action for so tilted an affair.

'Sex is only a by-product of what I mean. Sex, love, courting—at whatever level—can be used. But only to help a more general purpose. Nowadays we're used to hearing that people are mostly motivated, deep down, by two basic drives—sex or power. Right?'

Mark was looking impatient. I tried to help Geoffrey with a light: 'Right as a *fritto misto*. And as original.'

'The truth is not necessarily original. That's only for smarties, turning everything upside down to make an epigram. But there's a third drive in people, probably the most important of all, and which really includes the other two. And this is what I said—simply, making your mark on people. Usually, people do it simply for the moment, and having achieved it, let it go. Like any forceful conversation at a party—that face painstakingly trying to force its point home: the point itself is immaterial, it's the forcing of personality that counts, that works that face up. Same with business men together. Same even with a passing joke, say, from a bus conductor.'

'Aren't we a long way from our Contessa?'

The hors d'oeuvres came, wheeled up importantly on its own light machine. There was a lot of choosing, I noticed that a small yacht arrived, flapped down its sails, tied up and emptied itself before we all finally faced the personal little piles on our plates. Each of us watching the other's with suspicion—had we done well, had the others done better? More soused fungus? A little low on the anchovy? Those peas and rice must make a rare profit for the restaurant? It was like a card game where you dealt yourself your own cards and had nobody else to blame for this self-applied fate.

And Geoffrey, now between mouthfuls, went straight on: 'The Contessa has the make-a da mark complex very strongly. And, on a wider scale than most. She not only makes her mark on people but creates people and then makes a double mark on them.'

Mark munched: 'I wish you wouldn't use my name so. Isn't there another word?'

'Effect? But what I'm getting at is a quite technical matter. In a few words, she owns this newspaper, these illustrated magazines. Plus a film company and so on. These are all fed with news, with features: a large part of which is 'personalities'. Everybody knows the press goes for personalities, builds them up, runs them to death. Rests them, then in a few months revives them. Right? Well the Contessa goes one better, she doubles up on efficiency and creates a personality from nothing—or at least an unknown someone. Picks up a likely talent, grows it, trains it, feeds it, gets it in with the right people—who can't resist, since the talent is already being slowly made into news—and whoomp, you've got another perpetual headliner.'

I stabbed a group of faded french beans with my fork, Mrs Poseidon's trident spearing a batch of oily green eels: 'You mean—like Mark?'

He nodded. Mark threw back his head and laughed. A little too loudly for comfort or truth, I thought.

But then I was chilled, and with it judgement went: I really felt a cold kind of fright coming right up from somewhere inside me, a sudden overshadowing, or rather in-shadowing, the damned, condemned old dentist's waiting room feeling. 'How do you know all this?' I splurted through anchovies and egg.

'He doesn't,' Mark said. 'It's supposition, hearsay, nosegay. He doesn't even know the gay nose.'

Geoffrey quizzed his head with an extra tilt: 'One can put two and two together? After all, you were talking about that film already, those fleshy typewriters. Plus the fact of your, if I may be so bold, redoubtable good looks; plus even the fact that you work in advertising and therefore would be a jot or two less likely to foul the air with scruples against publicity. My boy, you're a cinch.'

Mark looked out at sea: 'Aren't you being a bit of a bitch, old man?'

'It's the modus vivendi of the Vilgense *dolce vita che far niente.*'

The only thing for me to do was to cackle with brittle laughter, to swallow fear with fun:

'We're rich!' I squealed to Mark. 'We'll buy a villa even longer than the Nose's! We'll dump this fearful *fritto misto* and have an immense whiskery *aragosta*, a crayfish fat and red as a cardinal. Mark, what will you do when you're rich? Geoffrey—what would *you* do?'

And as on holidays, hysterical with heat, cheaply hilarious with oh-so-local wine, we played a game.

One of us said: 'I'd take the slow one to China. And back.'

'A garden, a small one, and cultivate it.'

'Give it all away. It's too much like hard work.'

'Rape. I'd rape Miss Universe and pay her so much afterwards she'd keep her mouth shut forever, should such be possible.' Geoffrey, of course.

'And how,' I said sharply to Mark, 'does Mr World Tape feel about that?'

A helicopter came to our rescue. Like a giant hoverfly, intestinal as an insect, it roared over very low dropping what looked like silver tin-foil in the glare.

People on the beach below rose and ran for the droppings of this huge fly, which now swung round a slow tail and hovered off and away. Nobody, of course, on our élite terrace moved: except a couple of young waiters, who came back delighted with their find—in fact brochures again commending the celebrations for Santa Vilga the following week, together with a particular aperitif with which to drink the saint's bearded health.

(I have not yet of course recorded the nature of our curious lady-saint. She was in fact a Portuguese princess from the Dark Ages of such consuming beauty, and of such consummate purity too, that pursued on all sides by carnal suitors she prayed for a beard to deface her. The Blessed Virgin granted her wish. A fine beard afforested itself on her ivory cheeks, round her cherry lips, and this was well and good. However, one enamoured swain proved too capricious. This powerful fellow, a Sicilian prince, was so enraged at the hirsute dousing of his love, that he had her crucified. Some say he lopped her breasts off first. Her real name was Wilgefortis, not very Portuguese but possibly a Visigothic rendering? How she got to the Italian coast is unknown. But then, the ages were indeed dark, and saints seemed to travel everywhere in those little one-man open boats. Out of the horizon they floated, standing up in their coracles with long beards flowing, landed, and set up house. This would hardly have been possible with the crucified Wilgefortis: but bits and relics of saints came floating everywhere just the same, like the dead Levantine Torpetius to Saint Tropez. So, somehow, this pocket Italian fisherport received the remains of Wilgefortis, and naturally changed her name to suit their Latin tongues.)

So great was the noise of the now departed helicopter, so great the commotion on the beach, that our momentary contretemps over the rape of my St Mark was passed over; though deeply not forgotten.

Danger signals had been properly hoisted.

And there were more when, after a lunch too expensive in more ways than one, Mark and I returned to our rented love nest to find there an immense sheaf of scarlet lilies.

They were addressed to me. 'My gardener picked these for you. Kind regards and see you soon. R.'

5

By UNSPOKEN common consent, mention of the Contessa Renata between Mark and me was dropped.

The subject was plainly inflammable. Husbands and wives, convinced givers and takers by nature of their calling, must play a wary game. This is not dishonest. It is a tribute to the fine web spun between two people, a web too precious to risk tearing.

So mum was the word. Yet, of course, she was there. She was there palpably in the form of those ghastly great lilies. A natural regard for flowers prevented us from throwing them away. I even watered the things. On and on they lived, slap in the middle table of our room. And she was palpably there in the form of that borrowed miniature recording instrument, which Mark very naturally delighted in using at every opportunity, while he had it. Of the moment of its return we did not speak.

Meanwhile I had immediately sent her a note of thanks for the flowers, adding a final pay-off, a see-off, 'Will telephone you a little later on', which a rhino-skin would have recognized as goodbye-for-now.

And the long hot days sauntered on.

In the mornings Mark and I usually led a fairly independent life. We both agreed that too much pure lazing brought on a rich cafard, so that any individual pursuit should be encouraged. But we both liked different things. Thus, he was not much fond of walking with me round the churches, the local one and the little hermit chapel on high ground; and I was certainly not fond of holding a microphone to the glup-glup of those big-eyed fishing-boats as they nestled in port among orange-rinds, oil and other port filth.

For his part, he was not too keen on sitting staring at a pile of nylon fishing nets while I painted them. Sketching, painting is a small obsession with me; colour, as you may have noticed, part of my daily bread. That is what led me towards the junk-shop I run at home, an affinity with the arts if not much of a propensity for them — I'm not that good as a painter.

But I do love it, and if it was not say a postcard-writing day or a sandal-hunting day, that was the way it went, me sketching tattered palms or torn nets while Mark was away beeping and glupping. We met for lunch; and sometimes went down in the morning to bathe together. But the morning beaches proved too full for much pleasure. The late afternoon was best, when only a few ready-broiled bodies lay about, the devoted all-day broilers brown as old shoe-leather; and later there was the magically sad westering sun gradually weakening and saying, along with the tired beach-man collecting the day's deck-chairs, 'another day gone'. This was a moment tied to childhood, when the long sandy day was over and one was ordered home; a moment then of anguish, but now, since only the depth of the emotion is remembered, a time of stimulating sentiment.

Neither are our present days abroad, our holidays, truly remembered. They begin as falsely as they end. Before one arrives, the scene is anticipated far too brightly, the usual blue skies and sunny beaches, striped sunblinds and palms imagined altogether too clearly, as in an illustrated brochure — forgetting altogether the well-known body and personality we drag along all the way to our imagined paradise: and much later, when it is all over, one remembers at home usually the brightest moments, sequences and flashes which again quite as falsely resume that clean disembodied picture one had first anticipated — not the same detail, for one has now met with certain real shops, rooms, beaches, cafés, but all these are remembered in the same lightly-picturesque manner.

Nothing of this has to do with really being there at the time. The long-passing loaded minutes, hours are forever gone. The lungs, the stomach, the feet—flesh altogether evades the mind. I don't mean to labour asthmatically, but I am quite sure that for most of those clear golden days you never properly breathe, the hot air is solid as a shawl, it plainly goes in and out of you but never feels as if it does, never refreshes—witness the relief later of the first chill smell of autumn: but down there in the subtropical torpor you might as well sit with your tongue lolling out, everything is panting breathless, the mouth is dry and constantly calling for ices, fruit, drinks, which of course rinse the mouth but end in the stomach, not the lungs.

The same with clothing—an ounce too much, and a whole hour sweats; the same with eating, an avid pleasure because it is cooked by somebody else and, as in hospital, serves to demarcate the day—but it is usually overdone, and its heavy aftermath adds one further torpor to the other.

Feet—look under any cluster of café tables and see how many feet have slily disengaged themselves from even the slightest sandals. Those feet, swollen like everything else in the heat, have nevertheless walked further than they usually do, over rougher grounds, yelling with mouthless soles for fountains to rinse in.

Eyes? Goggles up, to be sure, against the worst of the sun. But the goggles are too often of a distorting colour, your sunny scene goes blue or green or fearful rose, and the good golden life takes on a quite absurd aquarium quality. And you sweat and cloud them, and sand and dust must be wiped away. They also break.

None of this is outwardly apparent. On the face of it, you look fine and well and cool, as do all those brown and light-clad others sitting or strolling about you. Nobody sees their insides, nor are those insides ever after properly remembered. Nor are packing and unpacking, the laundering, the hot sheets, nights that are sleepless, lavatories that are too suddenly needed, sand in books and blisters on newly-sandalled feet, that dreadful loading up of a day's necessities for the beach, sandwiches soaked in sun-oil . . .

Yet when you are there all these matters are there with you. Do I make it sound too grisly? That would be nonsense, one enjoys far more than such distractions imply — all I mean is that they are there with you, they represent the thereness which is seldom remembered, like the peeling stucco wall you face for an hour-long drink and know so well at the time, like balconies and washing and chimney-scapes, like the young man with an orange beard and matching orange shirt who once sat, so well observed and now so well forgotten, opposite.

Like the arrival at Santa Vilga of the Mafia. Even at this fairly close remove, I remember them only as a blur of three men in striped business suits, flash hats and shoes, who arrived suddenly at the World Whores' hotel and, since they were so often seen whispering with their dark heads together, were soon dubbed the Mafia, since the affair of the murdered manager was still much in the Vilgense mind. Always on holiday this parochial dubbing of people and things, these unrepeatable jovialities so easily acceptable at the time.

What the Mafia would be doing so far north, even of Rome, no one questioned. And doubtless they were no more than land-developers or propeller-suppliers from the big city — as Mark, more sanguine than most, proposed. However, there they were, glossy slickers in our undressed midst, and they conspired or sat glaring glum contempt at us the tourists, while we in our turn gave them some of our gabbling, giggling appraisal.

Since Renata's name, as I have said, was unmentionable between Mark and myself, it often cropped up. As usual with things unmentionable, brief and casual mention emphasizes them. Thus her nose and her name were the bone of

69

many a light flippancy. This or that small fish on a plate was smaller than a countess's nose; or when one evening a preying mantis alighted on a leaf in the little garden of our rooming-place, and began rigidly to pray, with a more soundless and motionless inactivity than could be conceived, I of course commanded Mark quickly to record the prayer, 'especially for the Renata, for her long winter evenings'. That sort of thing. But we never talked *about* her: and in the end, what with the jokes and the undying stare of those lilies, it became suspiciously uneasy.

Suspiciously uneasy? Uneasily suspicious, too. All my presentiments—which my God were later to prove real enough—compounded. I found myself on the look-out—though for what I had no idea. A sight of her in the street? A sudden coming upon her and Mark deep in conversation round some terracotta, sandal-hung corner? A telephone call—offering something irresistible, a voyage on the *Spada*?

Anyway, she never telephoned and I never saw her. Though one morning I did think I caught sight of Mark in one of the curious local taxis, three-wheelers with canopies like your own personal and private ice-cream wagon, busying along one of the half-seen roads winding up the fatal hill.

But it was only a head of hair which could have been his and since I was (am?) in love with him, any such even slightly similar head of hair made my throat gulp and stopped me in my bright-eyed tracks. An odd paradox about being in love is that you can picture the loved one's face less clearly than anyone else's; yet you recognize him wherever possible with the least provocation, I mean as a back view, as a figure at a distance. Or even a close face, whose similarities you instantly recognize, but could never have imagined for yourself. Why? Because his face is often too close for detailed recognition; or because your heart is so close it ceases to criticize? No wonder so many have a silver-framed photograph handy. That way you know whom you're married to.

However, Mark said he hadn't been up the hill. And then came the day of our splendid picnic.

We had heard of wonderful deserted little beaches along the coast. They were, for hilly reasons, inaccessible from the road, which was why they were deserted: but you could hire a boat, and row to them. This being too much of an effort for most people, they still remained largely 'deserted'.

So one evening we hired a boat for the next day: and I went shopping for salami and ham and cheese to take with us. I took special care with this, and, although the result was not so different from many another economic meal I arranged for our room, I felt especially 'wifely' while I did it. Perhaps this was due to the extra care needed for packing the stuff up, cutting it into sandwich form and so on; perhaps it was due to a daydream intention that the little beach should be a paradise, an Eden for two, with only Mark and me, and a long and leisurely love scene after lunch in the shade of conveniently-placed bushes and an umbrella pine. A pisolino with a difference.

To salt this daydream, there was a laughable little scene when we went to hire the boat. The owner had a very small shop, a kind of agency for local coach tours and steamer tickets from the larger port along the coast. It was little more than a hole in the wall, into which we went to talk to him. Though still young, he happened to have a stagey, old-fashioned Italian-type look—a long curly black moustache, side-whiskers, gold teeth in the right places, an operatic smile: altogether, the effect of some imagined Neapolitan impresario.

When it came to asking about the outboard motor, this impresario effect went into direct action. He drew himself up, and fixed me, particularly, with a mixture of leer and secret smile: then put his finger on his lips. A great secret? Something of redoubtable intimacy, yet also of impossible, sacred worth? It was a curiously tense, held moment.

Mark and I looked at each other nervously. Mark coughed, and began again to ask him: 'But where *is* the motor? Aboard the boat?'

Instantly the man's hand shot up, palm towards Mark, commanding silence. Mark stopped, astonished: and now the man, eyes blazing with excitement, rolling white eyeballs at us, twisting his moustache with one hand, and holding the other still to his lips, tip-toed with a dreadful archness the few feet to the back of the shop.

There he paused, turned to us with an immense gold smile, proud and confident and confiding, and very slowly pulled at what must have been a cord. The back of the shop moved. In the gloom, we had not seen it to be a dirty blue curtain.

At the same time, he snapped on an electric switch: and there, as the curtain drew back, a small alcove parlour was revealed, a secret living-room with chairs, a table, a clock, a pot of flowers—a little stage-set whose very curtained-offness suggested a privacy into which we should not have intruded.

It was suddenly, though his previous actions must have determined it, immoderately salacious. We seemed to be involved in some mixture of Eleusinian mystery and strip show. Now a blue film would suddenly be projected, now an erotically-clothed priestess would enter bearing an obscene priapus.

Nothing in fact moved.

But there, exactly in the centre of the table, exactly under the one shaded lamp hanging from the ceiling, in fact spot-lighted, lay the absolutely naked figure, isolated and explicitly exposed for show, of a marine outboard engine.

'*Ecco!*' breathed the impresario, with proud wonder. And one expected the pale grey metal to rise up and writhe its gleaming propeller into the measures of some appalling orgiastic dance.

Nobody spoke. The seconds panted. Nothing moved. It

really was the most highly theatrical, wildly improbable moment of shameless voyeurism—perversely the inhumanity and cold mineral qualities of that metal sculpture compelled a more obscene aura than if a real undressed body had been revealed to us.

It was then whispered that this holy Awfulness would be transported to the boat in the morning. And we paid and went. Once outside, of course, private laughter. We both giggled about the Dirtiest Show on Earth, or The Marine Venus, Good Clean Fun for Semen, and so unrecountably on.

A woman is hardly given to such private voyeurism: it's a man's world, poor unrestricted beast. Yet the little scene, since it was a kind of powerful pastiche of erotic display, stayed with me. And, as I have said, salted my disposition to regard our small seaward trip as a visit to Paradise, now with sex. Or in my case, less sex than love, that is to say, romantic intimacy.

So the next day we set out, loaded with food and wine, with the little outboard motor put-putting behind us. In the daywide sunlight, the motor resumed its ordinary proportions, a machine as innocent as a lawn-mower: yet, if from time to time I looked at it with concentration, it still carried an inner secrecy, something to do with its propeller active and hidden in the water, its vibration, and all those lightly associative memories of the little show of the night before.

So we curved round the coast, cutting the water, out at sea, at rest from land. Pleasantly independent, but still alert on this apparently benign watery element, as one would never be alert in a similarly comfortable deck-chair on trusted land. The sea was apparently flat calm, yet somewhere inside it a giant muscle moved, for the boat very slightly rolled. Our small speed produced a light draught, so that the sun's heat was cooled, we could breathe—yet another kind of breathlessness entered the eye from the heavy diamond glare of blue water all round.

73

The coastline passed coiling and uncoiling, showing differences within itself we had never seen before: it became alive. Mark steered, his arm lazy on the little outboard tiller, much the practised mariner. I was happy.

We passed several small beaches and a few sunning bodies. The first beach had a tattered thatched open hutment serving drinks—it must have been the last one connecting with the road. And now small cove after cove opened up, gentle places of a few yards of sand, edged with miniature red cliffs topped with scrub, and sometimes the steps to a villa above.

At last we came to ours—how we knew it I forget; by counting, or simply by elimination? Though I remember it was confirmed by the grey skeleton of an old wooden telegraph gibbet again, a sign Mark had been told about—so we curved round and into land with that odd sense of arrival very strong after even so short a journey as this: a feeling intensified by the sudden absolute silence as the engine stopped and we stepped into the shallows to beach the boat. At the same moment, since we had ceased moving, the sun also struck, hot and hard. It was about noon. We were quite alone in a silent place of tangible air.

Shade? The convenient umbrella pine? None. Just a semi-circle of ascending rocks and scrub, crescented below with fine whitish sand. On the sand were scattered tufts of what might have been scratchings of a wart-hog's hair, in fact clots of dried weed. A few bleached snakes of driftwood watched these like dinosaur creatures playing perpetual possum. Yet these were acceptably natural beach-litter: there was not a carton, not a can. It was in fact paradisial in a hot Saharan way. We settled the boat and the motor, chose a flat rock to eat off, stowed the food in the shade of a ledge, took the wine and laid it in the cool water's edge, and then, even such small actions increasing the heat, the sweat, the paradisial torpor, came the longed-for fresh moment of water and bathe.

Up the hill there was no villa; only hill and sky. I smiled at Mark: 'Naked? Why not?'

He laughed and looked down at his minuscule slip, at my two bands of near-nothing.

'Why bother?' he said, then pointed to the sea. 'Besides, telescopes.'

I remember him glancing quickly to the sea—now, it seems to me shiftily—a sea quite empty, and I insisted, 'It's that little much free-er that means so much, and what's a telescope anyway? Good luck to them—' when Mark laughed very loud, took my hand, and less dragged than bore me into the sea with the impetus of his weight, and we were splashing to our middles and flopping down delighted in the cool fresh water.

We swam a few yards into deep water. Trod it and floated, shouting, rather than talking to each other, as one unnecessarily does in the sea. And then for fun I took off the crutch-part of my two-piece, underwater, and waved it at him like a flag. Was there a shadow of a pretended frown on his face? At any rate, he instantly submerged himself in mock shame, and, his head gone I was suddenly alone. For a brief second, the solitude was complete; it's astonishing how one such second can embrace a world of time, even engrave itself on the memory—I can recall feeling delight in solitude, then a desperation of loneliness, then an animal alert to be isolated here in an unknown place apparently placid but charged with possible dangers, all these various emotions in the second before his face popped up again, blowing and gushing like some incontinent but handsomely wet grampus, and waving his arm high. Empty of a bathing slip. Not playing my game.

I love swimming. The freshness of water, the relief of buoyancy, the call for effort and stretching of an unusual kind, all this and the pleasure of motion through an indulgent, beneficial element makes for a sensuous small ecstasy—but for how long? Without an object, it soon becomes a bore.

75

Hence all those rafts to swim to, hence the pleasure of the sides of a pool: one would be better off with a floating tray and a book, as in certain spas. And holding a bathing slip in one hand hardly helps — I put the thing in my mouth like an old poodle and struck out for the shore.

As I went up the beach, top on, bottom still off, a motor boat chugged by, not too near in, but near enough for the faint echo of a wolf-whistle to come distantly across the gleaming eiderdown of noon air. 'Told you so!' came Mark's warning cry. But the boat was already gone — and what, in this lonely place which was ours, all ours, did it matter in any case?

So I stretched in the sun's heat, almost feeling it dry me second by second, and strolled thus still half-naked over to the food. 'Ready to eat?' I yelled to Mark. 'Bring the wine . . .'

And soon we had nasty little plastic cups of coolish good wine in hand, and I was opening the food on that flat slab. The rock cut a bit to sit on, Mark strolled round the beach like a surveyor, nosing it, and I felt thoroughly pleased with us, and our place, and myself particularly, since I had troubled to look for a particular old salami which Mark liked. Very housewifely and loving.

He came and stood over me as I laid the things out and I was just saying: 'Here, darling, here's your special bit of old sausage . . .' when he spoke sharply down at me:

'Put that slip on, quick!'

I looked up surprised. Normally he would have been saying to my pubic hairs, 'Quite a little orgy, eh?' or something silly — but now I saw that his head was turned away towards the sea. And then I saw what was hidden by his body, the varnished brown bows of a smart motor cruiser. Bent over the food, enclosed in my task, I hadn't even heard the sound of its motor.

Renata the Nose, of course.

There she stood behind the chromium rail, staring straight

76

at us, waving. The motor cut off, the cruiser glided nearer, the white-vested sailor with her threw down an anchor. I saw it all past Mark's hip, oscillating slightly as he too waved. Who had waved first? I had time to wonder, swearing and buttoning myself into that confounded slip.

She had jumped off into the water and was now wading ashore. Shouting back some instruction to the sailor, striding up to us quite unashamed of what was such an obvious intrusion. (Yet perhaps this was my British attitude? To her warmer senses, friendliness and casual propinquity were the most natural pleasures? Though against this, she was rich, and the rich value privacy above everything.)

'But I disturb you!' she carolled, disturbing us. And, by God, if that sailor was not already wading ashore with a huge basket raised with outstretched arms above his head, a slave bearing gifts or trophies.

She shook hands with me first, levelling in a smiling charm like a laser beam. The only defiance I could manage was to remain sitting: I had to smile back, I had to shake her glistening paw.

'What a coincidence!' And from Mark a brilliant, 'Two minds with but a single thought!'—as it transpired that she had chosen today to come here to picnic also. Her 'picnic' was already being laid out by the sailor on a carpet of towelling, a whole array of plates and cutlery and God knows what else in that vast hamper. The first infuriating detail I saw was ice, a whole bucket of it.

She was dressed in a bathing affair made up of what seemed to be super-elegant silver bicycle-clips circling her flesh like very loose chain-mail but carefully clustered closer together at the more provocative points. It gave her something of the appearance of a very large fish: mentally I fixed one of the bicycle-clips at the very end of her long piscine snout.

Pleasantries were exchanged. The weather, the presage of a heat-wave. Her motor-cruiser—a useful run-about. Then, believe it or not, from her own snakish lips, how *lovely* it was to be away from people, to be on one's *own*. Would we have a glass of *spumante*, it was at least beautifully chilled?

The sailor had spread out cold veal in a tunny-fish sauce, a large *loup*-looking fish sprinkled with dill, and other things . . . while I glanced back at our peasant sausage already melting in the sun, the bread toasting and so far untouched. All my loving care!

So we squatted in our treeless paradise for three and tucked into her grub. It was excellent, I hated every mouthful. At first I remember refusing and chewing on with a bit of our salami, but Mark seemed to find no such objection: a male attitude of simply eating what was put before him seemed perhaps a vague excuse, but I blamed him, and was soon blaming myself for guiltily following suit. Once I offered her a slice of dripping salami, which she graciously accepted. I did not do so again.

The boatman had gone back to the boat, where, enviably, he was probably enjoying a simple sandwich. The three of us lunched and talked in a supposedly relaxed manner. About the country behind, about the sea in front, about the absence of flies and about a film she was about to set up. The film lacked a musical score.

Once Mark got up and wandered a few yards off along the little beach. Despite the heat, and as people seem compelled to do, he began throwing stones into the water. I took the opportunity to put an oh-so-idle question to the lady bountiful.

'Do you often come here?'

She shrugged: 'From time to time, darling.'

'To this particular beach?'

'Oh, always. It is undoubtedly the best. And just too far for the other boats.'

'It's funny we picked on the same one.'

'But I told your Mark about it. Number seven along the

coast, lucky number seven. Anyway, it has that old semaphore
to point it out.'

A long pause to swallow this one, helped by a glass of her
iced wine.

Had he then secretly been counting coves as we sailed so
sweetly along? Uno, due, tre, quattro? . . .

I watched her profile as she lay watching Mark, her nose
trained on him like a guided missile. One could scarcely
blame her, there was nobody else to watch. But naturally now
I was fabricating hard, looking for little plots everywhere.

'And did you tell him — did he tell you we were coming
today?'

An infinitely light pause, but enough for her eye to glance
once, somehow slowly and unruffled, at the food I had brought,
before she said quietly: 'No. Why?' And adding: 'However
could I know? Why, we hardly ever see each other.'

Innocent enough? But I was now looking for trouble,
'hardly ever' suggested far more than 'never'. Though 'never'
would, of course, have sounded impolite.

Then Mark came back and I shut up. It was a matter to be
reserved for him alone later. And with emphasis.

'Hey, Marco!' she laughed. 'You haven't managed to throw
all our beach into the sea?'

Our beach! To my hot, sharp, dark mind that meant 'theirs',
I was excluded. It was, of course, quite ridiculous, but by
now I was ready to suspect anything. Mark was particularly
sweet to me that afternoon, attentive in all sorts of small
ways — and my reaction to this was equally negative, I saw in
it first a dark compensation for guilt, and then I even went so
far as to imagine he was flirting with me to make the Nose
jealous! With me, his wife!

So the afternoon wore on, the sweltering sandy beach
afternoon hot with longing for cool sheets and shade. I would
have thought our Latin companion had a parasol stacked
away in the launch, perhaps she had, but was at least polite

enough not to call for it. So she suffered the sun as much as we did. I lay there trying to fault her, the nose itself was a gift but the more I concentrated on it the more reasonable it became; I had to find a couple of reddish veins on one leg, a broken fingernail, a single unsightly mole—but these were trivialities compared with her general elegance and good looks, even beauty. The long dark tongues of hair in her armpits came in for the usual non-Italian criticism; and again the question rose up, do men like it? It seemed unashamedly pubic, a man of any finesse would be put off? But would he?

Nothing moved. The mid-day torpor had set in with no breath of wind. The greyish-green scrub-growth stared above its black underlying of shadow, heavy as a charcoal line, and the sky, if you stared hard, turned from blue to thunderous purple. The cicadas blared their electric song like one huge tautened nerve. We tried to sleep a bit. Then went in to bathe again.

The cool water put all those hot things at an immediate distance. It was enough just to lie in it without bothering to swim. But I saw Mark swimming out to where the launch was anchored—only a few dozen yards, no more—and then suddenly saw beyond his head a dark blue fin cutting the water.

It was horrific. One moment the diamond blue sea, wide and calmly innocent—and the next this shark-like intruder. Porpoise? Dog-fish? Did they have sharks?

'Mark!' I cried, 'Mark, come back!'

I was pointing in panic, I had screamed it high, the Contessa near to me in shallow water turned anxiously to look where I was pointing—I had enough breath to shout to her, 'Shark, shark!'—and then the fin rose further above the water and showed itself to be a long rubber flipper attached to a naked leg.

Her laughter seemed to echo and bounce about the cove, the calm sea, and then she was pointing and chanting: 'Shark!

Shark!' in imitation of me. Not unduly offensive, natural enough in the high-spirited moment — but to me in my mood sharply aggressive, so that, feeling a complete fool, I began wading back to the beach.

I turned back once to see the flipper change into the head and shoulders of a man; a hand clutching a harpoon-gun rose beside him, and he began to swim towards our beach.

While I went through the absolutely unnecessary motions of drying myself — the sun would have seen to it in a few minutes — the Nose came back to join me.

'I think your shark's coming to dry land,' she said. I looked back, and saw that now there were three heads making for the shore. 'But it's a shoal! Or is it a school of sharks?' I managed, trying to drown my fury and match her pleasant enough remark.

Soon three frog-footed men came high-stepping up the beach. Their flippers made them walk wide-legged, as if a most private accident had occurred; they raised their rubbery feet with difficulty, as if stuck to something on the ground, big blobs of chewing-gum perhaps.

They were big men, darkly sunburned and furry with hair, and they wore an armoury of knives and pouches over their near-nakedness. Rubber-strapped waterproof watches on their wrists; and one of them had an extra knife bound to his shin. They all carried harpoons, and on one of these a small octopus slewed its blind tentacles.

This meagre beast they threw on to the sand, where it lay bubbling and wetly writhing. The three men stood round it, like champions. It was a monstrous sight, they so big, the octopus so small, and all that paraphernalia of harpoons and knives to achieve this pathetic end of which they now actually boasted. The hair on their muscular chests rose and fell as efficient French poured out, they had even come from far abroad to effect so elaborate a victory.

Very very grave was their talk with each other, they struck

attitudes, hands to hips, feet splayed at an officer's parade ground right angle, brows furrowed with deep thought. I could not catch much of what they were saying; but the Nose did, and shouted to them to bite it between the eyes.

'*Vraiment?*' '*Vous vous amusez, madame.*' '*Un canard!*' Apparently they had been discussing how to kill it, and our Contessa had recommended a handy principle adopted by local fishermen.

'No *canard*,' she smiled at them. 'It's really the best way.'

The men laughed nervously. Now they looked down at the little animal with rather more respect.

'Shall I show you?' the Nose asked them, and rose, walked over to them and did so.

I remember so well that little walk of hers, the elegance of it, the short steps, her graceful carriage and animal poise—the metal bathing dress shining against her brown skin—and how negligently she picked up the octopus, whose tentacles instantly slid sucking round her arm, a sudden cluster of snake bracelets. The action was still so feminine, she might have been picking up a hand mirror. Then, very quickly, like a cobra striking, her face arched down as she bit into the rubbery head of this living fish-thing.

All three men had taken a step back. I saw one with his teeth bared, like a man flinching at a wound. The Renata now calmly began pulling the tentacles free from her arm, they still seemed to have some life in them. When at last she was free, and the tentacles all hung limp from the body, she offered it to one of the men. It now looked no more than a dark oily rag. None of the men liked to take it. Finally she reached forward and stuck it on one of the harpoons; with a slight deference of her head, a whisper of a bow.

My God, I thought, she's dangerous. It was not only the act itself, but the absolute lack of any hesitation, the sureness of it. Coupled with the thought—wherever had she learned to do such a thing? And the answer would have been simple

82

enough, it would go back to some childhood holiday among fishermen: but at the same time it was multiplied by the possibility of a hundred other expert capabilities, from stripping an engine to making sense of an Italian tax-form, from show-jumping on some fearsome foreign horse to managing one of her board-meetings, all the many accomplishments with which the idea 'native' bemuses the visitor on foreign soil, they know, you don't. And with her I had to add the fact that she was a woman.

Mark had now come up from the sea, blond and paler-skinned among the furry dark-haired Latins: he must have seen what happened for he was able to smile at the Nose and mutter of all things, and making it into a kind of understatement, 'Bravo'. I loved him for that. Reliable, unruffled Mark. Blond Mark who so easily salvaged my spirits, bolstered me.

The three French huntsmen squatted down in the centre of the beach, 'our' beach. Even when it was empty, Mark and I had placed ourselves a little to one side. Deference to reticence, I supposed; the reserved English. But there was not much reticence in my feelings as I watched those three take over so prominent a part of our paradise, lost though it was.

'So we have company,' Mark smiled.

I could only snort crossly: 'I wish to hell they'd go away. You'd think they'd think—'

'But it's a public beach,' Renata interrupted. 'And they must have swum quite a way. Though perhaps they've got a boat anchored just round that little *colline*? Still, they're not in the way . . .'

Which of course went further to deflate me, because people ought to like people, a theory I deeply subscribe to but never seem to practise.

Very shortly, however, the frog-footed frogs began looking at their waterproof watches, shooting these out self-consciously, as if their naked wrists were cuffed, and after a long and ferocious volley of discussion about the time, with upward glances at the position of the sun and horizonwards glances at presumably the weather, the light or the shipping situation — they rose to their frog feet and waddled down to the water. Without pausing, as if they were seals or sea-elephants, they wallowed into the water and swam off, their flippers forming a little white wake in the blue water.

It was not at all late, but the exodus was infectious. We, too, looked at our watches and discussed the time. By now I was over-eager to go. The day had been long and ruined. Writing of it now, in retrospect, it may seem eventful — but in substance thinking back, whatever happened was interspersed at tedious length by the hot blanket of a southern afternoon, an ever-drying mouth despite all the Nose's wine, a grilling on sand which became harder and harder, and for me a gritting of the nerves which drummed louder and louder, like a personal choir of cicadas, as I absorbed the horrible blue sea and sky, the dry vegetation, the Nose and my disarmingly deceptive husband, whom I was now intending to trick into a confession for which I thoroughly disliked myself.

But there was one more event in store for us on that long afternoon of paradise lost. We got up to go, and the Nose suggested we should all return in the launch, towing our dinghy affair behind. I was so relieved that the afternoon was not going to begin again — and it could easily have lasted another couple of hours — that I instantly agreed. And so the boatman arranged a towrope, and with a deep expensive gurgle from the heavy motor we set out.

We sat on soft blue cushions among polished mahogany and bright chromium fittings. Even the sun managed to add an extra sense of luxury; it had receded in its late afternoon way, the heat was mellowed and with the air of our passage all was cool and delicious, which of course I resented: to the absurd extent of sitting off the cushions on a hard bulwark to be, quite privately, less comfortable.

Renata pulled out a drawer-thing of drinks, served us, but took none herself, again marking us as guzzlers from the north while she dispassionately rose above such gross excesses. It was quite beyond me to refuse. Nor could I refuse the marvellous salty feeling after a whole day in the sun and sea, a sense that one's whole body is saturated with benevolent essences of salt and health, crusted with crystals which the cool air now gently fanned.

I must honestly add that neither then nor during the whole day did Mark and the Nose talk about his music, or refer to anything technical which I might not have understood. The talk, such as it was, was general. And consequently I was left looking for other things, glances, smiles between them: in fact, trying to make up what never happened; wanting what I did not want.

Now Santa Vilga came into view, at an angle never seen before, a mirage of façades disturbingly known and unknown: the church with its blue faience dome now rose far too much to one side, the large bastion restaurant where we had lunched looked negligibly small, houses painted pink and yellow and blue now exposed water-fronts we had never seen before, though we must have known each one intimately from the streets. The shadows of evening had not yet fallen, but a prescience of them seemed to engrave the whole place in a late afternoon hush, an essential heaving towards the end of day: particularly where the sea lapped against walls which would soon be in shadow. It all looked tired.

'Quiet,' Mark said, 'for a noisy little place.'

'Wait till tomorrow,' the Renata laughed. 'When the Bearded One puts to sea.'

'Why?'

'Every siren and hooter in the port is screaming, guns go off, bells ring . . . it's enough to sink the poor lady. For my part, I retire for the day. No doubt you will find it most picturesque.'

'Wouldn't you,' I said, 'if you were seeing it for the first time. Your Florentine friend found Manchester picturesque.'

And exactly then, before such a slight difference could be developed, even felt, the boatman was bringing us up against the harbour wall, and miscalculated, and crashed our dinghy hard against the stone taking the paint and one rowlock off. There was a certain amount of splintering too.

The good Contessa raved high with apologies. Mark stupidly said it was not much. I expressed hope that the outboard engine had not suffered. The Contessa joined me in my hopes. 'How desolating,' was her final pronouncement, but her boatman looked very glum, and I could see he was thinking what I was thinking—hours of explanation to the owner and the owner's voluble reply and who would pay what? Not, apparently, the Nose. I am sure it never entered her mind. Her life was so well organized and supplied that such matters were simply 'attended to' and that was that. She was certainly not trying to avoid payment; in fact, had she even thought of it, it would surely have been a useful card in the hand that seemed to be after my Mark.

Her chauffeured car was waiting to meet her. 'Probably see you tomorrow in the evening; there'll be dancing and so on. It's quite some fun if you can bear it.' And with a last light jangling on her bathing rings she was off.

Mark and I trudged off to the office of our boat supplier. Would he come down and see a little damage that so unfortunately had occurred? He certainly would, he had his office shut and locked in what must be record time for the entire peninsula, and down at the quay, when he saw what had happened, the explosion put that colourful blow-up at the hairdresser's nicely in the shade. I will not describe the opera that followed, it was long and tedious, and featured many a brave aria on no-claim insurance bonuses. *Pagare* was the profound thematic element. More than ballet was provided by the man's hands, which fluttered like a flock of birds

86

everywhere at once: while the whole production was enhanced by a Greek chorus of endless woeful nodding from Mark and me. The blessed Santa Vilga herself took part—it was Her Day tomorrow when she blessed the fruits of the sea, at the same time managing a more than usually fruitful day for boat-hirers. Finally we arranged a payment on account, with the promise of bills later. Luckily, the motor popped into instant and joyful action. My only hope was reserved for the launch's boatman, who would surely later have some say in the matter.

As it was, we were out of pocket to the extent of paying for a couple of the Contessa's picnics; the only profit of a horrible day, delightful food and drink, was dispelled. It was no joke to have an incursion like this on the holiday budget, necessarily limited by the amount of cheques carried, and quite beyond any further limits on the bank at home.

Altogether it did not break us, but we felt broke as we walked home. That well-known end-of-day walk home! Tired and usually satisfied, passing this and that landmark, this tree, this shop, that café, stopping to buy something, wedging yet another package in the carrier-basket, waving to someone, seeing people you've seen before, and always in some fantastic way noticing something or someone new—and the afternoon smell of cooking, far too early, from the pizza ovens, and the constant foof-foof-foof of your sandals on earth and cobbles and pavement, eyes so often down on the slap-happy rustic road.

The episode of the boat-owner had taken the edge off a so far silent quarrel with Mark. Perhaps I put it off in any case for more involved reasons, hating myself for suspecting him, hating my own deception more than his original deceiving. One always seems to hate oneself the most on such occasions, very unfair.

But it blew up later. Naturally enough we were talking about the day, what it was, what it might have been, and, 'Mark,' I said obliquely, my eye on a wash-basinful of shorts, and my other eye on him, 'Mark, who actually told you about that particular beach? Why did we choose it?'

'Oh, somebody somewhere.'

He was sewing a torn canvas shoe. There was no reason why he should not have gone on sewing. But he certainly did not look up at me. He went on sewing like a sailor or a cobbler, the way a man always looks with a needle in his hand.

'But Mark you were so definite about it! Where did you hear?'

'Really really really! Somebody must have told me. Geoffrey perhaps? I can't remember. Such a sea of faces in this salutary wop resort.'

'How about one with a nose?'

'Nose? They've all got—oh you mean Renata?'

'I certainly do.'

'Well—I suppose it might have been.'

Was he looking particularly vague? I watched his sewing hand. It continued absolutely evenly. Too evenly?

'If you want to know, she told me she told you.'

Now a most definite pause. Silence, and the sewing stopped. Then:

'I thought it was you who wanted to know? And if she told you she told me, why are you asking? Isn't it rather underhand?'

'So you did fix it with her?'

'I fixed nothing.'

'And let me go out buying all that bloody sausage and planning a day alone together . . .'

'Oh for God's sake.'

'You must say, to an outsider it does look a trifle connived.'

'You're not an outsider. It was not connived. Come to think of it, she *did* tell me, it was her.'

'When?'

'Happened to bump into her down at the port. Or was it that thing they call a marina? I see I must be quite sure to get my facts right. In fact, it was she who nearly bumped into me,

88

in one of her formidable four-wheelers. I'm *terribly* sorry that
I forget exactly which one. Or which day, come to that. Let
alone the hour. Further cross-examination, of course, might
reveal the entire detail . . .'

'Why didn't you tell me?'

'Do we report every small thing that happens?'

'Small!'

'Minute.'

'So she said it was her favourite beach and she'd be along?'

Mark suddenly flung the shoe across the room. 'For God's
sake shut *up*!' he said, almost shouted.

He never did things like that. He was always contained.
Too contained, perhaps. Or was that again my wifely frustration at not being able to get inside him, get at his ultimate and
hidden essence? The 'real' Mark? Forgetting that the 'real'
also included the frustration? Do men feel the same—or do
they get an illusion of entering the mind when they enter
sexually the body?

I suppose really he was behaving quite reasonably, but alas
I happened to love him so: so I was behaving reasonably too?
But the way he threw that shoe! I said 'suddenly'—but
sudden as it was, he still managed to poise it and direct it
exactly, as if it were a dart, into the angled corner of the room.

A silence while slowly he rose. You could have heard a pin
drop, as they say: but his needle dropped quite silently.
'Why in any case have you always been making such a fuss
about the woman?' he asked. 'Because you can't understand
these little matters of sound we talk about?'

Hitting the nail on the head, my sweet. So I produced an
alternative nail, as one likes to fight by exposing a weakness,
expensive diplomacy: 'I suppose because she's so rich. And
we're not.'

'How very human,' he said. 'And now, I'm going out. What
does the husband do in a holiday squabble? He goes out and
gets drunk.'

I managed a laugh, 'But darling, you're going to get drunk tomorrow. It's the festa, remember?' But the laugh was on me. However trite, his pronouncement had a traditional horror to it. Unfairly, because Mark in fact seldom got drunk.

But then without another word he left the room.

There was something particularly ruthless in his manner of leaving. It was so easy. No picking up of a jacket, no hat, stick, overcoat. No goloshes, come to that. Nothing delayed his movement from here to there. He simply loped out easily on the sandalled summer air. Not his fault, of course, but I lost my temper and went to the door and shouted after him a long volley of words, a good old nag, I forget what, except that of all things it centred on money, he and his blasted woman had already cost us a packet that day, and now he was going to empty his pockets around the bars, and what were we going to live on for the rest of the time? You see—'his woman'.

My temper was lost; but apparently controlled at the same time—for in the next instant the nag was cut short and I was through the house to a street window in the front from which I could see where he went, judge his bar. Something awful again about the way he walked along the street, quite normally, never looking back. But why should he have looked back? Why should he think the raging virago was at the window? Because he ought to have guessed? But the fact that he hadn't guessed was a compliment?

Not just then. I went back slower into our room with its messed-up bed, its strewn clothes, its us-ness, and wept. At least, the tears welled up like bruises but never really fell, it was as useless to cry alone as to be in the middle of a row, as I was, with the object bolted. In fact, a vacuum. The room itself, the empty reminder, was too awful and I went down into the little garden at the back. Quietly there the anger subsided, the blood slowing painfully like the blood returning to hands numbed by the cold: but here it was all warm, the garden was a happy little jungle of subtropical plants, yuccas and cactus and aloes and vines—roses and brashly bright zinnias too—and I hated it. I took it out on things normally hardly noticed—ash still piled in a dead barbecue oven, a frayed skipping rope, sun-faded cushions on a wicker chair. They all looked so tired, deserted, bored. Like me.

A beautiful evening, of course. The varying shapes of pink house-backs rose like sections of a plaster Arab fort, the sky's blue was gently purpling above them. Exquisite, but I managed to turn myself against all this in the same way—I was the only one left out in this loveliness of evening beginning. Someone, somewhere was singing. A woman came out on a balcony and arranged some washing. Cooking smells rose. Plates clattered. I was the only one with nothing to do.

I went out, and like a homing pigeon found Mark seated outside a small café in a back street we never usually visited. He was not drunk, but sitting with a lemonade and a piece of paper scrawled with the designs he used instead of musical notes.

So he had coolly and calmly come here and settled down to work? Quite unaffected by our quarrel? Here again was that self-contained quality, that most infuriating thing about him. My lips began to tighten, but I was so pleased to see him I smiled instead, we both smiled at the same time, then laughed. It can be as easy as that. Such a relief to love again. I loved him, I loved that place. A simple hole-in-the-wall café with a couple of tin tables on the trafficless little street not a hundred yards back from where we lived—quiet small biscuit-coloured houses, not an advertisement in sight, a haven away from the port. The roofs were overhung by the gardens of villas above, cypresses and hedges of roses seemed to sprout from the roofs —strange.

'You're pretty drunk,' I said pointing to the lemonade, and that was the only reference we made to it all. Except deciding not to dine: after all, we had had a good long lunch, had we not? And we still had our bread and sausage, hadn't we?

6

THE day of the Festa of Santa Vilga. A saint's day when a whole town's life seems to go dead—at the same time blossoming into greater life on a raised key. That is, most of the shops were shut, or shut themselves and reopened at erratic hours. Bus time-tables were changed. Effortful old trusties like the dredger stood strangely silent. Houses stopped being built, concrete mixers stood about with a dead look of disused agricultural machinery. In compensation, the beaches and bars were full, unknown buses brought in strange hordes from the hills, church bells pealed for a celestial field-day, and all the tourists, unhinged by these alterations to their routine, began to drink too much too early. I don't mean people got drunk. It was more like the atmosphere of a wedding reception, when a sense of occasion has already heightened the nerves, and a few glasses of wine at an unaccustomed hour make people more excited and receptive than usual, while clean and special clothes add their own intoxication.

A young bachelor once told me that a wedding reception was the best place to find a girl prepared, almost there and then, to go to bed with him. In the sanctity of the church, infected by a mood of sacrifice and tears, she would have been imagining the consummation of the approaching night. She did not want to be left out, she wanted to be loved too. With our festa it was not quite like that, although I would think there was a kind of eroticism in the air, nearer perhaps to the liberalizing atmosphere aboard a ship, a sense that the day was apart from ordinary life, a voyage of a dozen hours freed of restraint and responsibility.

A fine blue day as usual, but unusual a fluttering of flags in the corner of the eye. Overnight—or I suppose when we were away yesterday—people had strung up lines of coloured pennants across streets, shrines of greenery appeared at corners, one small street was entirely carpeted with a pattern of flowers. And in paintings set in many windows, and on little posters pasted on walls, the recurrent image of the saint appeared. As the various artists preferred, so the cut of the lady's beard was altered. Sometimes she wore a small goatee, sometimes a tailored charcoal line, at others a fully moustached and flowing affair. As we wandered down to the port, Mark agreed with me that there was something curiously familiar about these images. But what? We had never really seen her before?

'But of course,' Mark suddenly said, 'the boss!'

'Eh?'

'She can't look like any rank and file lady-saint, not with a beard. No, she looks like the boss—J. C. himself.'

And of course he was right. Robed in a neutral flowing garment, there was nothing to suggest a woman inside: if, like St Agatha, she sometimes bore her breasts on a plate, then these could have been loaves, fish-pieces. In a sense it was elevating, as if for once Christ had escaped the cross.

We met or saw everyone we knew. Apart from the two world whores, got up more tinselled even than usual, and the ubiquitous Geoffrey striding at an accelerated pace from errand to errand, and the Mafia-men still holding private court in their striped suits, we met our boat-owner who offered us the damaged boat for the Procession to the Sea at double the usual price, and many others we half-knew—people who had sold us sandals, the sausage-shop man, a strange woman who greeted me like a long-lost friend and who turned out to be someone whose face I had wiped on the day the hairdresser's blew up. All going and coming with a pleasantly pointless urgency up and down the shopping street with its dappling of young acacias, its shut shops and open bars, its flags winking against new concrete and old plaster façades.

The atmosphere was infectious, both full and empty, and we were physically empty soon, it was impossible to lunch anywhere, the restaurants were full, overflowing with huge family parties seated at sudden long festive tables. Not a corner for us anywhere, we could only buy a couple of pizzas which we took down to the dredger and ate sitting on the harbour wall.

A sky of buckets, a near vista of mud-caked boat, a mouthful of tomato-sodden nonentity, and I felt deliciously romantic, alone with Mark again. Warm and loving? Sweltering hot and loving. I could have taken him down into the dredger's hold and lain in his arms for hours. 'Well, it's one better than home,' Mark said, looking around. Which was another way of looking at it.

Still, such sanguine comments cover a mine of resolution, the reliability and strength for which finally we love the brutes.

'After all,' he added, 'there isn't a telephone.' How many different ways you can react to such simple pronouncements! At another time, I might have skinned him for managing to run down our holiday and our home in about the same breath. But not now — and I can see in retrospect that I was really then most concerned with keeping the pair of us out of danger. People, the innocent holiday crowd, had become danger. That Renata might always pop up among them.

Later, long after we were back on the afternoon sheets at home, with the shutters drawn and in the green aquarium half-dark, the first of the firing began. At first a few sporadic shots, like a group of jolly sports cars backfiring, then a longer fusillade. I looked round at Mark, he was asleep, a long naked figure lost to it all.

The firing grew nearer, then waved away, approached again, echoed from a muffled distance. I lay and lazily listened in the warm southern shadow. The slats of the shutters looked so peaceful, a single shaft of sunlight bore in on the mirror, discovering the usual rainbow patch of prism that shone like a jewel. Or like the rainbow ribbon of the general's medal, the general who was even now directing his coup d'état in the streets outside; for the shooting sounded exactly like a little revolution.

Could it be? . . . I suddenly opened my eyes wide, saw more clearly the china ewer across the room, its washstand, valued its symbol of past peace and thought: 'God, could it be an uprising of some sort? A risorgimento of strikers or something, anything could happen in a foreign country, for beside the plastic buckets and frog-flippers and holiday crowds it still was foreign? What had those close-printed Italian papers been saying these last days? I hadn't bothered to glance . . . and would all this room, this peace, be broken up, enraged men clubbing in with rifles, the whole bomb-splintered scene of plaster falling on a last tapping typewriter in a hotel room, that scene so often read of from foreign correspondents in the past?

Nonsense . . . I remembered talk of the Santa Vilga shooters, groups of men with old carbines who went round the town shooting blanks at the sky in honour of the bearded one . . . And the peace of our room went flat, not so valuable after all—so I dreamed a revolution back again, as the firing came and went, and it became a South American rising, Asunçion or somewhere, a hard Spanish-Indian affair with none of this facile Italian atmosphere and its facile wop contessas jingling their jewelled bangles in the eyes of innocent husbands . . . Spanish probity would forbid such female extravagances.

'I'd say the post office is occupied,' Mark's voice came quietly, 'and the water supply. No radio station here; but there's some strong action round the dredger, heavily defended till now.'

'The dredger! No!'

'Once those buckets are in guerilla hands, we might as well put paid to it.'

95

Mark turned and looked at me gravely, propped up now alert on one arm. 'You prepared to fight to the last inch of mud, little one?'

I promised him, by the ultimate strand of the sacred beard, that I would die happy. The two of us went on like this for some time, private myth-making which never bears repeating but is probably one of the sweetest binding agents in the lives of two together. It had been so warming to find Mark echoing my own thoughts. Not unnaturally so, since that echo of firing conveyed a pretty obvious allusion: but how many people would not have taken it up? Mark and I had always shared so much of this light daily thinking, frivolous in essence, but essentially of such intimate importance.

Then like an abrupt overhead thunderpeal a volley of shots exploded close in the street outside. We both sat bolt upright. 'The alarum for our excursion?' And agreed that the evening was on. The festa called, first with two glasses of tepid wine from our bedroom bottle, and two cool sponge-downs by the washstand before putting on the whiter and well-pressed clothes reserved for such a celebration.

Of that celebration I carry only one clear, intensely clear memory, a concise framed photograph in colour and its caption portentously spoken later. But of this, which pre-cipitated the crisis of our lives, more later. For the time being all was confused, as it always is on festival occasions.

Of course I remember much of it. But a heightened version of the morning's extra coming and going of more and more people, new faces, new laughter, a visual excitation of so many new and gala clothes, sounds of shooting and music, bright-nesses of extra little light-bulbs strung up everywhere, fireworks, sirens—all this and the flow of wine made the evening a vivacious blur, a brightly-shaded intoxication. Feet weary from plodding from bar to bar, ears dazzled by tran-sistor after transistor—so many people carried these, append-ages as necessary as handbags: and all in the violet dusk, the tinted night of a lighted town by the old lap-lap of the black salt sea.

Though before night fell, on the white waters of a then milky sea, there was a high moment when the saint embarked for her marine blessing. Her gilded and painted figure, with its extra-ordinary waxwork tuft of a beard, was lifted on its palanquin aboard a flower-decked motor vessel, and with a priestly bodyguard chugged off. Boat after boat followed. Thus a pointed arrow-head of craft forged slowly out to sea with the saint staring out in front. For the first few minutes it looked absurdly like the procession of boats following a sculling race. But it was not absurd, not at all. With that gilded figure poised like a conquistador in front, with the empty sea ahead and the safety of the town falling back, we were bound up with an errand of great sanctity and, with so many silent faces around, of a mysterious grave joy.

Mark and I went out in a large pinnace for a few lire with about twenty others. It was a shuddering great boat, everybody shook and quivered, teeth chattered, breasts shivered, it was like a boatload of epidemic locomotorataxia. Then the engines stopped and the lonely opalescent sea seemed to throw up a great cooling silence, as all the craft, boats of all sizes, simply drifted and only a very light whisper of lapping could just be heard.

The blessing began. For another year, the bearded one promised rich harvests from the fruit-bearing sea. All the water for miles around lay still, and one could feel it sort of filling with goodness. It was a holy moment. As it came to its climax, they let off a single red star into the sky.

A signal. As the lonely firework curved and broke, every siren and car-hooter and bell in the town broke into one single great high-wailing chord of sound. Such a chord echoes, the whole sky and bay seemed to fill it as the blessing had seemed to fill the sea. We all looked back at the little town dominated by the blue dome of the church, and because of this dominance it seemed that the whole immense chord of sound rose from the church itself, a vast peal from its unseen organ grown hugely resonant. It was a moment of great beauty. I put my hand on Mark's, and found it clenched tight. His eyes looked blind, I knew he was overwhelmed by the poetry of the moment. But even at such a time one side of me also knew that one side of him was counting decibels, harmonies, unheard-of atonalities.

Then we turned about and chugged back to the miniature town with its little puffs of white musket smoke, from that distance a museum model recording old battles with wads of cotton wool.

The lights were going on, the purple evening falling, and we joined the accelerated crowd. Two orchestras were playing almost within sound of each other, so that as you walked about different music came in gusts—the oom-pah-pah of the Town Band with its quick southern marches and its military patina of official caps above ordinary suits; and a mix-up of accordions and guitars on a space roped off for dancing. The Town Band sat in a semi-circle in front of the memorial statue of a wounded bersagliere expiring at the foot of a very blind-looking angel —in daytime, there was usually a gull on the angel's head, so that the soldier always seemed to be reaching starved arms towards this last chance of a meal—and the dance band in yellow shirts played underneath a bright cluster of red, green, blue electric bulbs. A warm evening, coloured balloons leading a tall faceless love-life above café tables, the first few showers of confetti thrown. Sunburned limbs grew duskier in the nightlight, laughing teeth whiter. We sat about a bit with Geoffrey, with the vivaciously innocent Green ladies, and there was a lot of inane chatter about the holy hormones descending on the bearded one, and once in the distance I saw a young man splay himself out on the quay while another brandished a parasol pole above him. It was the same youth who later appeared in a false beard and a long skirt impersonating the

Vilga herself, a travesty of doubtful taste resulting in the beard being plucked and the young man left smooth-shaven like a male transvestite in his embarrassing skirt.

And the wine went down, the waiters were so rushed it was easier to stand up at the bars, and when we did sit down it was usually with the half-known — a precise Scottish major more like an accountant, a tall dark Swedish couple without a blond hair between them, a young Belgian student and his Indian fiancée, a big butch from Walthamstow. As so often on the holiday run, no one ever added up to one's first impression of them: the consequent microcosm at a small table always emphasized how very diverse the world is. Homes might be mentioned, and you supplied from memory a passing picture of something like it you know — a small house in Warwickshire, a flat in a suburb like Walthamstow — and it would ten to one have no resemblance to where that person might really have lived. It was all inaccurate, all chat — but, of course, valuable as communication, and the less perceived the purer the communication. Hairless apes mouthing and blinking at each other, and very nice too. If the major talked of his water-skiing that day, he would be thinking perhaps of the strain and purchase of the tow-rope, while Mark and I would see a little figure swishing far out on the water. What could be more distinct than that? Even if that butch and I mutually approved our glasses of good white wallop, the experience might still be very different, the butch's gullet and antacid perceptions not mine at all. And if this were so between strangers, what about husbands and wives? Tales of so-called telepathic closeness were a mere nervous veneer covering a gross multitude of deeper differences.

When now Santa Vilga was borne through the balloons towards us, what were Mark's impressions? As a figure in some future opera? As a diminuendo of sound as she passed and people stopped talking to bend a knee and cross themselves? For myself, I wondered at the brilliance of this golden figure raised high against the night; and at the nobility of its staring eyes seeing further in their blindness than any of the humans below; and at the painted liveliness, a fresh look of life so unlike her shadowed dustiness in the church. And I was a little shocked that one of the bearers smoked a cigarette. And filled with disparate emotions when, not being a Roman, I didn't genuflect but instead rose awkwardly to my feet as at a passing anthem—emotions of guilt at no proper obeisance, yet pleased with myself for this formal politeness.

At one time later I left Mark and the others and went back to the room for something, I forget what. It was quiet away from the port. Out of curiosity, I walked round the back way through the little street where we had made up our quarrel the day before. It was deserted as before. In its humble way, it had dressed itself up for the festa—clothes-lines across the street with cheap little screws of coloured paper—but despite this it looked very different, as places revisited often do. The emotion was gone. The café looked even smaller. The gardens above dark now as a jungle. The houses not so much quiet as lifeless, depressing. I felt suddenly lonely for Mark, and hurried back.

He had gone. Nothing particularly out of the way in that, it was a wandering evening. Somebody pointed the direction he had taken, I strolled along. A little further on I was stopped by a firing party, three young men with antiquated guns and tended by a boy with a pramful of ammunition. They went very seriously about their business. Before the salvo was fired, the boy beat with his arm an uno, due, tre like an orchestra conductor. Then the deafening explosion, a sudden fog of powder smoke—from which emerged like a spectre a white-suited Italian who caught and pumped my hand effusively. I didn't know who it was. At a loss, then, I smiled wider than if it had been a friend. But then the mind, like the smoke, cleared and it was that wolf-faced Florentine we had met up at the Contessa's.

With inordinate expression he was inexpressively, he said, pleased to see me again. So we were still at Santa Vilga? So was he. He had moved from the Imperiale to a room in the town. Just like us. So we must meet again. He did hope so. Did we take a morning aperitif? What beach did we swim at? And so on. And he repeated to me his address, cinque via Dottore Urbino.

The odd thing is I remembered it. Perhaps even then I recognized an ally, or at least a friendly alien. Or more simply, because I've always liked the budgerigar bleat of that 'chinkwe', my favourite Italian numeral, along with respect for the euphonically urbane Dottore.

We ciao-ed, and I walked down off the main street to the port again. The dancing was going full tilt, and probably because it was in open air the movements of the separated couples looked more tribally African than usual. Beyond their lighted gaiety the quay itself was darker, with the ghost figures of half-lit people passing to and fro, a white shirt, a pale dress; a few of the boats showed lights, green, red, or the yellow of cabins, and here and there the greasy dark water swelled with a golden reflected rippling. Somewhere up the coast another town played its game of twinkling diamond lights: occasional glimmers in the hills marked a loneliness of farms or villas. It was all very quiet beyond the festa; natural, it looked unnatural.

Just then, as I stood for a moment absorbed in the great dark vista, wondering at its natural unnaturalness, the canteloupe rind of a huge yellow moon began to show above the hills, moving at a grotesque speed like a leviathan signal of light to come. And it certainly was. It was the moment when the fireworks went off. First a volley of lonely rockets describing the sky so high, so wide—yet drawing it close in at the same time. And then all manner of lights, green, red, yellow as all along the quay roman candles and catherine wheels began and more rockets soared aloft.

All at once, of all things, that dredger burst into flame!

They had set tinsel-red fire-candles in each bucket, and now the whole great iron thing blazed with ruddy light like an industrial inferno. A homely touch, indeed: and I walked back past the dancing and saw, very clearly, from a slight rise in the road, Mark and the Nose inside a café leaning up against the bar.

The doorway framed them absolutely. It was an exact rectilinear picture, their standing figures a little smaller but matching the upright jambs of the open door. The light flooded yellow all around them, I saw a coloured calendar on the wall behind, my whole inside dropped hollow. Mark had on his pale blue shirt and trousers — and blast her, she wore a blue blouse and trousers too. Their ensemble was emphasized. Other people must have been sitting out of sight inside the room, and the few tables outside were full — but they alone stood at the bar and looked isolated and private. They were laughing, and deep in talk.

I didn't know what to do. There was no real reason why I shouldn't go in to them, it was probably only a chance encounter. But I didn't, I took one step forward and stood teetering, like an idiot got set for a walking race. But above all I felt sad, as if this was a scene foretold, doom come true. I felt small and lost. What was happening was inevitable, and all around me life fell away empty into the dusk.

So alone I took several steps backwards, into shadow, against a wall. And stood watching, hating them, and myself for watching.

Suddenly she put an arm round his back — no, slapped him gently on the back — and with the other hand took his. It looked for a moment as if they were shaking hands. But then people holding hands would look like this? And then both their heads went back in laughter. They laughed, then nodded some sort of agreement. What the hell had they to agree about?

I turned and left. A mistake, of course. Much more satis-factory to go barging in, it can solve things and in any case you feel affirmative and avoid the risk of going off into a corner to sulk and worry. Which is what I now did, on a corner seat outside another café. Let him come and find *me*, I told myself, let the bloody man come and find *me*, I repeated to harden my attitude. But my attitude was pulp, I felt just squashed.

A couple of boys came near my table and brandished guns at the sky. It was a pretend salvo, like the firing of the afternoon, only their guns were modern and efficient, sleek and black: plastic, but grimly real. After routine mouthings of 'pow' and 'pfat' they screamed with delight at me, the nearest face. And I couldn't even raise a smile for them.

It seemed like hours sitting there waiting, wondering what he would say, whether he'd say nothing about meeting her, even perversely hoping this so that for once I'd be in the right —but in fact Mark must have found me in less than ten minutes.

'Hello! At last! I've been looking for you everywhere. Why so alone?'

'I was watching the fireworks.'

'You've been a time.'

'Just there and back.'

'Couldn't see you anywhere. Kept on going back to that café'

'Why did you leave?'

'They all got up. So I wandered about.'

'See anybody?'

'No. Well, everybody.' And he pointed all round him at all the people.

I think I said: 'They've set the dredger on fire.'

'Oh?'

'Cruel, don't you think?'

Then quite casually he said: 'Matter of fact, I did see somebody. I ran into the unmentionable just now. The Renata.'

'Bloody hell!'

This, I think, more in astonishment than criticism. His coolness was really astounding.

'Oh, she's not really so bad. We had quite a merry little chat. Matter of fact, she's just—'

'Let's merrily chat about something else.'

'But she's just—'

He paused as he saw my face. Then, cool as before: 'Sure, darling. What topics have you?'

'Oh Mark!' I'd suddenly burst into tears, and put my head against his chest, hating myself for suspecting him, wonderfully relieved he was there, wildly curious as to what 'she's just' but determined, with a tooth biting a lip, not to ask him. Which was why I had to wait till the next morning to hear the caption to that scene in the lighted doorway.

'There,' he said, 'there.' And stroked me better.

7

LOOKING back, it is far too easy to suspect Mark of being particularly pleasant to me the next morning—as if he were preparing a good soft mattress for the recoil of a little piece of news he had for me. Given a crisis, hindsight can always consolidate these foreshadowings, like remembering imagined symptoms long after the illness has arrived.

Probably it was all more a matter of tiredness after a late night. For long after my brief tears we had danced under the coloured lights, under the southern stars and all that . . . a little too feverishly, perhaps, retrospect again added. But he must have been somehow more attentive than usual—in small forgettable ways, pouring more coffee, closing the shutter against the morning glare, things I normally did, because I must have mentioned it to get an answer I do distinctly remember:

'Bottle fatigue,' he said. 'People are always nicer with it.'

'Don't headaches mean sharp words?'

'Haven't got a headache. Just got glut.'

'Ugh!'

'No ughs about it. People are always nicer nicely tired. Give me tired and ill people every time. The accelerators off. They just course along. Everything's easier, nobody trying to force things.'

There exactly might have been a nail hit on the head. Perhaps that morning he was all there for once, not self-absorbed, planning nothing, just there with me and his bottle fatigue.

Only, within a few minutes he was saying: 'Ready for some news? Had your coffee? Done your duty like a big girl?'

'Mmm.' I expected some very ordinary nonsense, 'my left big toe's gone to sleep', something intimately inane.

'She's offered me a job,' he said.

Knowing quite well whom he meant, I said of course, 'Who?'

'A very good job, with millions of lovely lire. What about that? Stay in Italy and write the score for a film, a television series, and for god's sake a sort of opera-ballet into the bargain.'

'But Mark—this is tremendous!'

He smiled.

'It's what you've always wanted, Mark—I mean, it's the break-through, it's *it*!'

He still smiled, lazily.

'Unfortunately,' he said, 'there are unacceptable strings attached.'

'What! I mean, what?'

'It would mean working for about two years in Italy.'

'Oh. Oh but why not, we could—'

'That's just it. There's no "we" about it. That good lady is either stark mad or terribly, terribly sane. It's just as Geoffrey said—do you remember, at lunch in the Torre?—she wants to own a person completely. Once under her wing a twenty-four hour devotion is obligatory.'

'I say, I say!'

'No, not like that. She went on to explain that an employee such as myself became an investment. Apart from all the necessary sound-equipment, machines, special studio and that, the main factor was the public build-up, I'd have to be on tap for news stories, be seen in a specialized social whirl, also lecture, be constantly interviewed, travel, America, Germany and so on—'

'My God, she'd got it all worked out!'

'Quite preposterous. She wasn't going to take on a family, she said. I said there wasn't a family. She said she meant it differently, she wanted a personality, a talent, a genius and no strings attached. I laughed, but she then lectured me on the Russian ballet school, on men who built dams in jungles and how often did I think an international oil executive saw his wife? Occasionally, at least, I said.

'So might you, she said. Only she must have the last word. You never knew what cropped up in this game, she said, you could make all your plans and then something happened and loyalty to the project must come first, she had had it all before time and time again . . .'

I was thinking. Two years. All his ambitions realized. The coffee was cold in the cup, the sun outside getting hotter. It was going to be a sweltering day: the heat carried with it a heaviness of the years, all the hot days of childhood added together, a sense of time standing still, and with it all a kind of doom. The day would be endless.

'Still . . . Mark . . . *it is* what you've always wanted, what *we* always wanted . . .'

'It's ludicrous. You'd think you could write a bit of music without all this kind of nonsense.'

'Perhaps we're too innocent? You never know much about these what—highly-geared circles?—till you're there. Anyway, surely there's some compromise?'

'That's what she was most emphatic about. None. Of course, it sounds very, very bald the way I've repeated it—in a nutshell. But there was no nutshell about the Nose. Out came the old vermicelli, she piled on every detail and even made it sound convincing. The words put me to sleep, I kept waking up. And the funny thing was, of course, that though she was inviting me and trying to convince me, I had to conclude that in the end she couldn't want me very much.'

'Why?'

'Surely the chance of anyone accepting such conditions is pretty slim?'

'We don't know that world. Perhaps it isn't. And perhaps she's a gambler? Perhaps you're a way-out chance, worth a million if it works, but sort of replaceable—I mean, in some lesser terms?'

'She can use an old brass band, for all I care,' he yawned.

Yawned. I don't like yawns at such a time. They can be just nervous. Or they can all too easily be a cover-up.

'In any case,' I said, 'how does she know what you can do? Just from a couple of tapes you took up to the villa that night? Don't tell me she can read your kind of score.'

'No. I lent her a lot more stuff. *Membrane*, and—'

'Lent? When?'

'Oh, I promised them the night we went up there. She sent a man from the yacht.'

'You never told me.'

'It wasn't much to tell, really.'

'Why from the yacht?'

'I suppose it's stuffed with apparatus—at least it only needs a player.'

'Oh.'

I can't say that then we let the matter drop, it was hardly the kind of matter for that. I remember quickly getting out of bed and going to have a shower—wonderful cold water to wash it all away, that kind of inconclusive impulse.

The water came stinging down, blinding like the confusion inside me: after all, he had refused it? Whether he should or not was a longer matter—but his plain reaction had been to refuse. But I felt things had been going on behind my back, there was a very intangible sense of conspiracy. Yet it could all be explained—particularly since this music thing of his was not all that comprehensible to me, what they had talked about from the first was technically way above my head. But that only added to the feeling of being excluded.

That morning we went down to the ordinary beach to bathe. I didn't want to paint, he knew I was upset and I should think he had plenty to worry about too and on top of everything there was the sense of exhausted aftermath following any festa. We were in for a heatwave, too: the air was breathless, a solid torpor pressed down, even the shop-keepers were fanning themselves.

So we went to the relative cool of the beach and got tar on our feet like all the other holiday-makers and lay there sweating among the transistors and beachballs. I had with me the usual paperback stained with suntan oil and the bloody bodies of squashed mosquitoes: but it was impossible to read, this awful predicament kept spinning round the hot little mind with an insomniac insistence of night-worry. A decision, a decision, it yelled—but then Mark had already made his decision?

It was not as easy as that. Nothing could be. I could see a mounting pile of argument, discussion, compromise, a ziggurat of talk. In my immediate line of vision the wide fat bottom of a white woman from the north, grilling herself for the first time, red as a lobster by noon, red as my mind. Two naked little girls in white sunhats ran to and fro saying 'Bye, bye' to each other, always 'Bye, bye'. A handsome Italian-looking couple in plastic leopard briefs and bikinis lay and kissed as solidly as they might have at night, but now not only navigating noses but also sunglasses too. Every so often a wet sandy football came skidding at us, followed by urgent feet and never an apology.

We bathed among swimming Italians and archly splashing tourists—how *can* they, year after year, with such surprise and shrieks, as if it had never happened before? We came back fresher, but in ten minutes the sweat was running down the sunglasses as before. It felt as if my glasses were running with tears, as I buried too many cigarette stubs in the sand.

Like anyone with an illness, I was glumly irritated that life went on as if nothing had happened. And as very often happens on beaches, there was the morning's distraction by which afterwards you often remember a particular day. It could have been the coming of some special yacht, or a television crew, a half-drowned bather. With us that day, it was a big fish. A huge white devil big as a small submarine, grinning like mad and arrowed with fins. They drove a special lorry down to hoist it aboard with a block and tackle. God knows how they caught such a monster—about as big as what I'd caught.

It was to be indeed the day of the fish. At lunch I ordered an unusual item on the usual menu, squid unfried for once in some sort of sauce. Instead of the expected squidlets, my plate was draped with one immense brown cuttle-fish, it looked like a big leather money-purse. Its glaucous, reproachful eye met mine with mutual disfavour. Its leathery tentacles hung over the side of the plate like a dead spider's legs. Mark gave it a gasp of welcome—something about there being more fish in the sea, yes, and this was the kind of thing you got—and went on talking about that parasol pole murder. He seemed to have quite forgotten our beautiful dilemma—or of course he was trying to talk it away? Anyhow, my own mind was still swimming with it, and now insanely it lashed on to these fish as symbols, fish, fish, big fish—here was the chance to be a big fish and did big fish all end scuttled and dead on beach or plate? Round and round it went. While Mark was saying:

'I'll bet we'll never hear the end of it. It'll be like all those other Italian scandals. The unsolved mysteries we read of at the bottom of page two in our exciting press at home.'

'Shall I really eat it?'

'Have a go. But perhaps I'm unfair to the eyetie police. Only the mysteries get translated, solution makes no news? Do you think Geoffrey did it?'

'Have a go?'

'Yes. I mean Geoffrey the old Santa Vilga hand driven mad by change? By the spoliation of his old paradise? By new hotels? . . . And one morning bright and early the bloody and headstrong revenge? I wonder what it sounded like. Try it on the squid.'

I lanced the thing for him, it squirted inkily. 'Hardly food for a major theme,' Mark said bending a mock-attentive ear. But of course all I was thinking was 'have a go', 'have a go', 'major theme', reaching out for any coincidental allusion to the problem of being a big fish.

At some moment during the morning those two little girls in sunhats had settled down close to Mark. Something had upset them. They began to cry. And Mark got up and took them each by a hand to lead them back to where their huge family sat. It is his back view I remember so clearly—so suddenly the gentle father with his two little children, my big blond frizzed-haired Mark leaning down so patiently to soothe them, their little arms stretched high into his hands, one on each side, and the big figure between . . . he was always good with children, Mark . . . why had we not had any, why, why?

Money.

But others did? On less money than we had?

Well—selfishness.

As that day wore on, so also did the problem, but at least it clarified some of itself, it achieved perspective.

I saw, for instance, that really it was not our own unique problem.

In today's world, it was a problem which affected many, many people. At least, most of the many people bent on improving themselves.

Item one, now I faced it squarely, if squarely could ever be used of so angular an organ, was that the Nose would be sniffing Mark into bed with her. It would be too naïve to think otherwise. Especially after her first and most memorable glance at him. Well? How many wives whose men are sent abroad on new and responsible assignments faced the same thing? Selling electric switchgear by day, running the gauntlet of electric new women by night? Husbands in tempting foreign places, in romantic liberalizing atmospheres built into the job? Lonely husbands at night, or husbands being entertained by local business men who know that food and drink are not enough. And what do these wives do? They make a wry face, and turn it the other way. They put it out of minds crowded with new glories, bedspreads, curtains, run-abouts consequent upon a well-raised salary.

Nor in any case would they do otherwise than put up with it. Male ambition must not be thwarted. Even if there was no 'male' to it, ambition itself is sacrosanct: the pure motivation of the rat-race, it would be absurd to deny it. That was the number two item I had to stomach. Nobody gets in the way of a step up the ladder. The ladder is holy. All that cultivate your garden advice, sane and honourable though it might be, is simply out of touch with money-blooded life. Multiply all that by two if it is a particularly male step up the holy rungs. It is as if there is no choice at all.

'We are quite comfortable as we are'. Seven years married and a quite sweet success made of it? Indeed? And where are the children to prove it? And are we quite satisfied with our three-room flat in grey old London, white though the paint be just now?

Life is development, that's a further thing. Change for change's sake is important to most people. Even though the cost is risky, people risk it.

And I can see another point being raised by many a sweet forehead corrugated with critical thought—may not some new long absence of a hubby be *a good thing* for a marriage? Absence making the heart grow fonder? Distance making him realize all the things he took for granted, my arms at night, my rissoles by day? Clasped hands before the telly? The good home comfort of take-away Chinese food? So I can hear their minds at work, digging for consolation, looking everywhere for the best in the worst. Brave souls—besides, everyone loves a sacrifice.

Therein lies another force—wifely sacrifice. To suffer to heal. To immolate one's whole precious self on the altar of future content. To do this with a firm chin and a well-secured bra, quietly to oneself, not bitter but sweet, greeting the world with a smile. Or splayed out on the earth, pegged down to receive the blows of fate without a murmur (that is, sit in the kitchenette with a glossy magazine, passing the lonely hour with instant coffee) . . . but sacrifice, sweet sacrifice, woe for the weal.

Altogether then, I was not alone in my predicament. In other forms it was going on all around me all the time. Certainly it looked as though my case was worse. I had met the woman in question, her terms were unusually onerous, her attitude of possession extreme . . . but was this all not only a matter of degree, was it not the same as for other wives except apparently, only apparently more so, since it was so bald and obvious?

There is the famous old proposition, the other way round, of the stranger saying to the wife: 'If you'll sleep with me once, only once, I'll give you £500,000.' What does she do? That money will assure her family's future for some time . . . It's a difficult one, that. But in essence it's the same thing, different only in degree.

By the late afternoon, after our sleep, I was quarrelling with Mark about something quite else. A matter of his clothes strewn all over the room. This was their normal situation, particularly on holiday, and previously I had neither mentioned nor minded the fact. But that afternoon I went at him, telling him he was making a slum out of an Italian idyll, how beautiful our sweet Tuscan hide-out would be but for his slop and sloth and so on and on. He laughed at first. But in the end we were both morosely stuffing clothes into drawers, and there were not enough drawers, so they were piled up in different and less accessible corners. Of course, I was simply using this as an escape jet for the real problem. I even knew it at the time, but couldn't stop myself. I remember particularly walking about with a pair of socks, socks with holes in them, socks utterly unnecessary in the south, and wondering where to cram them, and thinking, into my mouth, into my bloody mouth.

So that by the evening the festering boil had to have its head picked off.

There is a special impulse at work in all evenings — a quality of renewal, of putting the day aside and of cleaning up for the night. An animal change from sun to moon, night-hunters preparing themselves, and expressed in human terms by baths, changing clothes, scent, the pouring of the first iced drinks.

Which is much intensified in a heatwave. An English heatwave brings memories of strawberry-tasting days, of evening lawns long with shadow, dew about. But a southern heatwave is solid as golden rock, it weighs the whole body and mind, the air's truly like hot flannel, the effort of fanning even a light breath from it is too much. No relief all day from the breathless zebra of glaring white sun and hot black shadow: until it all fades pearly into evening, the diamond blue sea turns now to boiled milk; from nowhere a fake coolness springs up, but it is not really a coolness, certainly not a breeze, it is only a lowering from torment to something a bit more bearable. A wash refreshes, but its effect is gone in a minute; the same with a fresh dress, hot and clinging the next moment; the same with the iced drinks, calling to each other like a glass flock, going and coming with no quench about them, only the anaesthesia of alcohol.

So Mark and I sat in a café with our glasses and our melting ice and our baby flies drowning in the vermouth and hammered it out.

Only hammering is not the word, we went at it with a light play of soft felt drumsticks. Round and round we went, in and out, and of course adding to much I've said above about the predicament, I had to bring up his vocation as an artist, his aesthetic probity. It is not enough only to be good, even great in a matter of creative endeavour—you must develop it, broadcast it, and to do this you must seize your opportunity. Nothing ever happens without that seizure. When something comes along, grab it. It is one of the big qualities of success—to be able to see an opportunity and act.

I began arguing against myself, and for him going away from me. Looking back, I can see I was really testing him, fishing for an emphatic refusal. Mark in fact did refuse, and went on refusing, although his idea of emphasis was not mine. He countered my arguments with others, he continued in fact to *discuss* the matter. What I wanted—what of course I would have done in his place—was for him to give me some drastic big black blank No. Tell a lie. Say it was *not* the kind of work he wanted. Say he could *not* work for a moment with such a person as the Nose. Even say he was not up to that kind of work—that at this stage of his development he did not feel capable of canalizing all his energies etc. etc. etc. In fact, sweep the glasses off the table with a word like a stick.

But soft kind understanding Mark simply went on saying 'no' with vague logic about it not being the right thing for us, not really helping our life, which we liked enough as it was, didn't we?

All this 'we', when I wanted a good old masculine 'me' from him. 'We' made me an accessory to the crime of not seizing an opportunity, 'we' made me a drag. I don't think he thought I took it that way, I think he was simply pedalling along with his male logic, being 'sensible'.

Like: 'You see, darling, we've got a nice enough flat. It's near to your shop. You like buying and selling your antiques —I mean you like the feel of those things so it isn't just business. And not having to travel to and fro, and having somewhere comfortable enough to live are big considerations nowadays. My own job's pretty secure, and it doesn't tax me all that much. I can still experiment in my spare time—much of it, in theory at least, in the office itself. So all in all we're pretty well off. It would be a pity to knock that all up for something unknown.'

'Mark, I could kick you. Where else are you going to get a break like this?'

'Why not at home? Sometime? You never know.'

Humble and patient. Or playing the contented stick-in-the-mud, whichever way you like to look at it.

It was still like this when the two Green ladies came by, stood for a while at our table chatting, and had to be invited to sit down. They had had 'Oh such a marvellous day visiting the Etruscan tombs' and 'they're really the coolest place in this hot weather'. The taxi, though, overcharged. The usual touring twaddle.

I remember the paint on those very painted, very innocent faces was in one way distinguished. The younger Green labelled Sprout had put white on her upper eyelids. The light from a naked bulb strung in the tree above her head caught these two white blobs. They looked exactly like pigeon shit.

There are times, as in a dream, when physical impressions seem to repeat themselves, to recur after a few hours in quite a different place. Say—the distant sound of gunfire practice on one afternoon, followed a long time later in the evening by someone making meat tender with a hammer over a particularly resonant table. The two sounds, without coincidence, are heard as the same, as if your ears beckoned them to do so.

It was the same with the Sprout's pigeon shit eyelids. Sometime in the middle of that night I woke up. Moonlight was shining white through the window. It was very bright. You couldn't say 'clear as daylight', as they do: it was just clear as itself, slightly diffused in a way you could hardly judge, but made up of whites and silvers and greys—occasionally burning a warmth rather than colour into some normally brightly-coloured object, a yellow shirt, a red vase. And, because it was less fierce, the lovely grey-white glow seemed altogether steadier than sunlight.

I raised my head an inch quietly to look at Mark asleep by my side. His face was full in the light, and turned towards it. That white, white moon had placed two blobs of pigeon shit on his closed eyelids. He looked like a blind man, or like a statue with stone circles in the blind place of eyes.

Then, in sudden horror, I lowered my head again. Very slowly, hoping he had not seen.

For his eyes were wide open. Their blue had been melted by the moon to its own cold white. He was lying awake and staring; thinking. And it was such intense, lonely blind-looking thought. He looked the oldest and loneliest person in the world—not physically older, but graven, like a dead man, like the effigy of all men troubled to the core of their souls by silent thought.

Why didn't I simply say: 'Mark—you awake?' It would have been easy enough?

No. There was something terrifying in his immobility. And, of course, after a second my own mind had put into his mind what he was thinking about.

And he did not even look sad. He simply looked lost. I suppose I mean lost in thought. Not there. Gone.

8

'HE LOVED her so much. And there she was, naked, and cold, and laughing at him. Married to him, enticing him, there for the taking, and always refusing. Poisoning him with her delight in it, and secretly giving him the other poison too. Week after week, month after month. He would have gone mad, she watched him going mad, her smile was as fixed as a sneer. Can a snake smile? That is what it would have been like . . . cold, biting, disgusting . . .'

It was Rinaldi speaking, I had gone to visit him the next day to find out more, if I possibly could, about our Contessa. I had to know more of some sort. Something to bite on—not that it would do much good. She would never be quite comprehensible—a foreigner in her own foreign country. But somehow I had to act, even if only for the satisfaction of action.

It turned out to be an altogether extraordinary visit. In the first place, though I had remembered the *cinque* address, I only realized when I had rung the bell that I had no idea of his name. Professor was all I could think of. And who should answer the long thin tingling of the old-fashioned pull-bell but the short fat figure of that butch we had so often seen about the place. As usual, she wore purple trousers and a purple military-style top. Both emphasized her square purplish face.

'*Il professore?*' I said.

'*Sì,*' she smiled with her huge man's mouth.

And we waited. For a long time. Grinning at each other. So I repeated my professional enquiry. And she 'si-ed' me again. Impasse. Then she pointed to herself. In fact—I won't go into the long interchange in Italian, mine so lame—in fact she was a professor too. Well—who wasn't, unless they were a Dottore? So that I had the awkward job of saying to this man-woman that I wanted the man-professor.

She looked sly for a second, then must have digested my dejected innocence, and threw her bull's head back in a huge laugh. Amused, thank God, not hurt.

It was the laugh that must have alerted the real man-professor upstairs. For now his voice called down, a waterfall and waterspout of Italian followed, and then followed the footsteps and body of the man I had called on.

He was surprised, and acted enchanted. Up I went to a room breathless with books and furniture, fishing rods and papers. I thought as usual: How can they, in such a hot country? But of course it was a home. He had rented a room in a home.

After a few minutes of tortuous politeness as formal as an Arab coffee-party—he wondering and possibly hoping about my intentions, me wondering why we weren't squatted praising our ancestors and flocks—I came to my brass tacks, asking his understanding and, please, confidence. What kind of a woman really *was* this Contessa?

'Kind of a woman?' he asked, astonished. 'Rich,' he smiled, the easy way.

'No—I mean, what's her record? Is she honest? Does she fulfil obligations? And what in any case drives her to do all she does, these projects one hears of?'

'Questions! My goodness, questions! Well . . . in the last place, I would say—she was an artist manqué, her own hands and mind cannot create so she creates situations, organizes true artists—'

'I know, and does she do this well?'

'She is only interested in success. Her position is to judge. And naturally she backs her judgements to the hilt. It is a very powerful hilt.'

'But if she made a mistake? I mean, choosing an artist, I mean choosing a composer, like my husband?'

'I thought that was it. No, she wouldn't let him down. She would have, what—identified herself too much. Her protégé would never be wrong—only conditions or something outside control could fail. Is your husband then to work for her?'

I told him. And we went on talking of her in the same general terms, of her ambitions, or her as an egoist, a supreme egoist but at the same time a generous, outward-thinking egoist: the paradox, her egoism was other people. 'Ownership?' I bluntly asked. 'I'm afraid so,' he said. And then went on in the same vein, but rising in some sort of vehemence: it was plain from the beginning that he did not like her, and now the vision of her seemed to compound in what he was saying, she was steaming him up, his emotions were fuelled, so that in the end they took over and he was not discussing her at all objectively but beginning almost to rage against her. And then in fact to rage, as suddenly he launched into this extraordinary story of her second husband.

'He was my friend, Paolo, my very good friend. We had the same years at the university. We were close, like brothers. And then the fool goes and marries her. When they first met, he told me, he scarcely noticed her. That might have been because she was, well, so rich and separate. Although Paolo wasn't doing at all badly, he was an architect, and brilliant, with plenty of work and a great future. I think she must have felt his lack of interest in her. So she went after him. And carefully, cleverly—at any rate, he told me she grew on him, he saw a thousand things in her he had not immediately noticed, she became finally an obsession which quite naturally he translated as love. Oh, a great, great love. He found himself obsessed—I would say rather "possessed". But some men are like that, Paolo was not a weak man, but something in him welcomed this possession—what I don't know, vanity, the wish to relax into another person?

'Also, perhaps a sadness appealed to him, too? She was a young widow. Her first husband had died in tragic circumstances. An accident—but an accident which might well have been suicide. But of course it was, of course he killed himself.

'So they were married, Paolo and this Renata. And from the very beginning it did not go well. I only saw Paolo after some months, six months—but he was much changed even then, thinner, pale, nervous, abstracted. At first he would tell me nothing. But eventually I got it out of him. And what he had to say was very terrible indeed. He was—how shall I say it?— undergoing a form of provoked and malevolent sexual torture.'

It was about this point that the professor put his hand on my knee. We were sitting at an angle, he on the bedside, me on a little chair. And now as what he was saying aroused in him remembered anger his hand kneaded at my knee, softly, then suddenly clutching. His brown eyes looked hurt, his eyebrows raised in appeal. I didn't move my leg in case it would stop him: poor Mark, here goes number one deception, I thought. His wolf-face. Was he a wolf beneath it?

'I can speak about it? The sex thing? We are all free nowadays—you English, of course? Liberated, what you call womb-lib, I think?'

'Women's Lib,' I said quietly. It was odd how these wonderfully-fluent English-speakers always get one word, a word or two wrong. Always. It stuck out because you never expected it: of course, it was not odd at all.

'To put it simply, she refused him sex. Oh not at first, the marriage was well consummated and Paolo had never known anything like it. And he had known a lot of women. But this one—he could not describe it, she was the most animal, the most human, the most inventive, the most utterly abandoned yet carefully controlled lover he had ever known, or could have believed to exist. I won't go on, such matters are beyond description, too much of personal experience. So at any rate she made sure she gave him a good taste of herself. Then, quite suddenly, arbitrarily, for no reason, she stopped. Refused herself absolutely.'

The hand clutched. But it could still have been construed as a friendly hand, a hand gesturing confidence, trust. If it were not—but I had always heard that Italians were predominantly romantic lovers, they were seldom physically predatory, like the French, the Spanish. No race of bottom-pinchers, no maulers, the eyeties. Their singing minds shied off the touch. But I suppose that's a generalization, full of holes as a sieve.

'But, you see, she still made love. Still made seduction. In fact, she intensified this. She made herself as attractive and charming as possible, made all possible advances to him, paraded herself for him in the bedroom—and then said no. When he was in high excitement. You may ask, why did he not take her by force? First, it was not his nature, Paolo was gentle, always gentle and considerate. But finally he did. When after a few exercises of this hot-cold seduction he lost control, he did. And she lay there cold as a corpse, staring at the ceiling, a look of disgust on her face. Of course, this was no satisfaction, worse in fact than the simple physical satisfaction, worse than nothing. After what he knew she could really be like.

'And so it went on. He tried to be wise, tried to appear disinterested, went out—but always came back. He could not help himself. And at each small resistance, she grew more subtle. Every man has his small fetishes. She knew his. And she would purposely do her hair this way or that, show him special clothes and jewellery and other things she would wear in the bedroom later. And finally—this he only found out later—she began secretly to feed him aphrodisiacs. A little at first, more as the months went by. These things are not always powerful, but some are. Cantharides. Poisons, irritants. She put them secretly in his coffee, his drinks—just like any little murder story, and like any little murder story it was by the empty bottles that he discovered much later what she had been doing and the amount, the awful malignant amount horrified him as much as the whole conception of it.

'So my poor young Paolo withered. He tried all the palliatives. Of course, you know he masturbated: but that was only a temporary relief, and although he felt no particular guilt about it, the solitary enactment was always a blow to his pride. There he was, a man married to a beautiful woman, and yet he was reduced to the state of a lonely powerless youth lusting with himself on the quiet. It was a further emasculation. And so he went out after prostitutes. A mistress? An affair? Not so easy, easy in theory but in practice not necessarily available, not the right person, not at the right time. Besides, they're complicated, they need a relationship, and Paolo was too distracted to be able to provide this. He did, in fact, have one: but after a week or two the affair failed, it was simply no substitute. For in the meantime Renata kept up her game. Always inventing new pleasures, always refusing them. You could scarcely believe a woman, or anyone, to be so purposeful, so remorselessly what, hard-working, devoted? Diligent? But of course she loved it, she revelled in it, it was her idea and by God she was making her mark on someone, wasn't she? You see what I mean about her egoism, her drive?

'And she was delighted that he went with prostitutes. It was a further abasement. She saw it, of course, only as sordid. So did Paolo. But who knows whether he was not beginning to enjoy his own abasement in some perverted way? Of course, Renata was playing with murder. In the end he would kill her. Or kill himself. Was that the reason for the first husband's death? Did the something happen? I don't know. All I know is that Paolo might in the end be driven to one of those acts of terrible, sad violence. Yet she did not seem to be afraid. She liked the risk. She was all-powerful. It must have been like gambling at some high and fevered pitch . . . yet she lost.'

The hand stopped its clutching, it now rested very gently on my knee, as if to implement what next he saw to say. His voice softened too.

'It was by the purest chance. An outside chance that few gamblers could conceive. I suppose Renata must have considered it possible he would fall in love with someone else: but not seriously, she was too convinced of her own power. However, Paolo picked up a girl one night and this girl was very young and it turned out it was her first time. She had never been on the streets before. She was innocent, it was poverty drove her there. On that particular night. She was gentle and sweet, Paolo said, like a little sister. She had not eaten for two days. He took her to a restaurant, he'd never seen a girl eat so much before. Afterwards, in a hotel, she was very sick. Paolo made her stay, took a small room for her, he was very touched. And he looked after her. As the days, weeks went by he fell in love with her. Not from pity, but from absolute appreciation of her gentle nature, her innocence, the absolute antithesis of the cruel Renata.

'And that was that. They're still living happily together; and the dreadful Renata simply had to take it.

'For she *is* dreadful!' he suddenly shouted. And abruptly stood up, and went on shouting, 'Dreadful! Inhuman! Ruthless! Cold!'

It had been rivetting. It was now embarrassing. The more so since I felt I could not look him in the face while he was shouting so. I was left looking him straight in the fly buttons, or zip or whatever it is. So I stood up too. And caught the full blast of his breath, which was not clean.

Did he think my standing up opposite him an invitation? He reached out and took my shoulders, pulling me towards him. 'Horrible! Terrible!' he was shouting. 'You asked me and I'm telling you, that's why, she's *evil*, she's a . . . a . . . she's the opposite to you, my darling, who are so sweet, so beautiful—'

And his mouth came close.

There is that phrase about being alone with a man in a room—'being chased round the table', it runs. But what if there is no table? There often is not. Like lightning I picked up the nearest thing—a copy of *Oggi*—and held it between us, a poor enough table indeed, but at least an object. Better a vase, an épergne. But in default of these—the malleable *Oggi*. At the most, a symbol. And Rinaldi recognised it as such. Whether he was startled by whatever illustration the cover carried—a bikinied starlet newly-murdered, a bikinied HRH taking a holiday tanning, I never knew what—or whether he thought I would scroll the thing and club him, whatever it was his hurt brown eyes popped out their whites and he began to scream:

'Cold! Cold! Cold like you, like all damned women—'

And I have no idea to this day what might have happened, whether *Oggi* would have saved the day or whether he might have lost himself and struck, embraced, raped, even I suppose killed me . . . but just then there was a heavy-handed thumping on the door and the butch's purple face swung round it.

'Excuse me, but what a noise!' she rasped, and strode in like a gladiator. 'Is there something wrong?'

Rinaldi, plucked the *Oggi* from my hand. 'Something wrong?' he yelled. 'Look at this!' And he opened the thing at random and flung out a great stream of rapid Italian about the defacement of Venice and industrial gases, while I could only marvel at the quickness of his mind, at his assumption of my conspiracy (quite right), at the flexibility of his passion (as untrustworthy as the Contessa?). I was also relieved and while nodding agreement, soon said, 'My, the time! I must go!'

All of which the butch saw through instantly, a slight smile on her great lips. She took me by the arm, 'I will show you down, dear', and we left with Rinaldi's voice still following us down the stairs: 'Come again, signora!' 'How long are you staying, signora?' 'I'm in usually in the morning until eleven!' the way they can never say goodbye without trying to stop and talk for another five minutes, as if they can't bear their personality losing its grip on you, as remarkable a social acrobatic as that moment a few minutes before when the butch caught Rinaldi at it and all three of us pretended nothing was happening—why? A deep instinct for decorum? Or as deep a curiosity as to the next move, the next human ingenuity?

The butch squeezed my arm before letting me go. 'Don't believe a word that man said,' she smiled, giving me all her teeth and a generous helping of butch-breath. 'He's a little . . . you know, up here.' And a great fat forefinger tapped her forehead.

9

WHY I've repeated at such length the dreadful story of Renata and her aphrodisiacs is to explain why that late afternoon found me sweating up the road to her villa. She had to be spoken to face to face, and alone. She had to be tested and judged. By me, with every ounce of instinct and intuition I might have.

No appointment, I wouldn't risk being put off. I was even carrying a sheaf of sketches, so as to look in some way official to the servant opening the door—you see all planned. Even in that heat? It was the heat that hired me one of the three-wheeler taxis with the little striped canopies, those we called ice-cream trolleys, so that I rattled up to her formidable gates like a red-hot vanilla wafer.

The gates were open—had she gone out? No point in waiting, I strode in and past a man hosing one of the cars who first quietened two fierce-looking guard-dogs and then turned with the beginning of a 'signora?' before, my head in the air and my sketches at the ready, I was well ahead and ringing the bell. I rang the bell to get the duty-servant to the door—while now I edged off round the house looking up at the roof and down at my sketches like a surveyor (for the hose-man's and his guard-dogs' benefit). Then out of view raced round to the back with all its windows and doors leading on to the terrace. They were all shut.

So she was out? And I was a common burglar? Or an uncommon one, with sketches for sale—all of which could be explained later, of course? I fingered the catch of one of the doors and it swung open with a blast of fresh air. Of course—air-conditioning, hence the reason for this great closed shop.

I went quietly in and looked round. The big sitting-room. Then the sound of the front-door beyond opening, the servant's voice talking at speed to the man with the hose, and I was hurrying up the open stairway to upstairs where with luck the Nose was risen from her afternoon sleep.

And there she was, sitting in a bath-wrap by a huge palette-shaped dressing-table, and a maid was with her. The maid's presence melted the Nose's first fixed glare into a long smile of charm, not quite matched by her words: 'What a pleasure, Signora Forster, to see you—unannounced!' She sang the last word upwards, like all delight: of course the maid spoke no English.

Then without pausing she dismissed the maid, and I steeled myself for the storm which never came, for in that short time she must have weighed pros and cons which included Mark, and had decided to play it cool as the conditioned air. First she reached forward for my sketches: 'You've brought them to show me? How kind!'—and began appraising them, praising them: 'How lovely—yes, what *line*!' 'There are the yachts! And there's my *Spada*!' 'A simple agave—yet how much you see! Or feel. Ferocious—you like spears, then?' And so on: but not for long, suddenly she put them aside, as people so often do with, say, a bunch of photographs, as if the stint were done, honour satisfied, and introduce some new topic you feel they've been thinking up all the time.

Pointing to the windows, she said: 'I've thought of having a rainfall put on them, the way they do with flowershops. A sort of air-conditioning for the eye. Or would that be too deceptive —avoiding the truth?'

It was plainly my cue for entrance. Spirited by my material entrance, and possibly the fresh cool air, too, I took it:

'I hear you've made my husband a proposition,' I said, particularly not smiling, 'and the conditions seem a little hard.'

She increased her smile: 'Have you ever made a film, my darling?'

'I have heard of them being made. And usually employing husbands who return to their wives at night.'

'To their wives camp-following in hotels everywhere? Travelling? Doubling—if I might say so—the expense?'

'Yes. Hotels are not always expensive.'

'Your husband, my darling, surely explained that this was also, mainly perhaps, an operation in building his personality? Making him a figure. Only the best hotels, then. The finest and most peculiar studio to live in. But that is not the real point—'

'I could live in a peculiar studio, too.'

'The point is not this. The point really is concentration. Absolute concentration.'

'I've never stood in his way. Have you ever lived with a man who returns from his office and dives into a tape recorder for the rest of the evening?'

'But you are *now* standing in his way.'

'I'm simply saying I think it's unnecessary, the way you intend it.'

'My dear, you'd be quite lost. Waiting in the wings all the time. He out to dinners, receptions—flying off to America, Hamburg, Utrecht at a moment's notice—quite apart from his actual company. You know, I'm thinking of you, too, a little.'

'A "little" expresses it.'

'Let us then keep to the point. I have to have absolute control. It is the only way I do things.'

I took a deep breath of her expensive air. She was still smiling, still playing graciousness. But I was going over her face again, the way one does, and thinking, 'why snake-like, why a snake?' Small head, long neck, wide eyes, down-drawn mouth—that must be it? The body too, no hips, narrow shoulders, a kind of coiling thing? Snake seemed such an obvious concept—yet there it was. She'd never sweat, I thought. Smooth, cold.

'The way you do things? I heard about your husband today,' I said. 'The second one.'

She lowered her lids slightly. Usually lidless too, I thought. 'Rinaldi?' she asked.

Of course, of course. Yet it was a shock, I could only nod.

'And what did you hear about that disappointed man?' she asked. 'Though I don't see what it has to do with—'

'One of your less successful products,' I said.

'Really, signora, such things are private. I am not discussing—'

'But I am discussing *my* husband.'

She chose to do a little bright belling of laughter. 'But really, I am not marrying your husband! What *is* this?'

I shrugged. 'A parallel,' I could only say.

And then, do you know, I flopped. All the attack went out of me. Perhaps I simply did not know what to say next—after all, I could hardly resuscitate all the detail, which she would obviously deny? But I think, too, that other frustrations arose: the fact that really I was only enquiring about something I knew nothing about, that my real instinct should have been simply to say: 'Your conditions are unacceptable. The deal with Mark is off.' And slam out with a smile.

All hindsight. We are continually saying what we would or should have done. The fact is that just then, faced with that woman's well-kempt elegance, I became suddenly conscious of beach-tar hidden on the sole of my foot, of a still raw 'V' on my chest from the first days' sudden sunburn, of my ear-rings pinching and of my hellish hair clotted with sand and sea and God knows what else. Wine and paint stains enlivened my trousers, my sandals had a buckle missing. All very hale and hearty for quay life—but not here, oh no not here. I just felt awkward, inferior, gross: and instead of increasing resentment and fight, as it might quite easily have done in other circumstances, it deflated me.

Why? I suppose really it ran deeper—that I did not really know what to say. I mean, I couldn't blurt out: 'What do you want of my husband, Contessa?'

Nor could I go whining into a plea: 'How could you want to

upset two young lives, madame? Do you *know* what you are doing?'

Nor did it seem, after all, the right moment to theorise: 'Whether art copies life or life copies art, my dear Renata, is hardly the point—without life first, art can be of no use. And where would be our life etc., etc. . . .'

So I sat speechless while she rose and began to move to and fro—it was hardly pacing with her—and described to me the conception and quality of the film she projected. She plainly wanted to excite me creatively with the thing. Personally, I find that any description of work in progress is no damn good at all. It is not so much what you do, as how you do it, that makes a work of art. No synopses with me. So while she went on moving to and fro, emphasizing points with a flutter of her hands, turning on me suddenly to declaim—all of it done, I must say, rather beautifully—all I did was pick at a callous on my finger, undress her, and dress her again in the kind of erotic decorations she might have used for the entertainment of the unfortunate husband number 2. (Why had Rinaldi said it was a friend of his? When he must have known I could find out—or already knew—his identity? Delicacy? Shame? Even habit—telling the story to strangers, loving it in a perverse, or even still horrified way? People are not predictable, not at all.) Anyway, I dressed the unsuspecting schnozzle's naked body in all manner of furs, jewellery, silks and leathers, straps and chains and, growing wilder, the sudden tall hat of a chef—at which I must have made a little gasp, for I remember she rounded on me and said:

'Ah, that interests you! A combination of essences from both Hamlet and Faust! But for the truly heroic, the heroically human, this is conceivable—'

I did manage: 'Why not throw in Ben Hur?' so that she threw her arms wide, embracing the whole wide world to say: 'You laugh! But why not? Everything is at first conceivable. You try, you reject. I am no miniaturist.'

Nor indeed was she, with her theory that all truly great works depend on a central hero, and she would build such a figure tremendously indeed, and project it not only in one film but all over the place in different media. Mark had mentioned a television series and an opera ballet, he had not said that they were all to be repetitions or extensions of one theme: and now this woman was saying, why, over the years they put this or that historical fiction—like your Hamlet—into ballet form, modern dress, this that and the other . . . why should I wait? Why should I not do it all now? And have him painted, she added. And feed him into advertisements. Everything, high and low.

And bore the tits off everyone, I was thinking.

'You think it would bore people? Not on your life. Things go so quickly nowadays. You must create a vogue and slam, slam, *slam* it . . .' and on and on she went, while I sat cursing myself for even listening to her.

She was doing me the honour, I supposed, of working quite hard on me. I was being given my due position as a hurdle of some eminence. Then erect yourself, girl! Say something, do something! But like her reiterant Hamlet I was irresolute and dilatory: and Mark was like her bloody old Faust selling his soul to the devil, Art, Mammon . . . yet Hamlet had finally gone into action, schemed, planned, acted—and what had it gained him?

'So you see, darling, it is a truly great enterprise! You would not want to come between your brilliant husband and this fine future for him?'

My little voice was surrounded by silence. 'Yes,' I said. It was so small, I might have been saying 'no'.

'Then you will think about it,' she smiled,'I know you will.' Cooing to a child.

And the awkward, dirty big child rose to its feet and put on a last petulance:

'I came here to see if we could compromise. I don't see any

one good reason why a wife shouldn't follow her husband's work wherever he goes. Good God—it's too absurd to think otherwise!'

Softly, very softly: 'But, my dear, I *am* otherwise.'

I left. She came downstairs with me, a final act of gracious propitiation. As the door closed behind me, I did at least hear a sudden crescendo from her as she began screaming at the servants for letting me in. Drearily I congratulated myself for upsetting her, and faced the blanket heat and the long road down.

The little town looked beautiful from up there. Neither sandal-shops nor little grey cars visible, only the apricot roofs, the blue dome, the blazing blue sea. It made me feel more lost than ever.

10

WE SAT by the crayfish cases. When the beach was too full, as now in this heat wave, we often climbed out over the rocks past the yacht harbour and used this reasonably depopulated part as our watering place. You could dangle your legs in the cooling sea above the long wooden boxes with their clawed prisoners, wondering that your defenceless toes stayed safe with so many pincers just a few feet away: but the cages were planked and submerged, you couldn't see anything.

Other pincers awaited you, though. Sharp pincers of rock, the needles of sea-urchins. Rock bathing is never what it sounds, the diving in delicious but the clambering back awkward and dangerous, and that morning I both cut my ankle badly and got an urchin needle in a toe. Mark was sweet about it, bending down to suck the needle out and carefully wiping my blood up at the same time.

But the little black point wouldn't budge. 'Don't know how they do it,' he finally gasped. 'Sorry I'm such a poor sucker, though the blood's naturally delicious. Come on, let's get you back to the iodine bottle.'

'They do a lot with their mouths round here,' I said. 'What with Renata and that octopus.'

It slipped out. We hadn't mentioned her for a whole day. This was unnatural enough, considering the issue involved. But I had never told him about my visit. And the guilt was mounting. I can see now that this was not only wicked but foolish. Inaction can be as active as action. I was nursing a hate that grew and most importantly I was being dishonest. Quite obviously honesty between husband and wife is not only the best policy but the only one. Yet at the time, absurdly, I excused myself because of the hot weather . . . later, later, I said just as dishonestly to myself.

Mark now said nothing, but grunted about iodine again.

'Oh, it can wait,' I said. 'It's too hot to go back now. You know darling, I've been thinking—about Renata and her splendid job—and I've really come round to your point of view, perhaps you shouldn't take it after all.'

He nodded. But gave me a quick shrewd glance which as quickly cleared to a vague look out at the horizon. 'Oh?' he said.

'Perhaps we're better off as we are. Besides, you'd be going very much into the unknown. You wouldn't really know whether the whole thing might not collapse. Films, foreign soil—all that.'

'That's not the point. There'd be a firm contract. An even firmer advance payment.'

So he had indeed been giving it further consideration? And why not? Surely it was natural enough with such a momentous proposition, even if you're still going to refuse?

'The point,' he went on, now making his voice lazy again, stretching back, gazing out into the blue, 'is surely still us? Our life together. Of course,' he added, 'one must also think about children.'

'Whose?'

'Ours. We could have them.'

'With you in Italy and me in London?'

'I mean afterwards. I mean, we could afford them.'

'But Mark—other people afford children, in any case?'

He nodded vaguely. And abruptly tacked.

'Of course, when you come to think of it, it would be a tremendous chance, too. I mean, giving one's ambitions a chance, leaving the rat-race, too.'

'*Exchanging* the rat-race.'

Again a ruminative nod.

'Of course, one could get round her ridiculous conditions, I'm sure.'

'Are you?'

'Of course.' And 'when you come to think of it'. Phrases denoting discussion, life in the abstract: I added them up and calmed down inside me. My old Mark was only doing what a million husbands and wives do — keeping a discussion going for its own sake. I mean, previously he had been against the whole thing, and now that I seemed against it, he immediately became for. It was academic, and shortly I let myself be led to the iodine.

A long hot bad day again. Everyone in the place was weighed down and listless. Bad temper abounded, even among the natives. Women pressed their heads, men sweated and glared. The tobacco shop woman was more pleased than ever to have no stamps, the salami shop was deserted. The pizza-baker came up for air, found none, and went back; a lot of little fans like ping-pong bats were selling like cool cakes, and the holiday-makers had stepped up their drinking, proving at least that this was possible.

The Mafia had their striped city jackets off, we passed the boat-hirer and even he was too hot to give us his usual spate of admonition. Only Geoffrey de seemed normal, giving us a busy wave and going tilt-headed about some nameless business — but I expect he was simply pretending, an old hand knows heat.

We passed the butch and she gave me a huge wink. Mark saw it and said, 'Hello, a new little friend?' in a facetious way, and that buttoned me up further. The sky was dark blue with heat, it pressed down like a painted ceiling, the whole place seemed to be getting too small.

A long hot sleepless rest, the shutters still closed against the morning sun and so stifling any breath of air that might have blown up. There was no iodine, I put brandy on my cut, tried to dig the needle out with a scissors point, put scent on the resultant mess. The scent then stifled the room further, and by the evening, which was for once not much cooler, I was saying to Mark: 'And you think you can compose in a country like this?'

'It's not like this all the year round.'

'This or something else. Smog in Milan.'

'You're speaking as if I've decided.'

'Isn't there a "we" about?'

And then I exploded quietly, bringing up the unmentionable:

'You realize, of course, you'll be popping into bed with her? In the course of duty?'

'Julie!'

'It's pretty obvious that's how things go.'

'Don't be silly.'

'Don't be naïve.'

'Christ, you're making a fine mountain out of a molehill.'

'Some molehill. It's like being married to a male whore.'

'For God's sake.'

And then I'm afraid I went on about gigolos and heaven knows what else and it all blew up into a row with more edge on it than usual, and dinner that night was a silent sulk. I drank too much wine, nervously, repressedly, and then the ice ran out, and then I ran out on him — or at least, swept up saying I was going for a walk.

I went down to that bar where on the festa night I had seen them together. This time I stood inside looking out through the same door frame at the dark square of night.

Into which, like a doomed moonbeam, there presently walked the figure of my dear Renata in a silver pyjama affair: walked past.

I gave her three minutes — three hot swollen minutes in that desolate bar with only a poster of a sizzling Morocco on its empty yellow wall — and then hurried back to the restaurant where I had left Mark. We had been sitting at a table on the street. He was gone.

So I went on back to our room, looking in all the cafés on the way, smiling grimly at people I knew, on and on, limping now, sweating as hell, until home—and again no Mark. The room, strewn as usual with clothes, felt suddenly, tearfully empty.

Then I heard the sound of the shower outside. I ran to it and flung open the door. Anyone might have been in it. But it was him. And there with the water showering down I almost fell into his arms, hugging him and kissing him in a kind of slavish relief, drenched through and happy again.

The water itself was lovely, not only refreshing but a kind of turbulent other element. If you have ever made love outside in the hot summer rain, say in a thunderstorm, you will know what I mean.

But the next day he was really gone.

II

LOOKING back, it is difficult to see what was or was not planned. For instance, the next morning we got up early. This was natural enough in a heat-wave, to enjoy the first few coolish hours. But then we decided on something not so natural in a heat wave, in fact to fight the thing, to force ourselves to go about our previous almost daily routines, to work separately in the morning and not meet before a late lunch. The last few days of heat had been all slop. We had to discipline ourselves again—to be able to enjoy the free hours the more.

But who suggested this first? I can't remember. Most often such day-to-day ideas come out of general talk, with no one acutely proposing anything.

And then our love-making the night before—this was suddenly, how can I say, *voracious*. It had about it a wild hunger hardly to be expected from a couple devoted and regularly satiated over our seven years. It had about it a tragic grasping of the minute, as I see it now—something like those fiercely yearning embraces of lovers parting on a railway platforms. That night I put it down simply to emotion following our row. Plus the heat, plus that evocative shower: plus my feelings of guilt. Now, of course, I can put it all down to Mark. His own and much darker guilt. Or, if I like, to his intense love.

We had our coffee at seven. I said I was going up to the little votive chapel on the hill to sketch the interior. Cool, at least, I said. 'And what are you up to?'

'Oh,' Mark said vaguely, and his following remark I do remember very clearly: 'I've a number of things I want to do.'

Or do I remember it clearly? It was the kind of thing he

often said, his kind of work being so difficult to explain at all, let alone in detail. Anyway, off I went up the parched and scraggy hill to the white pimple of a chapel, leaving him to get on with whatever beep-and-glup he had in mind.

The votive chapel was, of its nature, touching. Simple pleas for divine help were hung about — bandages, a war medal, a handkerchief, a long bent nail, flowers of immortal plastic. Objects of intercession or trophies from miraculously-avoided accidents, they hung humbly — yet because of their incongruity, and a kind of nameless isolation, they had an oddly hapless look for symbols of good fortune. Yet each contained a heart's whole desperate desire. This was made clear by paintings crowding one wall, many of them primitive pictures of small boats in a storm, one of a wall collapsing just short of a human figure, another of an overturned motorcycle, one simply of a severed rope with a noose and emblazoned with a military escutcheon — some failed hanging of a prisoner in the war? Simple paintings, some gifted, some grotesquely lifeless — but all, all touching in the fervent measure of wish or gratitude that inspired them. As a non-believer it seemed to me that I would be more affected by them than a regular Roman, who might, though devoted, take them as part of a sensibly practical routine.

But I might also have identified myself with them, just then, as one who had narrowly missed a disaster. In any case I sat and drew happily there that morning. The chapel was not big enough to be chilled like a church, but it was coolish, and quiet, lonely and nourishing. Though there were problems, particularly in trying to reproduce the effect of those other paintings — which was quite impossible. Try to be naïve and you end with a double layer of sophistication.

The noon bells rang out, one tolling beautiful and silver — no, golden in that heat, and why 'silver' in any case? — another the stipulated few minutes later from far up the hills, dead and poor as a dustbin lid; and I packed up my things and began the long stroll down in the heat. Stroll it was, I was definitely limping now with that urchin needle.

I was back by twelve-thirty, early for us, and naturally enough Mark was not there. But the room was different, marvellously cleaned up and clear of the clothes he always left lying about: that's that Angelina, I thought, being truly angelic for once, and I was so pleased with her I went straight down to the street again and bought her a bag of chocolate bars. No good giving her money, I thought, Mamma mia will only get that.

I found her, pale and tired-looking as usual, swabbing out the shower. When I thanked her, in my lame Italian, she looked surprised and even shook her head — but I put this down to our very usual incommunication, and she was plainly delighted with the chocolate, going so far as incomprehensibly to hope the signore would have a good journey.

Which became abruptly comprehensible in the next few minutes when, back in that orderly room of ours, I found Mark's letter to me. It was propped up on the table where earlier there would have been light, but now was in shadow from the drawn blinds. As soon as I saw it the doomed feeling struck.

For a whole minute I let it lie there. And went about stowing my sketches away in a chest of drawers, to conform with our new neatness. I kept on looking back at the letter, wondering. But of course really postponing it.

My darling Ju,

I don't suppose you will like reading this letter any more than I like writing it. So I'll begin by saying I'm sorry, oh so very sorry that it has to be like this. But I felt that if we talked any more on the subject, we'd still be going round in circles. The only consolation I have is that, thinking of all you've said, you were more in favour of the project than against it.

So this morning I went up to Renata's and signed the contract. It meant leaving immediately. I think I would have left immediately in any case, as we both dislike tearful partings and only further indecision would have followed. I go by train to Rome, and fly to Milan in the afternoon. What a pisolino, my darling!

I'll send you my address in Milan as soon as I know it. In the meantime, you *might* get me at the above—though it is probably a forwarding affair, it is just the office where I am to show up.

I don't of course know what you'll be doing. Staying on or cutting it short. But since there's only a week more, I'll write at length to home.

So, more soon. Don't take this too badly, my heart. It's horrible leaving you like this, but I do think I'm doing the right thing.

All my love, always, always,
Mark

Well. Well, first the desolate emptiness punches at your stomach, a hollow drag like the curse, and so you sit down and then you stand up and walk about and then you sit down again and read it through. And again.

No time for tears. Only a desperate now-ness about it— disbelief in the thing, yet a dreadful desperate realization that this is happening to me, to me now, this kind of thing that happens to other people and just couldn't happen to me, now, yet has happened to me. Now.

Terribly alone suddenly, loneliness striking like a storm. A friend to talk to? None, Mark was the friend I talked to. And then, in those first not numb but small hunch-shouldered moments, I didn't blame him at all. I felt he was doing the right thing, I felt it out of habit perhaps, I felt he was simply dealing best with a bad situation. I went to the wardrobe and took the brandy bottle out, then put it back, and read the letter again.

In ten minutes I was saying, blast the bloody man, the stinking bloody double-faced man. How on earth could he do it, with me and our trust? Our lovely trust in each other—and write such a letter, with its bloody awful excuses all the way. He *couldn't* have really thought I wanted him to go, I'd only said that at the beginning. He *couldn't* just say we both hated tearful partings, and just slip away avoiding them. He *couldn't* . . . but he had.

Then I was blubbing to myself, my Mark, my Mark, my lovely Mark, it must have been my fault, I've let him down. I've been dilatory and not put my foot down and I kept things from him and perhaps she even told him and objected to my interference and demanded a yes or no there and then. When? Had she telephoned us earlier that morning? I had left Mark there. But then—

—but then, and this was the worst of all as the thought really rammed home, it was most unlikely and that left the likely thing that Mark had known probably all yesterday and all last night, and it was all planned and he had acted at me, kept it from me, held this all in secret from me . . .

And for a moment I was thinking, how dreadful for him, how *dreadful* for him to do this, but that was only a brief moment and I was really mostly thinking of myself, how I was betrayed and how it was he, my dear love, who had done it to me, and then again how much of the betrayal was mine?

And on and on it went, round in circles in that terribly quiet and lonely room, and I crumpled up the letter and threw it away across the floor, and then picked it up and uncrumpled it, just as they do in films, and on the way I saw a sock of his, a single white sock, left in the shadow underneath a chair and this I picked up and held and looked at for a very long time and then stuffed it in my pocket.

I had that brandy then and the little fire in it braced me and I went downstairs and rang the Renata palazzo. The Contessa had left. I asked where to, when, to what address. And I couldn't understand the answer, and had to call our landlady to speak for me—the first demeaning blockage, this, underlining in a second how materially alone and vulnerable I was. If the landlady hadn't been in, that would have been that. But she was. And after it seemed talking for hours, she handed the receiver to me, saying that here is the secretary who speaks English.

A man's voice, and after a few seconds I asked: 'Surely—that's Professor Rinaldi?' And it was. But it was a different Rinaldi, cold and evasive. Certainly the Contessa had left. For where? For Milan. And what was her address? A pause. 'I am sorry, I am not permitted to give her address.' And he added the address of the office at the head of Mark's letter. Its telephone number? 'Ah, that was difficult. Unfortunately it had just been changed, and he had not the new one to hand.'

Pride, of course, stepped in. I could not appeal. So I made it into a know-all statement: 'As you know, my husband is flying with her. And he forgot to leave the number. It is very urgent that I should know.'

'You must then ask the directory of enquiries. They might give it to you. But I do not think your husband is with the Contessa, she is driving up to Milan. She left very early this morning.'

So nothing is as simple as it ought to be. No, no. Blockages like simple traffic blocks. A world of communications, beautifully wired, usually working—until one fault intervenes, and you are left impotent, quite impotent. The whole habitually innocent but really so intricate world becomes the machine it is, and a broken machine at that: you long for the simplicity of a village street, just walking down it and calling on somebody with your enquiry. But not so, not so.

Any wife worth her salt, one may think, would have boarded the first plane and followed her husband, somehow bearded him in his new lair. One may think so indeed. One would indeed like it to be so—action is so much preferable to frustration? But was I really in the position of a bearder? Nothing was clear-cut. I had not been abandoned. I had been asked to co-operate in a mission finally to benefit both of us. By following him now I would simply nip the thing in the bud. That was how the writing ran.

But reading between the lines I knew quite well I was being asked for sacrifice. Privately I was being asked to let him bed down with the appalling Nose—at least, that was my private opinion. Publicly I was being asked to stay on ice for a very long time; not only to live without him, but to live alone, to face loneliness. Well—like a woman whose man has gone to war, and expected to get on with life? Less stringently, like a woman whose actor-husband has been given a chance in Hollywood, or touring Australia, and has to lump it? And who would have found the South Pole, if wives had not agreed on a stiff and homebound upper lip?

But I hadn't married that kind of man, I had married a man with an ordinary job, and life had simply taken this turn. Or is any job ordinary, safe from some future twist of this kind? And if I now went to Milan, would I not just be a virago or a helpless drag, according to the attitude I took?

Beneath it all, of course, was a feeling of having been tricked. And this was really what I didn't like to face. The thought that Mark had foreseen and willed it all along, despite all our discussions, despite indeed any objections he might have fabricated inside himself, deceiving himself as well as deceiving me. Intuition is a dark perceiver, intuitively I suspected him and hated myself for it: while instinct told me to protect him against everything, including now myself.

It was a bog, it was clammy. And here was Angelina standing in the shadow by the now dead telephone with an incongruous moustache of chocolate on her upper lip. Well, I thought, at least she's done well out of it. And then viciously I wanted to grab that chocolate back from her. I was being just as mixed about her moustache as this whole huge predicament: and I stood there goggling at the poor child's moustache, while from somewhere in me came chuckles of hysteria, a horrible heartless sound but near enough to laughter for Angelina to think it was and so start chuckling with me, both of us standing there laughing with each other, shaking with it, letting it get louder and louder, soon helpless with it in our absolute different ways, she delighted, me in a sick stream of release, a laughing let of poison.

I went out and sat in the garden. I had to be alone to think, and I wanted most of all what anyone and perhaps particularly a woman wants at such a time, someone to tell it to—in fact, not to be alone. But who was there? No one. It was too humiliating a story. And if I'd been at home? I ticked off in my mind a couple of close friends, but quailed at the thought of confessing it even to them. It emphasized how close Mark and I were—marriage had simply cut out others.

I sat there just alone, alone, alone.

Yet gradually found myself in company of further disquiet. It was the hottest time of day, the heat was vast. Yet none of the garish plants about drooped, they stood there in their tropical-looking spikes and curves in absolute green and yellow vigour, carved. The coloured flowers hissed brilliance. They seemed to be forcing themselves under a glass of heat. And yet were slily moving—from one or two bushes heavy seeds dropped. They dropped with the absolute plop of a ball. At long irregular intervals. For long moments, the early afternoon quiet, then—plop, the dark thing somewhere dropped. Soon it became a hammer blow. A ticking clock can be bad: this was worse, it was a kind of water torture in pure sound, you waited in silence, the suspense ballooned, it would never come, the whole air and everything and time expanded to breaking point which did not break—and then it did, plop, a release and a heavy blow at once, and then the whole thing, the silence, the expanse, the blow, began again.

Seeds dropping in a Tuscan garden—I fled upstairs to that

dreadfully-ordered room, then out to the street and somehow there was only one place to go, up to that chapel where I had been that morning, in some kind of innocence. Before the fall. And so by back streets, away from people, I plodded up. I expect my shoulders were hunched, I felt at least small and lost as a fly.

Up in the chapel I tried to pray. But it wouldn't come. Not a believer, a self-condemned lonely one, I just stood there and caught myself shaking my head slowly to and fro.

But at least, at last, the slow tears came—at first I thought they were sweat—and I found myself appealing to the pictures themselves for help. Each one contained a miracle, I was pleading for the same miracle to happen to me. Obliquely, not addressing the saint, addressing some kind of essence of miracle. I suppose it was a kind of prayer. And my hand found Mark's sock in my pocket. I took it out and hung it in a corner. Far down, away in shadow, for I was an interloper, I felt I had no right here, except perhaps if I did it very humbly, on the edge . . . the first day with the begging bowl.

I SUPPOSE I intended to go home. I even got a case out and started to pack. But just then—with my tail between my legs? The urge to act, to do something was intense—but there was also the need to sit down and think things out. There was also the heat, and by evening hunger and the need to see people, to talk to someone, anyone, about anything.

So when night fell I was down in the street again, in Tonietta's central café, and sitting—of all people—with my two lady-friends, the spangled Greens. But, with my worm inside me, how I loved them then! They were having a postcard session—scribbling away at quite a pile of those turquoise-skied glossy cards, and when first I came up the daughter had brandished two of these at me, asking me which I thought best. One was more unusual, she said, but the other really prettier, didn't I think? She asked this with tremendous concern. The decision was momentous. Instead of being irritated, I was touched—my God, what wonderfully simple lives, really worrying about these little things, worrying about choosing a ribbon for a dress—do you like the reddy pink, or would the pinky pink be better?—or whether something happened on the Wednesday, or was it the Tuesday, no the Wednesday. Whole simple lives made up of making molehills into mountains. (And I suppose they would be complaining bitterly, inside themselves, that nothing really ever happens.)

So they were refreshing in their innocent way, and the more restful for the writing, company without much talk. All the others around were a different matter—there was the usual excitation of evening, everybody was busy about having a good time somewhere, and this indeed I resented. That they should go on, quite ignorant of my troubles: the usual feeling of someone with an illness, or in pain. The opposite, oddly, to what I felt with these Greens, also utterly concerned with their daily interest.

The postcards they had written were stacked address-side up. Some were scrawled full with words, others had very a short message written diagonally to look longer—you could guess at a glance who was a friend, who an acquaintance. Then I noticed that several were addressed to our own postal district in London. The numeration looked now immeasurably sad and distant, as if it belonged to another time altogether, and without thinking I pointed to it and said, 'That's where we live.' At which both Lettice Green and her Sprout gave 'ahs' and 'ohs' of wonder, exclaimed that the world indeed was a small one, and that they lived there too. A nice little flat above their shop, a hardware shop. Hardware and these two—their spangled nicety against mops, nails, buckets, hammers! The picture almost raised my spirits.

Then followed that usual holiday tear-jerker, the exchange of addresses—honest enough wishes which will never be taken up; the holiday would soon be so distant, the daily round at home too insistent. But what daily round would I have now? My shop, my meals-on-wheelsing, the very slight seeing of scattered friends, the closer company of near acquaintances—your own part of London being as much a village as anywhere, many of your other London friends perhaps five miles away. 'You *must* come and see us! We're in the book! I'm afraid I wasn't too nice, I told them my street but not the number. On the safe side, making it difficult.

For, once at home, what of all this would remain? The detail would go. A vague sensation of blue sky and sea, a pink house or two, a few isolated incidents would be substituted. This red tin table, with its parasol-less hole in the middle, into which one neatly put scruffed sugar wrappings which instantly fell through to the ground. This background of faces, brown

laughs, glass clinks, blue smoke, opposite balconies, straw
hold-alls, pink oleanders, sand, concrete, people, cars, big
Italian words in capital letters, sandals, bracelets, hair . . . all
so immediately known, all forgotten forever under a grey
London sky, to the sound of a well-known traffic hum, to the
routine of making a well-known bed. Making a well-known bed
one side only. *That* should remind me of dear old Santa V?

'Where'th your husband?' asked the raised pigeon-shit lids
of the Sprout, very wide-eyed.

'Didn't you know?' it came out naturally. 'He's been called
away. He's left.'

'Oh you poor thing! And left you all on your lonely-ohs?
Will you stay on?' the mother cooed.

'I don't know—I, yes, I'll be going.'

'Then we'll all join up and have a meal before you go! My,
we never *knew*.'

Very different from Geoffrey, who soon came up.

'I hear Mark's gone,' he said, watching me closely, the
tilted head giving its usual quizzical effect. 'Milano, eh?'

He sat down. Why do these perpetually busy old-hands have
so much time to spare? Not to spare, but to dig for gossip. I
gave him some, more in self-defence than from generosity. 'I
think we told you the Contessa up above might offer him a job'
etc., etc. 'Well, he's gone off to sniff things out, a preliminary
sort of reconnaissance,' I went gamely on.

'Yes, I heard she'd gone, too,' he said.

Bitchy? I doubt it. Simply keeping tabs on his material. But
then I saw the two Greens whispering together, and Lettice
giving a little laugh which she quickly suppressed. The
beginning of it! I saw miles then of comment, comment,
comment, everybody, anybody talking about us. The dark
weight inside me dragged lower. I looked at them sharply,
stared to shame them; but then Lettice lent towards me and
said a most peculiar thing. Coming from her silvered eyes, her
spangled niceness:

'That's him again, over there,' she whispered. And pointed at a young man sitting across the café, bringing her orange-lacquered finger up to her cherry-darkened lips to hide the gesture. 'You do know about him, don't you?'

I'd seen him about. A good-looking young man, too good-looking in fact, stiff with it, a kind of tailor's dummy. He moved like a dummy, too, something altogether artificial about him. He was always alone. And always about, carefully dressed, when most people were on the beach.

'No?'

'Don't you know about his notebook? It's a real giggle! I don't know whether I should tell you,' she added archly, a verbal blush. 'It's rather awful.'

'Oh *do*,' I said.

'He's got a notebook full of the dates women have their you-know-whats.'

'Their — ?'

She whispered very low: 'Periods, silly. He sits up here in the mornings and watches to see who's dressed and not down bathing! Why, we're probably in it! Tonietta told me, a friend told her —'

It was so incongruous I had begun to titter, 'But why?'

'So that when he makes a pass he won't be caught out, I suppose,' she giggled, 'wasting time and money on a closed shop,' and the giggle grew, we giggled together as I felt that awful hollow glopping laugh coming on again, while Geoffrey, who saw us and hadn't heard, leaned forward to cap it, as cap it he must: 'Did you hear? Two English in Emilia, hiking — and run over by a cheese!'

'A cheese!'

Already laughing at his own joke, 'A cheese, and it broke both their legs, I mean a leg each. Of course, it was a Parmesan, a sixty-pounder.'

And we were all laughing now, it was infectious and awful, while he went on: 'But can you see it? The thing dropped off a lorry. And came spinning at them out of the blue? Can't you see—awful yellow disc coming at you, flying saucer, object from inner space . . .' and terribly we were all bellowing, but me more dangerously than them, it was that appalling hysteria again, I could hear it coming up out of me with that insistent mechanical glop, like a hot water tap bursting against an airlock, and in a second I would be raving . . . .

I was saved by a blow in the face. And I mean it literally, a sudden sharp blow of wind—it seemed to strike up from nowhere, an abrupt cyclone pretty low down, gusting up straws and paper on the street, whistling up spirals of sand and earth, shaking a pink confetti off the oleanders, and of course all very startling in the middle of that days-long windless torpor, so that the Greens were shrieking: 'Object from Outer Space now!' and Geoffrey: 'The Cheese-man cometh!' and things like that, and one great drop of rain fell spat as bird-drop in the middle of my forehead.

'Rain!' I squeaked.

Geoffrey immediately: 'Didn't you know? It clouded over hours ago. We're in for a pretty big storm. It's usually pretty fierce hereabouts when it comes.' And I looked up and saw no stars, only a heavy purple sky somehow lower than before, a little reddish with neon, and the yellow light bulbs strung in the square's two eucalyptuses were swaying now and making their lovely luminous swathe in the green leaves shimmer and shake like silk.

The rain came down like rods.

Silver rods against the purple night, drumming down hard, rattling anything metal, heavier it seemed than the wind it came down so straight. But then the wind rose too, and blew it sideways, and awnings were pulled, and drenched with rain, and formed torrents, and a hundred rivulets began gurgling down the street like instant mountain streams.

Of course everyone rose with yells of panic, there was a great gathering up of glasses, cigarettes, baskets, and a rush for shelter in the café. Inside it was just like the day the hair-dresser's blew up, only now instead of striped madonnas in slips there were mostly tourists in all their eccentric holiday travesty, terrified of getting this wet. Half of them were still in beach-clothes, it wouldn't have mattered a damn if they were soaked through, well within reach of a change of clothes in their hotels, pensions. But all piped and squeaked disaster, as if Jove himself were above, and the bar itself became packed with bodies and reaching arms and all the frustrated panic of a theatre bar in its dreadful interval. It was like an earthquake, rather than a drop of rain.

My cigarette was soaked through, I stood there sucking at the grey thing and tasting wet tobacco and feeling my hair clammy and flat. While beside me the Greens gave out the inevitable, 'Nice weather for ducks', as brightly as if they had just thought up this monumental cliché, and Geoffrey was going on very gravely about the maize crop and the vines, and I—I of course was in a mood to take it personally, as another stroke of a now inimical fate, a further dimension of something ended. Holiday and heat. All now changed.

Out of the corner of my eye I saw that handsome young wolf of notebook fame go up to a girl and brandish a stumpy little brolly at her—had he carried this so symbolic means of introduction throughout the heat-wave? And the awful mechanical laugh started up in me again. Luckily Geoffrey stopped it by asking me what I was going to do now, stay on or go, and could he perhaps take me for a spin into the country sometime, there were the Etruscan tombs, and a quattrocento walled townlet of some distinction? It was very kind of him, and I felt suddenly that, knowing all, he would know of my unhappiness. I had at least the sensation of an ally—though in practical terms useless—and felt calmer for it.

The rain drummed down steadily outside, it set in quite plainly for a night's downpour, and the crowd in the café settled down with their drinks for a night's pour-in. It soon became as animated as the festa-night. A few left, women going out into the rain with anything to cover their hair, newspapers, baskets, like women with classical amphorae on their heads, only bent forward and running not so classically. The men absurdly put their little shirt collars up, if they had them. The rest stayed put and made their abysmal festa of it. Naturally, after the first excitement, they who had previously grumbled about the heat now cursed this refreshing downpour; it would spoil their beach life. Then, as the conviviality increased, they forgot to grumble. I left.

It is a familiar dichotomy with loneliness—you want company desperately, but in despair you cannot stand it. It is also familiar that even when you are in deep trouble yourself, and suffering, with no way out, an inane sense of drama can possess you beyond the suffering. Perhaps this even is a kind of way out—anyway, people are always jumping out of themselves to watch themselves play the scene set for them, and goddammit if on that night as I walked back through the pelting rain I did not straighten my body to it, let my arms hang straight to my sides, stare very straight ahead, raise my chin, relish the sacrificial drenching, welcome the turbulence of the elements.

So like a lost girl-figure in an old Belgian film, I strode the lonely street home to loneliness: a sludge of wet grey concrete dust, sand and earth made a bog underfoot; once with my head too high I slipped and waded calf-deep in a sudden lake, and then the drama changed, and I saw myself limping hunch-shouldered through the drenched dark like every forlorn waif the world has ever known.

All the time I was thinking—twenty-four hours ago I was drenched through, too, with my love, under the shower, my dear good bloody gone love . . . .

At home—upstairs in the curiously dry room, the sodden clothes on the floor round me—a cramping and material emptiness reminded me I had forgotten to eat. All right, the hell with eating? Lost, abandoned, I had no appetite? But I had. I thought of Angelina's chocolate, blast her—but no, they all went to bed at nine. Not a bite since breakfast—if I didn't eat, I wouldn't sleep. Would I sleep, anyhow? The only thing to do was to dress again, and make the long plod back to buy a pizza or something.

So like a cold wet bathing suit the clammy clothes went on again, dry ones would have been absurd, and I walked all the way back. No drama this time. It was just a long dull chore, like all the worst times—missing a train and waiting on a country platform at night, running out of petrol and walking miles with a can. It would end, one always thought, sometime. When I did get to the pizza-shop, another rain-festa was going on. It was full, the oven-heat had attracted the rain-sodden. Among them, the purple professor-butch, not so sodden in a white plastic halo all over her face like an ogre's in a pixie-hood. But she was charming and kind and made a fuss of me in my so obviously half-drowned state. It was what I wanted, it nearly made me cry. When she asked me home, just round the corner, I very nearly said 'yes', I wanted to crawl into anyone's arms.

That was avoided; but then there occurred a little scene which was to presage one of the silliest acts of my whole life. Not then, the next day.

Two men burst in out of the rain. Locals, fishermen or port-workers, the capable type you always saw dressed in workaday blue trousers and white singlets—but now they seemed incapably excited, gesticulating wildly at the pizza-man and streaming with words as they steamed with rain. Near to the ovens, a little white mist rose from them. I kept on catching the word *aragosta*, crayfish. Over and over again, that word which to us sounds rather ridiculous, making those angry-looking whiskered creatures so arrogant.

The butch looked startled. 'That's bad,' she said, 'very bad.'

'What? What's bad?'

'The what-do-you-say, lobster-pots? They've broken. The sea's risen and broken them. It must be rougher than I thought. The lobsters have escaped. That's very serious for these men, they're very valuable, those creatures.' And with her finger and thumb she made the lire sign at me, gravely indeed.

That night I slept badly. Worry, of course, and the sudden weight of a couple of pizza. But whenever I woke up a strange new sound came echoing through the dark from outside—the surging crash and roll of surf. Distant, a momentous soft-shoe shuffle. The Mediterranean blue receded, I was alone in a room in a grey Cornish fisher-town, dark and threatening.

The surf echoed insistently, terribly regular, tolling a kind of doom from the wide black endless sea outside. And doomed it certainly was.

13

OTHER lovers slash clothes, wardrobes full of them. I slash—
but let me try to explain what made me do it.

First, I was up early again. Badly slept, but unable to go on
sleeping, I went down to the port to have coffee. The rain had
stopped, but the old blue sky was now grey-white with cloud;
it was like a dismal northern day, warmer of course, but
stripped of colour and radiance. Ochres and pinks looked
oddly drab, and everything, café-tables and awnings and
gutters and pavements were still wet. Not glistening, no sun
for that, simply dishcloth wet.

But busy as usual in the cool of early morning. No beach-
clothed tourists about, only the natives putting their shop in
order. In this sense, a refreshing sight—*real*, as one says.

And I sat there in a real temper. Badly slept, which gave me
a cloudy head, but nevertheless with the vigour of a new day
and at least some sleep. I had woken with that empty place by
my side in the bed, my stomach had fallen, but now, alone in
the grey air, my gorge was risen. God damn him, I could only
think, that was not the way for a husband to behave, not under
any circumstances. As one does, I sat there chewing over all I
had thought the day before, over and over again, perhaps more
clearly in this rinsed air, but more bitterly too. I broke a nail
opening a little sugar bag, the urchin needle in my foot was
still painful—it never rains but it pours, I growled glumly at
the wet grey, and let hate grow.

It was all somehow busier than usual. Why? Then I
noticed a sort of coming and going towards those rocks out by
the yacht-harbour, the rocks Mark and I used to go to. And in
the sea by them, a diving of bodies and a bobbing of heads. Of
course, the broken crayfish cages.

'All men out today,' the café waiter said, pointing at them. 'Catching *aragoste*—' and he made a pincer sign with both his hands at me.

'All men in Santa Vilga—go swim today like tourist. Why you not go too, missy?'

This seemed to him a huge joke, he bubbled with laughter, making his nipping movements.

To cut it short—I did. I don't really know why to this day—a need for action of any kind? A way of avoiding the day and its misery of indecision? Anyway, I got up abruptly and prepared myself for the lobsters.

I'd already got the habitual swimsuit on under my jeans, and now I stalked off to that boat-hirer to get an aqualung. We'd done it before. 'You're in luck, signora,' he said, 'the last one. Big demand today.' Grave, and probably double-grave at having had to hire most of his apparatus out at cut-price, even lending it, to the unfortunate crayfish catchers.

I didn't go right out to the rocks, there was too much of a crowd there, I'd only be in the way, stick out as a woman and a nuisance of a foreigner; I worked it out that if those bristling slow blue crawlers had got free they would have had plenty of time by now to get much further away from the rocks themselves. One would have a chance of finding them anywhere.

So I dropped off my clothes and began adjusting the equipment. The sea was grey, with a long sullen swell. No longer pitching, but rolling and grumbling inside itself like a great grey body recovering from fever. Yet it was all fresh, refreshing. The heat-wave lifted, the air rinsed. I took deep breaths of the air and felt better, felt better too for doing something, even swimming after crayfish; and it was good, too, to feel one might be of some help to these people in trouble.

Over by the rocks they were diving in, disappearing, bobbing up again, very occasionally brandishing one of the black-looking beasts in a raised hand. All to a wild sing-song of excited cries, a high-pitched human music that was blown

157

across to me like the cries of gulls. Suddenly it all seemed very funny, a comic opera event: every able-bodied man in the place throwing up everything to go diving for blue treasure. A panic, really, of greed. I thought of the arrogant charges they made, remembered the many succulent beauties we had seen in restaurants and been unable to afford. And here was the whole place gone mad for all this money crawling about the bottom of the sea. I suddenly yelped aloud with laughter.

Then I saw the *Spada*. On a blue day, without distraction, she would have been the first thing to notice. Instead of being tied up with the other masts swaying together at the quay, she had been anchored alone and a little way out. Why? No room? Or had something happened in the night? Anyway, there she was, isolated, still sheltered by the harbour promontories of curving rock and quay, but all alone and, of course, magnificent. A long black hull, expensively polished brown teak above, a winking of brass and of white equipment. She was bigger than anything else there, and very beautiful. I envied and loathed the thing. For one aberrated second I saw myself climbing aboard with a tin of kerosene and a good dry match — a scene from a television film. Just then a dinghy put off from her, it had been hidden on the other side. The sailor we knew rowed, the back seat was weighed down by a fine fat mamma with a shopping basket, probably his wife. Lucky I didn't burn them too, I thought; adjusted the harness and knife belt, fixed the mask and dived in.

Down below, the water was no clear fairyland of aqueous green. It was like a Victorian pea-souper. The storm, of course, had whipped up sand and mud. There was the rain, too, that would have sent rivers of earth through the drains and into the sea. For a few blind seconds, I didn't know what to do. But automatically swam on, and then, as my eyes grew used to it, began to see a little more clearly, see vague foggy shapes of weed and rock and sudden clean patches like dells in a wood — but much-picnicked-upon dells, scattered with old cans and bottles and ghostly drifts of paper. It was a sad, muddy sight.

I weaved about, keeping as close to the bottom as I safely could: there were occasional quivers of small fish, once a small octopus coursing along like a sodden ball of wool, but no crayfish. I wondered whether I could have spotted one in any case. Then in a clear patch a short white conch-like shell moved—I saw the leg of a hermit crab dragging from it, and knew that if this was visible then surely a crayfish would be. So I swam on.

The breathing was going well, the easy scissoring of legs invigorating—I felt sinuous and lulled and for the moment free, that upper world cut out. The mists of mud about, I was encased, and much of it was beautiful in its strange way. On an ordinary day in still clear water, things had a glassy, artificial look—too highly-coloured, too good to be quite true. Now there was mystery, strange shapes came and went, weeds weaved indistinctly as shadows; there was a khaki reality, all the coloured uniforms changed for the mud-coloured dress of battle action. Then I swam against a rope, a line.

At least, I first saw an anchor. It was a double-pronged affair, its black legs grappling into the bottom like a big crab-thing—which I first thought it was, a monstrous sort of sea-spider, too big, too horrifying, so that I swerved quickly away and then brushed against the line securing it at a diagonal stretch. There was a heavy black cloud overhead. It could only have been the *Spada*.

I clung onto the line and without a moment's thought drew the knife out of its sheath. Why without thought? The odd isolation? An onrush of expertise, power? The temptation of all lines—to fray and cut them? Even the very tautness of this one? Or was it simply the ease of it, being handed the whole thing down there on a watery plate?

Whatever it was, down in the cold water I boiled over and slashed and sawed hard at the hempen thing. It parted, the top floated away, and with it, instantly on the move, that cloud above.

I was exultant—sly too. I swam fast for that line again, caught it, and began to fray it with the knife. A clean cut would have looked obvious. Then I flicked myself back to fray the end by the anchor. Obvious, too, if anything afterwards was to be suspected.

I kicked off as fast as I could in the direction of the rocks, now looking wildly for a crayfish, praying hard for one, my whiskered alibi. And I got one. There are times, when you are full of spirits and will and desire, riding high, when things do at last go absurdly right, when you seem indeed to will them to be right—like catching a train by the skin of your smiling teeth, like a taxi from nowhere in the small of the night. Like getting the last aqualung, like this navy-blue laggard just sitting and waiting on the sea-bed.

No difficulty in gripping it, but hard to hold underwater. So I bubbled to the surface, and held it high, paddling along with my left hand—not far, and then as they saw this blonde mermaid in the gas-mask holding up another couple of thousand lire a great cry of welcome came, hoorays and gold teeth all round. I got up the rocks all right, and gave it them to a chorus of thanks. The only woman there, I certainly made my mark. Alibi complete: I was only there for the crayfish.

I walked away, and only then risked a glance at the *Spada*. She was well away from her original position, drifting steadily seawards. No one else seemed to have noticed: but then she might well have been dawdling out under power, with the helmsman just popped below for a second or two. The sea was open.

Then, as I got to my clothes, three things happened. First, I saw the *Spada*'s sailor rowing as fast as he could out from the harbour quay, shouting something at the top of his voice. Then a woman, the plump signora from the dinghy, came running along the quay waving her basket and also shouting. 'Bambino . . . Bambino! . . .' came out shrill and clear.

And the *Spada* had turned in towards the outer arm of the rocks. She had simply swung round—a gust of wind, a current? —and was already only twenty feet or so from the sharp piled-up grinders, concrete blocks, jagged rocks. A moment ago in the clear, as if to sail forever out to sea, and now her length swinging round had eaten half the distance from the rocks.

I stood nailed. A wrecked boat, a baby aboard, the sea not rough—but that powerful swell . . . and me, *me* to blame . . .

The men out there were already clambering over the rocks further out to where the boat would strike—there were many of them, thank God. Then I found myself dressed, with the lung strapped up for carrying—instinctively I must have started running away then. And now I did just that. But slowly, slowly—running away inside myself at a most studied casual walking pace.

The small yacht quay had never seemed so long, I didn't dare look round. Then at last at the end I stopped and pretended to fix a sandal, squinting carefully back. The *Spada* had struck. Her bows were perched up and tilted on the rocks, like a toy boat. How so high? Striking on the top of the swell? But the men were already there, a couple of them easily aboard. The baby would be safe.

I took the lung back, paid, and began to walk quicker home. There was no question now, I had to get out of the place, and fast. I was frightened, the guilt was greying up inside me, I was a worm, I was lost, I was alone in a foreign place among enemies . . . and there was the post office, and I nearly ran in to do what surely I ought to have done yesterday, telephone Mark.

I began to explain about the number. But already the man behind the desk was spreading his arms and saying, impossible, impossible. The lines were all down. The storm. No service until the afternoon, perhaps, perhaps. Then he looked at me closely—'Signora Forster?' And smiled. 'You are fortunate. Last night, before the rain, a telegram, no, two telegrams.'

I scrambled them open, read them in the street still walking, still running inside myself.

'ARRIVED SAFELY ALREADY BUSY MUCH COMMOTION WRITING ADDRESS HOME HOPE YOU ALL RIGHT ALL LOVE MARK

And the second, just:

I LOVE YOU MARK

They had their effect. Buoys, life-savers. My eyes filled, I felt protected, I walked home faster.

I paid our bill, endured the woman's near-tears and interminable distress at my leaving, told her I was following my husband to Milan (already diverting my pursuers), ran upstairs to get my frog-feet and goggles to give Angelina, sent her for a taxi, ran up to pack. Never so quickly done, an hour's packing flung in by the end of ten minutes.

A last look round that fatal room, a long look through the window at the garden, the pink houses about. They looked strangely reserved, all concerned only with another day.

Angelina and her mother came out to wave me away, I cursed them smiling, this was not the quiet slipping off I wanted — but it was a real taxi, no ice-cream three-wheeler, and I settled down at a sly slant in the back to hide myself.

I wanted to tell the driver to avoid the main street, but felt it would sound suspicious. Early still, a few people about. Tonietta's empty — except of course for Geoffrey. Hidden as I was, he spotted me and waved. I nearly ricked my neck looking the other way, and we were past.

Then the brakes screamed, we had to stop and start edging past a parked van and an oncoming car. It was terribly slow. I suddenly found myself staring into Rinaldi's face, he was driving the other car. He never smiled. He must have been telephoned and was driving hard down to the yacht harbour, in any case he was distracted by this precarious edging past — but of course I made it into an accusation. He had seen my luggage, was all I could think.

Out of the town and up the hill and on top the driver

stopped again. He brandished a parcel at me and asked whether he might please deliver it to the house just there? I had to nod. He even turned the engine off, and I sat to wait in silence. Actually, now there was not all that hurry. It was a twenty-minute drive to the station inland, and the Rome train would not be there for an hour yet.

So poised above my dear old Santa Vilga again, I looked down for the last time at the sunny rooftops bathed in grey. And despite everything, my guilt, my hurry, all my unhappiness, that curious regret on leaving a holiday place took charge and shed a private sunlight over all that scene. Just there, we were above about the only olive grove in the place. But now it seemed this little Italian port was all olives, and palms, and flowers on the balconies and coloured houses . . . concrete and traffic were forgotten, cola signs and sandal shops never existed . . . false romance burgeoned like an old photograph of the place on a sunny day, and the familiar feeling came of never, never again. Already in the past, it was treasured and bathed in golden regret.

Until I made out the yacht harbour, and a minute black hulk like a dead blue-bottle lying out by one of the rock pincers, and smaller boats all round it like ants . . . and my heart and stomach bumped, the taxi-driver came back, and I was only glad to be off and out of the dangerous, inimical place.

A bad journey home. The train was late, and then crammed with laughing soldiers. A uniform of any kind was just what I didn't want to see. Charmingly, I suppose, they tried to flirt with me, gave up a seat for me. Among the kitbags, it was a long two hours. At last left to myself, I read and re-read those two telegrams. And by now read between the lines, they were no longer buoys but only messages of Mark's guilt. They were saving him, not me.

On the Rome station, a long trudge to the central hall carrying my two suitcases. No sign of the handsome, polished stranger who steps up and charmingly offers to carry your bags, dear young lady. No, only falling into step with a pleasant young Scot with a whole tent on his back and what looked like a couple more in either hand. But at least he knew where the post office was, and managed to jerk his head in its direction.

Post office full. Debating whether to taxi to consul, embassy, to ask them to telephone for me. No, a private matter. Then taxi to Central Post Office, all the way down to the pot-boiling centre? More bag carrying. And at first no telephone number to be found for that address. Then the number found. And found to be engaged. And while waiting a sudden panic about a seat on the plane. Postpone the telephone, another bag-laden search for a taxi. In one at last, interminable traffic blocks – all Rome driving to and from lunch in sheeplike herds of little grey humpbacked cars. At the airline office, taxi can't wait, out with bags again. But at least a ticket available – on an early afternoon plane. I could get it if I rushed right now. Taxi-search again, giving up, hopeless, then hope as I found one, and the long miles of clock-watching to the airport. Checked in, with a quarter-hour to spare. At last baggage-free, a rush here and there to change a large note for coins. Into a phone box, dialling the Milan number. Clicks, buzzes, half-heard voices from all over the miles of Italy. A journey into space. And suddenly I was through! And the girl spoke English! A Mr Forster? She didn't know, she would find out. A long, long wait. The silence was very dead. Had the line gone blank? No way of telling. But then she was back, it was desolating but Mr Forster had just gone out. Was there a message, who was telephoning?

No message. His wife. Just his wife.

I wanted to ask when he would be back, what was his private number, where was he, was there any other number – but time was running out, I saw delay after delay as the girl enquired, and then probably nothing of any use – for where was the time? – so I put the receiver down.

I look back on all this now, the taxis, the baggage, the tele-phones, the long effort and frustration, because it was a blue-print of much that was to come. You cannot simply slip about big cities in foreign countries, or even your own country, with ease; you cannot get hold of people in offices when they are out half the time. You have to wait. Time and money run out. You can fail.

The plane was all right. There was one bad moment with the passport officer, bad of my own making as I suddenly envisaged the Santa Vilga police circulating my name. But once in the plane I felt safer. Until imagination started again – what had actually happened to that baby aboard the yacht? Had it been thrown off its cot, injured, killed? What fearful little stove and scalding water had been left on? Bambino – baby, small boy? Small boy on legs? Baby on floor?

14

THE grey skies of London were blue, a warm September radiance gilded everything, trees, houses, the solider streets, with an obliquely Italian afterglow. It seemed unfair.

At home, the furniture was waiting with its familiar doglike devotion. All the chairs pointed in their usual ways, the dead telly stared a blank grey eye in its corner, the wardrobe door was half-open, just as I had hurriedly left it. Two coffee cups stood unwashed on the sink. I looked at them for a long time, and superstitiously did not touch them for days.

The mail was strewn over the doormat, I saw with horror that some of it had been chewed up by famished supermice. Mark's letter eaten by mice—that would have been it! But there was no letter from him. I was only offered a few bills, some with their totals gone forever into the tummies of my four-footed friends; also a few turquoise-skied postcards from people away on their jolly holidays. One with an Italian stamp made me nearly vomit.

So I had to face another evening alone and waiting. And this one was much worse, first with the anti-climax of home-coming, edgy with the double wishes either to go to bed for a week or get out and grasp the dear old reins of life, and secondly for me the strangeness of our empty flat. Plus now a vertiginous horror of what I had done in the long-ago earlier hours that day.

I still had a fear of being found out—though I don't think I ever really believed in this, now I was out of Italy: much more was a real terror of what I had done. When I thought of it I shivered, I could see my cigarette shaking; it was like look-ing back at some dangerous mountain road you have climbed, and icily wondering how you had ever done it; or like a missed car accident—but worse, much much worse, with no real parallel, for I had never done such a violence before, it was mad and not me at all, more like a photographed figure of someone else deep down under water with the cans and the weeds, and yet it still was incontrovertibly me, and it was me who had to live with the thought of that baby. But it was impossible to find out anything about it. In the next few days I bought Italian newspapers and searched for any yacht disaster. Nothing. I wrote to Geoffrey, slipping in a thousand-lire note for Angelina as a pretext, merrily asking him to write and tell me 'all the news'. That, if it ever came, would take days.

That night all I did was smoke, go to the window about a hundred times and stare across at the Victorian terrace houses opposite, brown brick and nothingness in bright new lamp-light, and otherwise watch the level in my air-cheap bottle of whisky go down. The telly was doing roughly what it had done three weeks before, anyhow I couldn't stand it. I couldn't telephone anybody, I hadn't made up my mind what to say about Mark yet, or I didn't trust myself to say it with the right enthusiasm.

It was intolerably lonely. I went into the kitchen and stared at the coffee cups, I went to the wardrobe and stared at his suits, touched them for some sort of morbid consolation, found a button hanging off and got some cotton and a needle but did not sew it on. Nothing seemed worth doing. The only thing was bed. But no sleep there. After a black hour I got up and unpacked. At least I could get the débris of that lovely holiday cleared away. Or fooled myself I could—holidays recede only gradually, there was stuff for the cleaners and laundry, to be returned as reminders of it all in a week's time, and then all the friends who would ask me about it. And all my private memories and fears and misery.

Mark's letter came the next day. I walked around it once or twice, as if it were a bomb, before I dared open it.

At least it was a long letter. And with a reassuring address at the top. But no telephone number. I read it not slowly like a love letter, but fiercely and fast, like a detective story, greedy for the dénouement, the solution, the way out. There was none. And by the time I had gone back and read it three times it came to no more than a long recapitulation of what he had written before, in fact a labouring long excuse for what he had done; and followed immediately—though he could not have helped this, it read most selfishly after the excuses—by a long description of how promising things were in Milan, how good the equipment was, how efficient-seeming the organization, how wildly luxurious his accommodation and how considerate in every way Renata had been. 'I've got a sunken bath, my big dove-grey bedroom looks out on an old green garden, statues, the lot—pretty good for Milan' and 'Renata drove all the way up, she says she plans as she drives. She certainly arrived here with a heavy schedule for me, all correctly ironed out.' Did she, damn her? There followed a bit about the actual work involved—he never said much about this, it was in its way unspeakable—and a bit about money. He would be keeping most of it in Italy, he said, not to spend but because it was financially 'advisable'—I could hear the soft grey click of a Swiss bank account—but he would be sending me over monthly twice and more what he ordinarily gave me. (I saw instantly it was not enough to board a plane to Milan without a dozen second thoughts, and saving up for it.) 'Early days yet,' he ended, 'to work out how we're going to see each other. But I'll soon be sounding out the possibilities, once I get to know the ropes.' 'Ropes' I shied at. And the love at the end looked now particularly useless in the circumstances, if not a downright untruth. A postscript: Would I please send on his pin-stripe and his mouse-coloured suits?

I must, I *must*, I told that letter, try to see it his way. Why? Because, for the moment, there was hardly any other.

For the moment. Anyone reading this might say, why in the hell didn't the silly bitch take a plane from Santa Vilga to Milan in the first place? Answer, bewilderment on the first day, on the second crime and its punishment of fear. Then why didn't the cow come to her senses a bit later and go over there from London, by train if necessary, during the following week? Answer not so simple, mixed up like the whole situation: firstly, money—broke after the holiday and overdrawn at the bank; secondly, pride; thirdly the unadmitted suspicion that all this money in the offing was perhaps, in the end, a good thing. It would solve a lot of things. (You will notice these answers no longer include the consideration of Mark's aesthetic ambitions: they are all *me*).

In fiction, I imagined, things would slide into place more simply, but in fact everything—like borrowing the money with a financial squeeze on, or from friends also short after the summer, or selling something off at a loss in the shop, nothing was as easy as that. Nor indeed was my mind as easily made up—in life one dithers, argues round things, sees a question first one way and then another, makes a decision in an energetic mood, discards it a few hours later in a moment of renewed doubt. None of that if the issue had been clearcut—if, say, Mark had been ill. But he wasn't, he was far too bloody well.

There were minor material problems, too, like opening up the shop again. It would be bad to open up, and then shut it again to go away: I'd get a name for irregularity. A minor matter indeed—but one of many such which added up to staying where I had put myself. So I went round and unlocked the thing. I had to go there in any case to check that everything was all right, no burglary. That meant telling a friendly colleague a few doors down, to whom enquiries had been relegated, that I was back; and a long little chat about what a good time I had had away. Fortunately, she didn't ask after Mark.

And fortunately there were few customers that morning. It was agonizing to praise a chipped Regency tray and watch that usual face fumbling about in the glaucous wallets behind its price-saddened eyes. So mostly I sat among all those familiar objects, some so well-known I loathed them—a grinning Buddha nobody would ever want (but . . . perhaps?), a merman's orgy I was sure (hoped) was a Boecklin—and mentally totted up their clearance value and how many tickets to Milan that would make up. A useless little exercise—I mean, what was the future, was I going on with the shop, what was Mark's new money going to mean? So instead I set to and wrote him a letter. I meant it to be long, it ended up short. But sweetish. I couldn't be honest now, even with him. I felt, too, I mustn't put him off his stride, not just now. I still felt that given a few days I would adjust, face things more clearly —steel myself, as they say. I wrote things like: 'Of course it was a surprise, and rather horrid at first. But understandable.' And: 'I miss you, the flat's very empty, but I'll ring up everyone I can.' It is impossible to write such a letter without the bitterness sneaking through; but it is also possible to read such a letter and not recognize the bitterness, if you don't want to. Simple phrases like, 'I miss you': anyone would say it, but who could know how deeply I meant it? Unless they wanted to. In early love letters, say, these would be phrases to be lingered over and infinitely treasured: or now in Mark's case, to be read with an access of guilt—that is, if he still had time for guilt. As usual, a series of 'ifs'. I did end up by telling him to telephone as soon, *soon* underlined, as possible, in case I couldn't get through to him. And I scrawled a P.S. 'By the way, just before I left someone told me there was trouble with the Nose's boat. On the rocks, or something. Hope no disaster?' Then crossed out 'the Nose's' and put 'her'. I didn't know who might read his letters now.

Twice, morning and afternoon, I telephoned that office again. Both times he was out. In the evening I tried to get from the directory the number of the home address he had given me. There were no less than ten different telephone numbers. What name? No, no one of the Contessa's name. Wearily I took down all the numbers. In case of emergency, I thought. What would be an emergency? I didn't know what to say to him anyhow—it was just a matter of contact. In spite of everything else, this lack of communication was the most crying frustration.

The next few evenings I had to stay in, just in case he telephoned. No great hardship, but an unnerving one. I even left the loo door open, in case the thing rang.

It was the same in the shop. Never before had I spent so much time there. I lunched off sandwiches by the telephone, even feeling the few minutes spent buying these might have been critical. The same with the few streets' walk between the flat and the shop, and with shopping and posting his damned suits at the crowded post office. At such a time you simply don't think the other person will ring twice, as he would if he really wanted to: rather, you fear your own telephone might be out of order, and you make calls to people to test it, and even that's nerve-racking, for they must be quick calls so that you're not engaged. People must have thought I was out of my mind. I was. So I took to ringing people up and putting the receiver down when they answered. They must have thought the district was running with burglars.

On the fourth day I got in a piping temper. I rang a man at Mark's London office, a friend, not his boss, ostensibly to ask how his absence had been settled, whether I could do anything? Apparently everything was all right, though at first it had been 'a bit of an upset'. Then casually the man told me he had been speaking to Mark only that morning. So! I didn't ask about what, only strained myself to sound double-casual too. The bastard, I thought, the lousy selfish bastard.

Which didn't make it any easier when finally Mark did come through early that evening. I was cut in half—one part of me in a joy of relief, the other cool, very cool. Before he said it, I knew what he'd say first:

'Hello, darling—at *last*! I've been ringing and ringing. Where have you been?'

'Here.'

'But you *can't* have been. I've put call after call through.'

'Then they must have got the wrong number. Or the line's been blocked. I've been here, here, *here* all the time. Every evening.'

'I simply can't understand it.'

And so on, the first vital minute spent like that! While I was thinking all the time, excuses, excuses, and receding further and further from him, which was in one way absurd, his voice seemed to be in the room, it was so clear.

'And how *are* you, Ju?'

'I'm fine thanks.'

'No, I mean *really*?'

'Fine.'

'And how's everything?'

'Everything?'

'Shop? Flat? All all right?'

'Nothing's wrong. Just pedalling along as usual. Fine.'

And more of that, our own voices, but a kind of telephonic caution, like strangers.

A furtive chuckle: 'And how are the mice?'

'Fine.' And I told him about them eating the bills. 'I always knew they were on our side,' he said. But this valuable interchange did seem to break some of the ice for him, he began to bubble on about how things were there, all very good, all very hopeful, and I wanted to scream at him you-told-me-all-that-in-your-letter but instead I bubbled back at him a lot of trivial stuff about the shop and friends I'd spoken to, making half of it up. Which he capped, and I capped back. It was absurd. Too absurd, so that soon I let my voice drop away. Then the crunch:

'Ju . . . Ju? You sound—sort of distant.'

'You don't. You sound in the room.'

172

'I wish I was.'

'Do you really?'

'*Of course I do.*'

'Oh Mark . . . miss me?'

'Terribly.'

'Mark?'

'Yes?'

'Mark—*when* are we going to see each other? When and how? It's really so silly this, so artificial—I mean, other people don't have to behave like this.'

'I know. But in our case—'

'Yes?'

'Well—we just aren't like other people. You know the conditions.'

'Yes. But I don't *believe* them. Even if you're up to the eyes just now—can't I just pop over? For a day or two?'

'Pop? Look Ju—please, darling. Let it ride just for a little. I'll find out soon what's the best thing to do.'

I suddenly bawled: 'But I must see you! I *must* come!'

Silence. Then very quietly:

'Darling, *please*. Please be patient just for a little. I'll work things out.' A pause. 'Anyway, I may not be here. Talk of having to go to Germany. Hanover I think.'

'Oh?'

'I'll let you know.'

'Hanover should be splendid.'

'I really will let you know.'

Then, by God, he changed the subject, 'I nearly forgot,' he said bright as a dozen buttons, 'to tell you about the *Spada*. You asked in your letter, didn't you? She broke her moorings, drifted on the rocks. Something about a small boy aboard at the time—but no bones broken. Renata was in a fine old rage. At least, it showed me how *she* can be when things don't please—regular volcano, wouldn't like to be on the wrong side there.'

It was infuriating, that change of subject trick—but still a relief. At least the *Spada* crisis was cleared up. And then his tone changed again, he said how he hated telephones, it was lovely to speak to me, but frustrating, and we bumbled on about this for a bit, and then said goodnight. 'Goodnight, my darling.' 'Goodnight, Mark dear.' And that was that. I listened for his receiver to click first.

Telephones are no good.

I suppose if you live on them, like those international figures you hear about speaking to each other across the Atlantic every night, usually in a foam-filled bath or lying across a bed of white fur—I suppose it's all right then. But not us. We weren't used to it. And when his next letter came, a day or so after, he added a P.P.S. about not telephoning often, he could hardly run up a huge bill, nor could I. Of course, it would be all right now and again. The exception, he generally added, proves the rule.

So then for a long time I didn't go to Milan. There the matter rested, and I was introduced to what is deceptively, the most dramatic thing in life—the passing of time, empty time.

Retired men die of it, teenagers are driven to violence by it. Housewives, I suppose, bed with plumbers of it. I didn't. No plumbers nor anyone for me. The days simply dragged by, punctuated by meals which grew more tasteless as I took less trouble with them. A little hope each morning, born of sleep, and then after coffee slap down came the blank feeling. The long look round the bedroom where nothing moved, same pictures, same door, same dressing-table, same window with a separate world outside and a blue sky beckoning everyone but me. Yet how often I had lain there alone before, with Mark tinkering at his tapes along in his workroom at the end, absolutely secluded, yet *there*, and in his partial absence absolute presenceful company. He was there. This odd figment of absence-presence even worked in the weekdays when he was away at his office and I was in the shop—we were connected across the town.

Then I made efforts. Friends came to dinner. I went out with people from time to time. But the variety of this quickly palled. In the first half hour or more it always worked, seeing the faces, the clothes, listening to what was trivially 'the latest', and *liking* them, even now and again disliking them. Then sooner or later Mark would be mentioned and I would have to play the bright young heroine. An airy little grin:

'Yes, I had a letter from him only yesterday. He's fine. Working very hard, of course, poor dear.' What a canary, what a cat . . .

And the usual wife-husband jollity: 'At last I've got time to get down to a thing or two, not tied to the master's nose-bag all the time.'

And their always optimistic encouragement:

'After all, it's just for a time, Julie. I'm sure you'll be going out there soon.'

Or:

'I'll bet that Mark'll just pop in when you're least expecting him . . . it's not like in the past, nowadays he can be here in a couple of hours, rolling in with little triangles of jetted cheese and a bottle.'

And even:

'You must be proud to have such a brilliant husband.' That woman who always said *husband*, I could have gouged her! The only pride I knew was in myself, my battle of saving face. Only in a much removed way had I ever been proud of Mark's composing: more astonished than proud, intrigued by the mystery of what went on in his separate mind – as one might be momentarily proud of a child winning a prize, wondering how the little mind had ever managed it, satisfied and pleased but feeling also that it had no real connection with everyday pick-nose life.

The shop naturally took up its part of the time, but again I was mostly alone there. Customers became unbearable if they chatted, became faceless and unfriendly if they simply bought or sold and went. No longer did there seem any point in doing those few creative things which used to pass the time – making those lampshades, refurbishing this or that, even drawing – and I began to develop what I had always slightly despised, the press-button life, radio, telly. As in a hospital, I turned on the radio at unusual hours and found its variety and persistence astonishing. The voices with their bright affirmative energy weighed, yet morbidly attracted me. How ever could so much be going on? My own pointlessness was emphasized. Only sometimes in the cinema was there some relief, in the big dark, engulfed in the very size of the huge dream-scene. Then the lights would go up, and if it was late afternoon I would find myself in an empty theatre scattered with a few old age pensioners, and with waiters taking the weight off their feet.

The Monday meals-on-wheels round, when I closed the shop and visited the elderly, was the only other relief, and a perverse one at that. Particularly with an old Mr Trillet. This poor white thin old man lived alone in a linoleum room with neither a telly nor radio. He had several pieces of brass he polished and polished, and a few strands of rope he knotted and unknotted. He was absolutely terrified of going out. Picking up his pension was the weekly horror of his life. He was one of those who never answered a knock on the door – you had to sing out your name and say who you were. There was no solution to him, but temporarily he used to solve me. I came away comparing my own loneliness with his, and seeing how well off I was. A comfortable kind of job, a pleasant enough home, health, friends, youth . . . what the hell was I mewing about? He would give me a few moments' respite, enough hope to go out and buy myself a pair of tights with *interest* . . . but little more.

Daymares sometimes intervened. I got lost in terribly real scenes with Mark knocked over in the street, being unable to explain to the Italian doctor where he was hurt, a bone badly set for life . . . and often with the Nose, once Mark alone with her on a wide balcony with a stone balustrade, cypresses, candles, the romantic lot—her backless evening dress and his hand, very gently, politely touching it, the finger with the ring I gave him slowly caressing a brown knobble of backbone . . . and the Nose on another occasion dancing languorously backwards pulling *him* by the nose, as a tango played . . . and then a Rinaldi with her slipping a powder into Mark's glass and Mark glazed with lust as she walked to and fro naked except for three very small tape-discs flapping against her breasts and wiry black bush, Mark squeaking: 'Beep! Beep!' from where he was tied up to a great gleaming coffee machine with his own coloured electric wires.

But mostly their lips meeting, and his big protective body all over her, his security. Security—so I myself entered the scene here, my loneliness squirmed between them?

Yet such ludicrous visions were in themselves a kind of relief. They gripped me entirely, they put an edge to life. They were far, far better than cutting my toenails which like other dull recurrent chores seemed not to come round ever more rapidly, somehow managing to compress the acreage of passing time, delineating it, and each chore although previously a half-pleasurable 'something to do' now weighing heavily, each a ridiculously phenomenal bore.

The lunar thing came on apace, too: though this had its compensations, I could make it my false excuse, attribute this great grey well of self-pity to the dull drag of pain and menstrual nerves.

I had to snap out of it. But where do you snap? Where in the long grey world that glassed out the blue September sunlight then the turning gold of October, was there a snap?

The palliatives in the book had no snap in them. Go to art galleries? The pictures had lost their gloss, they tried, they even succeeded for minutes at a time, but finally always failed. So go out of your way to help other people, lose yourself in others? I tried—not in the mealsy-wheelsy way, which was laid on in any case—but among friends, baby-sitting for instance. Though alone with a sleeping child and the well-furnished imperturbability of a smooth settled home, I got myself into a deeper depression than ever. And on the one occasion when somebody in trouble came to me, a girlfriend whose boyfriend was in love with a waiter and would always take her to the same restaurant—it seemed so trivial and passing, beyond the first conspiratorial laugh, the real consequent tears, that my own trouble only rose to boiling point inside me, boiling to get out and pour all over hers.

Nor was there any snap in the bottle, the old alcohol, only a deadening sweet gurgle. Then see the vicar, get a cat?

No. The only thing, of course, was to tell it all to a friend. I had to do the obvious, and unburden myself. I kept on saying that no one was finally trustworthy, that even the most conscientious ear had a mouth reserved for one other person, one only, of course. But in this wasn't I equally involved myself? Telling it to one ear, when pride had decided to bottle it all up?

Failing myself in this, like everything else, I finally unburdened myself to two other people.

Confession number one began well by saving me from a dog. I was in a pet shop playing with a puppy, finger in the wire netting, tender little nip, ears back, rolling eyes, reel away, rush back, over on back yelling with laughter—and by all sainted lamp-posts I'd have bought it if Pat Edgworth, fiftyish, friend of my mother's, hadn't seen me through the window and burst blue-rinsed into the shop saying, 'No, darling! Think again! Think!'

She lived round the corner, and thither we went: to a screaming new kitchen made up of plasticized wood and chromium, Provençal red ochre paint and jolly herb-jars, instant coffee in thick striped mugs—and instant tears out of my own thinly-striped mug of a face. First the puppy, now the mother substitute.

Finally, after I had poured it all out, I was wailing:
'Not that there's no contact. He *telephones* me. He *writes* me.'
'*To* me,' she said levelly, a compulsion, but really to help.
'But I'm not *with* him!' I bawled.

She did that thing they do with her lower lips when the crunch comes: out with the lower lip, like a little springboard for pros and cons. Horizon eyes. And at last the verdict, delivered distantly to a late and unwitting finch up on the trellis through the window:

'Pack your bags and go!'

Firm as her haircut.

The next confession was to a younger friend, Sally Entwistle-Drew, whom I had known since schooldays and who was very close. I should really have confided in Sally long before. But as with the other woman, it was finally ordered by external circumstances. We were in a disco, dancing about with a couple of husbands, hers and somebody else's. I was flinging myself about in front of Mr Somebody Else, stomping and waving my arms, which I usually quite like. But I soon saw myself objectively as a silly sad figure, puppeting about the rather empty dance-space, gesturing, no contact, and suddenly I could do it no longer, excused myself, and lugged Sally out to the car park. We sat in her big old twenties' Delage with the antlers lashed to the roof, a kind of plush first-class railway carriage of a car, the very opposite to that old woman's new young kitchen, and there I poured it all out once again.

Sally was sympathetic and considerate, but finally said coolly to the walnut dashboard: 'Of course, it's finally a business arrangement.'

'But he may be in bed with her, in bed now!'

'Bed? That's not much nowadays.'

'But—'

'Ju, you've simply got to take it cool. That sort of bed isn't your sort of bed. We live in an age when people simply don't make a *fuss* about it. No, what you've got to do is to stay put and play along with him. Write to him sweetly, don't show you're upset at all. And enjoy the jack-pot when it comes. God knows few of us have the chance.'

So there it was, two entirely opposite answers from my two confessors. The older woman prompted by tradition and possibly an extra-menopausal aggression; the younger too much influenced by overblown sex attitudes in glossy magazines, and by the get-rich-quick ethos of success stories in the press. The only thing they had in common was a markedly stimulated interest, or plain bloody delight, in their four blue eyes.

But of course the answers don't matter at such a time—one uses one's friends not as sounding boards but as baffle boards, shoulders to cry on, good kind dummies to bawl out your burdens to. It is the unburdening that counts. Finally you will do what you want to do, only that.

And so what finally drove me to action was a letter from Mark enclosing a cutting from an Italian magazine. It showed him in a new whitish suit at a restaurant table with Renata and another man and woman. Champagne and flowers on the table, and all looked very sunburned and smart. The sunburn probably came with the dark ink of the magazine, but not the suit, which I had never seen before. Underneath it said about so-and-so and so-and-so at work on a new operatic film celebrating the score being written by that brilliant new English composer of 'flesh-music', Mister Mark Marcus. 'Flesh music is an organically new sound removed from all usual electronic connotations, an astounding revolution which at the moment remains a closely guarded secret.'

In his letter Mark said, 'So you see, the magic is already beginning to work, the plan in full fruition!' And he explained his change of name as a more marketable euphonism—'after all, I hadn't much of a sound already.'

But what started me was the atmosphere of the picture

itself, the luxury, the extreme elegance of the two women, even that suit itself. As with his name, this was a new Mark, different from the one I knew. He was smiling, plainly enjoying himself, and for the first time I felt frightened I might lose him.

Never for a second before had I thought this. The whole miserable predicament had looked simply like a long hiatus. Of course, I had vaguely pictured a similarly luxurious scene and its material excitements—but mostly I had imagined the figure I knew bent over secretive grey recording machines like those gathering dust in the backroom here. But here was the scene itself in all its detail, Renata's languorous brown braceleted arm tilting a cigarette, the other woman a far too pretty blonde leaning towards Mark, both the women's cleavages furrowed deep with printer's ink, a buzz of type-set words in the columns all around as brightly black and white as the animated talk in the restaurant where they and their bucketed bottle sat.

Yet Mark I knew didn't care much for the bright lights, the smarty life: he took or left it. It is a familiar defence to ignore what you don't have. But what if it was handed you on a silver plate, day after day—surely it would be very pleasant and tempting, surely that grinning young blonde with a damned butterfly in her hair would be very pleasant and tempting? I had already got Mark into bed with Renata: but here was another trap, Milan pullulating with anxious blondes, the other woman's other women. I booked myself on a morning plane the next day.

There was no vacillating, I never had a second thought. My mind made up, the whole body strengthened—I got back my old energy and interest, I was exhilarated and bulldozed my way through the bank manager and then went shopping for at least one new thing to wear. I decided not to let him know, but spring myself as a surprise on him.

Early next morning, though, I telegraphed. Best to make sure he was in.

15

MILANO! Sunny Milano in the smog! It was drizzling and grey and the poplars through the airbus window came and went like thin ghosts in the mist, like tall ostrich things standing on one leg.

So many raincoats at the terminal, so many people with drained faces in dull colours, brown, black, grey—it didn't feel like Italy at all. Though it smelled different. What of— vanilla, blacker tobacco, stucco?

I took a taxi to Mark's address, which was fairly central. No concierge, I had no idea which floor he lived on. Then I remembered the garden, the flat would be quite low down to be able to overlook it; so I wandered about in the sole company of my own footsteps echoing from the hard mosaic floor, and finally found the door with a hand-printed card saying M. Forster. But no answer from inside, a momentous kind of silence which seems to breed presence.

So downstairs again, very alone in a strange city. Suddenly the very little girl again, with a long walk for another taxi to that office. (After all, I kept making myself think, obviously he's out at work somewhere, my telegram arrived too late?)

It was a smooth and polished office, low settees, rubber plants, a few girls herded typing behind a counter. One of these eventually looked up and asked me, '*Cosa*?'

No 'signora'? My clothes cheapened all over me. I told her I wanted Mr Forster. She didn't know a Mr Forster. I told her I was his wife. Then I told her his name was Mr Marcus. She brightened at this, nodding—then frowned: 'But you are Signora Forster?' More of this, but at last she picked up a telephone. After a few words, put it down and delivered

the bombshell: 'Signor Marcus left for Munich this morning.'
Oh?

Then the Contessa? Could I see her?

Without an appointment, impossible.

But I had just flown from London! Especially! It was an emergency etc., etc.

And the girl was trying to say something, but I kept on about how important it was and then lost my head and went bashing through the first door I could see . . . they screamed out at me, but the door closed behind me and I was bashing on into office after office each with a startled man or woman and once a little conference of darkly-spectacled men and thick cigarette smoke . . . but no Contessa, and suddenly in the middle of it all I felt how hopeless it all was, and my spirits sank away just as a male secretary figure from back in the waiting room got to me and with arms extended, crucified, bleated: 'Please . . . please Signora . . . she is gone.'

But why go on? Other people crouch in service lifts and crash offices that way, others burst in erect and by their very momentum carry the day—but these are telly-people, not me. I was simply led back onto a smooth low settee and told that a sudden decision had called them both to Munich. Suddenly, that very day. Suddenly, I thought, as my telegram.

But at least my identity was properly established and I learned at least how to make contact in future, Mark's exact telephone numbers in studio, home, office, and the best times to ring and so on. But even then they told me his life was very fluid, he was often away. I was even given a specious genuflection as the great Mrs Marcus.

Afterwards, being in Milan I went to the Art Gallery, where the pictures I wanted to see were away on loan. The Theatre Museum by the Opera was closed. I did get to see The Last Supper. The haloes looked like tin helmets.

16

BEATEN and bitter, after a lonely dinner in a little restaurant and a bad night in a small hotel, I went out to the drizzling airport for home. I did think twice of going to Munich—I had the name of their hotel, and the money just about—but by now foresaw only further barricades and innuendo. After all, in Milan when I had bashed after her I had not even found her office, empty or not: top people are well insulated, secretaries and outer offices cordon the inner sanctuary invulnerably, my earlier success up at the Santa Vilga villa had been a villeggiatura exception.

Home—and two wires from Mark. One read, 'Cancel visit writing.' The second and later one registered apologetic horror at hearing of my arrival. The next day he telephoned. I gave him a kind of cold, hopeless talking-to. She had cooked it, I told him; he countered this with technicalities, some sort of film-processing only available in Munich. I told him about the wool over his eyes, sheep's clothing on the wolf, plenty of that.

Then I thought it about time I pulled myself together again: first thing was to clear my head, and so to the hairdresser's for moral re-armament. Under the drier, before the new brush which was to sweep me clean, I opened dear old *Harper's*—and who was there grinning at me from the Scala foyer but the flesh-loving Signor Marcus? I nearly blew up: an espresso bursting through the wall in the orthodox Santa Vilga manner would have been most welcome. But it was no good blowing up: and, as I discovered in the next days, this new nuisance was to be implemented—his face, or news items about him, appeared in journals and papers everywhere; the way-out new-look composer had erupted into news; the Nose had done her work well.

And not only news—there was controversy, too. Was this vaunted 'flesh' music to be a new dimension of pornography—'pornophony', the paper brightly tittered. And one snide indepth journalist pointed out at some length that despite all the hoo-ha not one note from this 'flesh' musician—alas, he was called 'carnal' now—had ever been heard! Well, I could tell him a thing or two about that. But didn't—my declining energies were spent on a female arm linked with his in certainly two glossy great pictures. I got out the magnifying glass on the rings on its hand, and compared them with that blonde friend of the Nose's. Answer frustrating as usual: in one case the Nose's rings, in the second the blonde's

By now it was absolutely decided that he had been to bed with one or both of these energetically distant ladies. Somehow —like those thousands of absentee executive wives I mentioned earlier—I both settled for this and tried to put it conveniently out of mind. But into this false vacuum—which in my case could not be filled with purchases of cretonne and three-piece suites, and was brought freshly to my notice week by week by new references cropping up almost daily—into this vacuum echoed the true material argument against a little light promiscuity. The dread that there would creep in romance or affection, or their combination in the word 'love', and that I would lose him permanently. So—to air the bedding with a smileless shrug? Or fearfully to watch the whole lot fly out of the window forever, forever . . . I began deeply to dread this.

You can't just wait.

Yet it seemed you had to.

I thought again of selling up the shop—financially it was no longer necessary for pin-money and the proceeds could have gone to an extended European chase. But I was frightened of losing a hobby-ish demand on my empty time. Finally, with a kind of excited hopelessness, a nasty new guile erected itself. It came of a talk with the blue-rinsed and embattled Mrs Patricia Edgworth. 'Responsibility!' she intoned. 'Arouse his sense of responsibility to you, his loving and devoted care. Get ill,' she snapped. Then: 'Flu won't do, something more serious. Psuspected psittacosis?' she asked, eyeing her stuffed parrot. 'No, not quite credible. Pneumonia? Has everything got a P? Better keep to flu—make it Hong-Kong, no, Chinese, that always sounds sinister.'

'But won't it all just make me a drag?'

'What the hell? Main thing is to get him over here. After that it's up to you. But I'd better start it off, it's better from a second party. I'll cable him today. Now.'

And so it was. I gave her his number and there and then she picked up the phone and wired him a moving SOS sob story. I just sat there in dumb acquiescence: no arguing with the blue-rinsers. 'And now,' she said, 'lock up the shop and off to bed with you.'

It was a beautiful day. I felt at least physically very fit. So it was with an absurdly frisky tail between my legs that I did what I was told, got home and got out medicines and so on, undressed and rumpled up the bed. I remembered something someone told me about London's firemen during the blitz. What was their first scramble of true-blue action when the evening air-raid siren went? Answer: the whole lot scrambled off to bed. Yet it made nicely perverted sense—it was really to get an hour or two's rest before being called out for the night. So that's what I felt like sitting muffled in a thick dressing-gown with all the fires on and wondering how quickly, with luck and an instant jet-flight, he would be through the door. I blued my face about a bit with eye-shadow, lip-rouged a dangerous flush to the cheeks.

But four long hours later there came a long insistent ring on the bell, no fumbling of a latch-key. I coughed my way over— he must have forgotten the thing. But he hadn't. It was a friend of his from the office, best friend I suppose, a pinstriped Peter Metcalf urgently and capably ordering me back to bed, to bed, to bed *quick*. Only then could we talk. 'And how're you feeling now? Mark rang me about it. Said he didn't want to ring you in case you were asleep. Sorry to get you out of bed — thought there would be someone with you. Now, how really are you? What's the doctor said?'

The bastard, I thought, delegating this pinstriped lifeboat. Then — doctor, I thought. That'll spill the beans. You can't bribe a doc — better get him in tomorrow?

'Peter,' I said in bed to avoid the subject, 'there's the whisky bottle over there' — pointing weakly with a healthy fat forefinger and a carefully strained voice — 'so help yourself.'

After his first pained concern, he soon cheered up. And, like most sickbed visitors, began joking about God know's what. When the second whisky was down he got up from his chair, sat on the bed and in a most considerate 'friendly' way held my hand.

'Now what about food?' he said. 'Let me fix you something. I'm famous for my tinned soups.'

'No, Peter,' I said, now properly hungry and looking forward to a meal as soon as he went. 'I couldn't — I couldn't manage a thing.'

'But you'll have to,' he said, now stroking my hand. 'Starve a fever — it's really the other way round, isn't it? Starve a fever and you'll get a cold. Or is it Feed a Fever?'

A quarter bottle and he was commiserating with me quite tearfully about Mark's built-in indifference. 'Cool and calculating, that's our Mark all over,' he consoled the invalid wife; and near the half-bottle line made a grab at my left tit and lunged all over me. There's no one like a best friend for that kind of thing.

The usual struggle, gripping his wrist, turning my head hard away, scissoring my knees together — yet all the time using an absurdly apologetic language. '*Please*, Peter!' 'Peter darling — No!' 'Peter — I'm ill!' as if the lousy bastard had paid me a sort of compliment. Which, I suppose, in his whiskied way, he had.

Of course it was a bit awkward after that; and he soon left, quite overlooking any expertise with the tinned soup. I suppose I had rather too brightly tried to put him at his ease, for his mumbled farewell was both absurdly gauche and totally deflating: 'Well, old thing, better get back to the better half, she'll be pawing the mat with my slippers in her chops, the dear girl. But she'll be glad to hear you're looking so well after all. I'll let Mark know of course. Look after yourself,' he gaily added.

Fat chance of anyone else doing so, I thought, and shouted at him in a hoarse, foot-in-the-grave whisper: 'Don't worry Mark,' and went into a right Dame Camellia of a coughing fit to make him double-worry, if he could see straight.

However at least he passed the word on to another friend of ours in Mark's office, a likable young man from Design, queer as a coot and sweet as pie.

'But this is *too* ridiculous,' he squeaked next evening when he called and found me up and dressed, having forgone the whole charade. 'You're ill! It's too soon. Back to bed with you prontissimo, have you eaten, shall I make with the Ovaltine? Get those clothes off while I turn my back, it's not *at all* a bad back . . .'

And so on. I gave in to put him at his ease, and he really did cook me a meal, a sole he'd brought along with him and now expertly and quickly *bonne femme*'d. No trouble with *him*, whisky or not; this Curly McAllister was not only safe bedwise but also the best of bedsiders, one of those affable bitch-boys who love to play the attentive mum and ply the girlish gossip at the same time. Later on, because he was so kind and considerate, I came clean with him: Not ill, a Feminine Wile to get Hubby back—he loved it, and the next night brought his stuff from the launderette for a good old natter and an ironing too.

Curly was indeed the best of antidotes to my muddled despair. If I've sounded overbright about him, and even Peter before him, I suppose it's because looking back on such a time one can see most clearly the odder side: the shapeless pain of it all recedes, memory rejects a fog, only retains the momentary flash of a headlamp—but by heavens it was a bad time, unendurably frustrating, and with worse to come.

I've heard men say quite honestly, and without male malice, that there's nothing more soothing than the company of a woman ironing. Degas knew it, with his lovely and never sordid *Repasseuse*. So it was with Curly, who seemed to be an addict of the repassing board and every two or three nights arrived with his assiduous bundle and went equably to work. Perhaps it was really to help me, but he seemed to like it too, and sometimes, if it grew late, even bunked down for the night on a sort of sofa-bed we had. The flat got its little litter of his clothes, the odd shirt or two, pyjamas—and this gave it something of a 'lived-in' feel, obviating the empty absence of Mark's stuff.

That Peter had telephoned again, and said that he had spoken to Mark, and then I had a call from Mark, mainly to say how relieved he was that I was not after all at death's door, joking about Pat Edgworth's fussiness, but mostly enthusing about his own success. Had I seen the press? Ho!

And not more than a couple of dreary weeks after Curly's appearance I came home from the shop and, almost the instant I got in, sniffed something strange about the flat. So strongly, my heart jumped about: I felt someone was there, and in fact went slowly and fearfully from room to room very quietly, flinging open doors very suddenly, all with a large brass candlestick in my quailing hand. I don't know—who does?—about prescience in these matters. More likely, one's matter-of-fact side says, something like some last invisible, nearly unsmellable trace of tobacco smoke may be the real unconscious pointer, or perhaps the half-seen, undigested change in the position of an object, even a cupboard door left open—matters too small immediately to notice.

And there certainly was a cupboard door open. Also a couple of drawers. And a small pile of Mark's letters for forwarding gone. And, lying across a heap of Curly's shirts and pyjamas, a note. It was from Mark.

No 'darling', not even my name. It simply said:

'Had to come to London suddenly. Called in to see you. It seems I've intruded. Apologies, Mark.'

Christ, how long does one stand there?

Certainly I remember looking round, and seeing what must inevitably to Mark have looked like the scatterings of a lover's impedimenta. Certainly I got on the phone to Curly as soon as I could. He came round immediately. Then we phoned Peter to see if Mark had contacted him, and find out where he was staying. He said he had no idea: but it was very plain he was lying, no tone of surprise, and a rather outsized bonhomie about his professed ignorance. 'Bastard,' Curly said, and then we both saw the evening paper I'd brought in, unopened, and Mark and the Nose striding through one of those interminable corridors at London Airport.

Interminable, too, were the telephonic corridors now leading to a round-up of the ritzy hotels. Nothing doing. So they would be staying with friends? But who were friends? We tried the Italian Embassy, who knew but rightly refused information; the newspapers were equally reticent. I nearly went up to Fleet Street to get sloshed on the offchance of hearing something. Finally we went to work on possible film and stage contacts to try the next day.

'It'll be all right,' Curly consoled, 'right as a right little, tight little trivet. I'll see that ponce Peter tomorrow. He'll give. Unless, of course—' and he paused.

'Unless what?'

'Well—er—unless he's got it a bitsy in for you after the cold shoulder he got. Hurt pride and so forth.' He laughed. 'But not for long when I say it's me—after all, dear, they both know I'm safe as houses, as I believe they used to say down in the basement during the dear old Blitz. Come on, it's not so bad as it looks.

'But I want to *see* him!'

No word next day. A blank from Peter, blanks from the film

companies. Then I did the obvious – put through a call to the Nose's secretary in Milan. Curly, who'd stayed the night to be on the spot as an exhibit, snatched the telephone from me and told them he was the Director of Covent Garden Opera House and would they please confirm where the Contessa was staying, it was extremely urgent. Alas, the Contessa was already leaving London that morning for New York.

Only a few flying hours – but how very, very distant New York seems. It was November by then, I remember looking out of the window for the blessing of plane-grounding fog. Not a wisp. Of course, I rang Peter and asked him outright what he had said to Mark. He was still a bit guarded: said he had told Mark he *thought* the clothes were Curly's, leaving a good old question-mark.

Whether it was New York or marital anger, I couldn't tell – but Mark's letters stopped. And a week later, when I estimated they'd be back in Italy again, I got a noncomittal rebuff from the Milan office. No immediate knowledge of his whereabouts. I think they knew my voice by then, and the warning had gone out.

Days and days dragged by. Naturally I had written to Mark explaining everything. And indeed tearing a strip off him for imagining I would ever deceive him. But still no reply. Either he was still offended, or didn't believe me, or even felt guilty for suspecting me – or, worst of all, had snatched at this for the excuse he needed, both to stop communicating and continue with a freer conscience his own affairs. Naturally I plumped for the latter.

And I got bitter and angry. A free conscience? The idea rankled, oh it rankled, and one wet and dreary night it went rankling right through a Western I'd dropped in on – a weird film, I remember, where a posse of brown-painted, stripped-to-the-waist cowboys wore enormous mustang masks and dressed their mounts in sombreros and chaps, so that the Indians were truly 'a-feared' as the ubiquitous Doc said, at a terrible night vision of horses riding men, nightmare indeed — and anyway, when I got out the rain was lashing down, and I went straight into a next-door pub for shelter.

Over a couple of drinks in a corner, the matter of his conscience rankled higher, and in fact became my own conscience. If he was free, then I bloody well was too. It might have been that film giving me upside-down ideas — I don't know, anyway my bitterness kind of burst, and I picked up the man sitting at a table next door to me. Nothing intended, of course. And by no means a habit with me. But now it developed from a mutual despair at the rain into a definitive chat-up, a nice-weather-for-supply-your-own-feathered-friend.

So why? One always looks for one clear-cut reason. But I suppose any old general, and we might include any old cook-general, knows that it usually takes many ingredients to create a battle or a pudding. Items, then, for this disastrous pudding: one, he was very good-looking, a sort of suntanned blue-eyed tennis champion who should never have been sitting alone; two, it was raining; three, I was rankling; four, he was pleasantly offhand, no wolfishness; five, when he diffidently asked whether I'd like another drink, pointing to the rain dribbling in the lamplight down the window, he said I oughtn't to get that rather unusual suit of mine wet — why in the hell does one so easily respond to these clothes compliments, as always it's surely the shop that does the work? Oh, but as always there's one's infallible, brilliant good taste. Six, the rankling had began to flower into *laissez-faire*, a piqued tit-for-tat too callow to be dignified by the redoubtable word 'revenge' — simply if Mark wanted to play, so could I. Seven, the safe glow of Scotch after all those horse-faced cowboys. And so on. And adding a lot that doubtless I knew nothing about — perhaps he had some invisible resemblance, in gesture or something, to Mark, or perhaps I had reached some unconscious peak of man-starvation anyhow.

I could see his eyes approving me, which was nice. In a word, we got on famously. By the time the pub shut, we had a number of Scotches beneath our belts — he had let me pay a couple of rounds too, which was good for self-respect — and then he said he had a car outside and considering the undiminished deluge could he drive me home? Courteously adding that he'd have liked to do so had it all been dry as a bone.

When I went to the loo he must have bought a bottle to take with him. Anyway, arrived at my door — I was rather gigglish about the wet, he sheltered me in with his raincoat — he pointed out that one of the coat-pockets was a bit heavyish, and what about getting our noses into it? A quick one, he quickly added, for the road. I must have been a bit sloshed, or just plain excited — I can't stand drink and driving — but now I said yes and soon we were upstairs and, with well-filled tumblers, aboard the sofa.

He didn't try to kiss me for a long time; which both relaxed and disquieted me — so that when at last he did, at a moment reaching for an ashtray when our faces were naturally close together, I let him, either from surprise or relief, I don't know. But then, after a stillborn pang of guilt about Mark's own roof, etc., the matter took its usual, but for me most unusual course, and what one says on such mumbling, mouth-wet moments I do not know nor ever shall. I only remember the first defences to the first intimate fumblings, and the pleasurable relief, tradition satisfied, of giving in a minute later.

And it was me, alas, the much-married sophisticate, who suddenly stopped the fumble, stood up and said: 'Let's go to bed.'

A flinging off of clothes, and the sophisticate clutching the bedclothes round her, abruptly modest again. And he striving at me, and nothing happening, and he turning the light out and striving harder while still nothing happened until he turned away on his back groaning, 'Oh God, God, God . . .'

Was this the much mooted-fear of failure?

'I'm sorry,' the darkness said. 'I'm sorry . . . I'd like you to know it's not you, it's me. It's over-excitement. It's the drink. It's the first time. It's — I don't know . . .' and he turned away. But I could feel he was crying.

I never knew his name. I never saw him again. He left in the small hours; and in the middle hours of the following morning I had almost forgotten him.

My mind efficiently erected its natural feminine defences, pretending to shelve the whole episode as unimportant, a passing event as undistinguished as an afternoon's shopping. I told myself that there had been no technical infidelity.

Men are supposed to dwell in memory on such 'affairs'; not me, I wanted to forget it, and forget it I did. As far as I was concerned it had never occurred, it was hardly even necessary to find excuses. Perhaps, though, I did dwell a little on our meeting in the pub — in fact, the rainy romantic side of it. But not much.

Though a long time later, like now, I can sometimes take the whole thing out of its neatly sealed pigeon hole and relish the fact that I'd been cleverly revenged, or I'd been a bit of a devil, or escaped a disastrous indiscretion, as the mood takes me, it is as removed as taking out an old photograph of oneself, and judging that distant and other person pictured according to the moment's mood.

All these attitudes may sound much too calculated. After all, it was quite definitely the first time since Mark. But in another way I tell myself it was a measure of my innate fidelity to regret the matter by omission, by refusing to fuss about it by putting it in its worthless place. Though we cannot control our sub-conscious reactions, I must confess that somewhere at that time I did dream I was being kissed by the big brown mask of an impotent horse.

Curly phoned that he had phoned Mark, and then at last Mark phoned. He apologized for his lack of trust — but couldn't I admit it was a bit of a facer for him at the time?

Then we had a long talk about nothing, or rather the everyday everything, the harmless drum of my own life, the drumming hum of his own. Things were splendid! Going faster and better than ever he'd have imagined! And during all this I felt not a moment's guilt, in fact if anything the episode of Mr Nameless probably strengthened me, put me guardedly on a par with him. He mentioned Christmas — like a war, one couldn't quite be sure he would be 'over by Christmas'. Anyway, Christmas in Italy, and particularly his kind of Italy, wasn't much of a pause, if any. What would I do? Dunno, I said — and then facetiously added I might blow down and pig it in Santa Vilga for a bit. For old times' sake, for auld lang syne.

In fact, as usual, the now predictable impasse. Though my glib little barb boomeranged back at me in the familiar coincidental way, the blind 'It never rains but it pours' — Santa Vilga did occur again in my life both before and after Christmas.

The first time was heralded by a ting-a-ling at the shop door. After it, in came a green echo of the summer, in fact the Sprout and her mother Lettice. 'We were just passing,' they said, 'we just *had* to look in,' and I could see from their faces, from something intent and suppressed there, that those 'justs' were not at all true.

I sat them down among all my familiar junk and brewed a cup of tea on the mad little bunsen thing (brass, Sherlock Holmesy, also for sale). And there in the failing light of a dreary November afternoon, we recalled the warm and long gone summer days. It seemed, well, a lifetime ago, didn't it? And how was the hardware business going? Oh, but a bit of a battle with supermarkets and a lot of a battle with V.A.T., but they did have their regulars who liked a chat, shopping could be such a friendly thing, couldn't it, and come to that friends would and should always stick together, rain or shine, wouldn't they and shouldn't they?

This was the trenchant lead-in. And they went on to say, diffidently at first, that they had in a way come to me for help.

There was a prescience of fog about, it was windless and over-still; those two summer figures sat grey and engraved, sombre in the vellum-shaded lamps, disquieting against the background of my familiar junk, making this in fact strangely unfamiliar. Their bright-coloured hair and overpainted faces glared harsh as gaslight against buddhas and barometers, an armadillo basket and an early humane killer—I remember wondering what they must have looked like against their own shopful of pails and wire netting, hammers and cement. Yet they were really just the same prissy mother and daughter we had known in the sun, now overcome by November and by a certain awkwardness, a secretive seriousness, which indeed the mother now put into words.

'You see—we're very, very worried, Mrs Forster. And we thought we could trust you. We thought you could help us. It's the matter of a—of an alibi.'

'Alibi? How on earth—?'

'It's for an alibi back in the summer in Italy. You see, the Italian police—we're frightened of an extradition order.'

She stared at me, I felt my stomach fall—so the *Spada* had at last caught up with me?

I stammered: 'But what on earth would I need an alibi for?'

'No. Not you. Us. We wondered whether you and your husband could say we were with you on a particular night. A certain night in August.'

'August?'

'Yes. We could have had an all-night picnic—'

And Lettice's young off-shoot put in urgently:

'Yeth. An all-night barbecue in the hillth. Or in a boat.'

'Not in a boat, dear,' Lettice said sharply. 'A boat could have drifted along the coast. The hills the other way would be better.'

'Oh mother!' the girl said, and I noticed her hands clasping and unclasping themselves, like separate little animals.

I waited. The mother went on, dropping her voice to a whisper.

'The night that awful manager was killed. On that hotel beach—'

'And the boy, mother.'

'Be quiet, dear. You see,' the older painted face said to me urgently, 'it was us.'

'What!'

'There were good reasons. That man attacked my daughter. Beastly, beastly—he tried to—'

'Mother, *don't*!'

Then it all came out, sinister and mad. They said the manager had been showing them round the hotel late that night. And he had got them down on to the beach, to the bungalow where he himself slept. There, he had offered them glasses of liqueur. And when she, Mrs Green, was out of the room for a moment—to spend a penny, she archly added— the manager had made the most avid and revolting advances to her daughter. That, Mrs Green, calmly and with a certain pride, said was, well—understandable at least. But when she had come back and surprised her daughter struggling against him, and he had desisted—he had burst out laughing. And such an insult followed! 'You think I was serious,' he had laughed. 'With *her*?' And had doubled up with laughter, really doubled up, hands on knees, exposing the top of his head, which Mrs Green had instantly struck with the first thing that came to hand, a sharp-edged little transistor radio. He had 'fallen like a stone'.

'I don't know how I did it,' she breathed to herself, but heavily, living her fury all over again. 'But I did. And then my little one here helped me. We dragged him out—and, well, you know the rest.' And narrowing her eyes, very primly added: 'You see, we thought we ought to make an example of him.'

'It was a pity,' she added with a lost, almost tender look, 'about the little boy. But he was a witness, you see. We couldn't have him letting on. Still, it was unfair to him really.'

I didn't know what to say, I was both terrified and amused—

they were plainly both mad. Mad, and weaving this absurd fantasy to fill the emptiness of their lonely lives?

Then a man came into the shop to enquire about a picture in the window. It was a peaceful oil of Edwardian sheep: now it only looked like the knell of doom. I reduced the price too heavily, took the money and wrapped the picture. The two Greens sat primly on, waiting with downcast eyes: Mrs Green sipped her tea.

The bell rang the man out as I was still struggling to envisage these likely ladies impaling corpses with heavy poles. Impossible . . .

'It took us all our strength to get them in—' Mrs Green said, reading my thoughts, looking through me— 'those heavy poles. But my girl's a big strong girl really. However, enough of that. The trouble is—we've got reason to believe the police are on to us, we *know* it.'

My head was spinning, I wanted to laugh, but a quiet and ruthless nicety about them held me. With their beads and thin painted faces, they were truly frightening. 'Look,' said the mother excitedly, and handed me a little newspaper cutting. It was blurred and ragged, much read. 'Interpol,' it said, 'alerted.' And went on that foreign police were now helping the Italian authorities with their investigation of the unsolved beach murders of last August. 'Disgruntled tourists, it is thought, may be involved.'

So this was the sad seed of their fantasy? One day they had read it, and seen themselves reflected in a vast network of mystery and blessed drama? Like all those lonely ones desperate for drama and identity who confess to other peoples' crimes? . . . But then Mrs Green went on all too factually: she described how they had found bicycles and pedalled quietly off at what was still an early hour—though just in time, for a clatter of plates showed the kitchen staff were up and beginning work. They had wheeled the bicycles over a little cliff near the hotel—deep water, but wouldn't a fisherman eventually find

them? And the biggest problem was their hotel night porter—
like most 'of his breed' he was asleep on a sofa when they crept
in. But could they ever be sure he had not woken, seen them
with half a sleeping eye?

And more and more like that. Until, against all my instinct,
I began to believe them, and was finally convinced when Mrs
Green said quite humbly, disarmingly: 'We know it was a
nasty thing to do. We're not proud of it.' And: 'It's asking a lot
of you—but even if you—if you disapprove, couldn't you help
to keep—I know it sounds a bit old-school and that—help to
keep, well, our Country out of the papers?'

But I no longer felt like laughing. Character clicked—I
could see her as one of those who rise for the national anthem
when it is played on a radio at home, I know because I've seen
it. And I thought of parasols, umbrellas—the traditional ladies'
weapon, poking the things at barking dogs, thrashing out at
crowded bus stops, sales. And, my God, hadn't they always
carried them at Santa Vilga? Without thinking, then, I said:
'I'll have to think. And my husband—he's away. I don't know
how to get in touch with him . . .'

'Away?' said Mrs Green. 'You can't—get—in—touch—
with—him?' A new glint in her eye, a loading of the words. I
was suddenly furious. Both with her and with Mark. This was
the first time that what I had always feared had happened—
needing to get in touch with Mark on some practical matter, a
death in the family, a fire in the flat, God knows what. Now
these two poor women had put me in this position at last. I felt
helpless, and bloody angry. Bitches, poor bitches . . .

Finally they went, with me promising to think of what best
to do. And wondering what the hell was the best way out—do
nothing of course; or ought I go to the police myself? I
couldn't even ring Mark about it; even if I got hold of him, it
was not the sort of thing you could trust to a telephone wire,
operators listening in. And those Greens would be persistent. I
knew I hadn't heard the last of it.

Fortunately, as it turned out, I hadn't.

I remember it was our local early closing day, with which ridiculously I had to comply. And I'd bought an early evening paper to help pass the time. One of those jocular secondary editorials I never usually read caught my eye. 'Any Umbrellas Today?' invited the headline. And then the message—Italian police had finally arrested those guilty of the Beach Murders, an all-Italy mystery ('all-Italy', I thought?). Since four beaches as far separate as Tuscany to Calabria, the Veneto back to Civitavecchia had yielded the same pattern of impaled bodies, it had first been thought that the murders were imitative, as with type-crimes following the fiction of a violent film. Theories had abounded: hotel staff rebelling against management; even, latterly, package tourists rebelling against lira-loving hotels. Finally the police had traced the matter to a first episode on the Veneto coast later capitalized by two anarchical members of a break-away union who had travelled the length of Italy trying to incite catering staffs to imitate the nauseous Venetian impalement! In three more cases they had been successful. Was this not ammunition for those campaigning for greater censorship of violence in British films, never an ill wind but blows good, etc., etc.

After a brief vision of our blessed Island shingle littered with chilled blue bodies riddled with what—not parasols, but wet black umbrellas? My immediate feeling, I regret selfishly to say, was one of intense relief. No need for this extra frustration with Mark, no need to fence with the hapless Greens—I tore the cutting out and posted it to their address, luckily still in my holiday notebook. And I was basely pleased that my first instinct about them, their sad wish for excitement, had been proved right.

But on the other hand, this whole and blood-red herring which had dragged across my path had revived a close mental picture of Santa Vilga and the whole disastrous summer. How often holidays are vitally galvanized by this or that parochial event, momentous at the time, seldom if ever thought of again. How long ago, how bitter—and it might have been this memory and its association which made me bring out my paints again. I'd put them firmly away, part of the lethargy which comes with sickness of heart. Now they'd perform an act of therapy. I'd paint this whole thing out of myself. And in the next days I began and finished odd canvases depicting frog-suited carabinieri in their melon-hats round a wrecked yacht; and a curiously grouped trio of striped-suited detectives like a concourse of zebras in the café on the square (who finally were these not so plain-suited detectives, the anarchical fomenters themselves? And even if so, were they in some way still connected with Renata, who could easily have a nose in every pie?). And then I painted a chilling study of the Greens in the November gloom of my junk-ridden shop. I put a lot into this one—I did feel now in retrospect deeply sorry for them and their crazily-coloured, lonely world.

This painting from imagination was new to me. Always before I'd worked from life on the spot. But now there emerged a curiously free capability, something I would never have imagined, and in complement my imagination ran riot on the canvas, producing some very odd scenes, primitive but contrived, either good in a Rousseauesque way or plain kitschy smart-aleck. But that was decided one day in the shop when I had taken the canvas of the Greens along to paint in a mite more detail of the background, my delightful antiques.

The picture stayed there for a day or two: and in came what the Irish would pointedly refer to as 'your man'. No local: but a well-heeled, overly-whiskered fellow with glasses on a gold chain. I'd already spotted him in my convex anti-shop-lift mirror; he was looking through the window in the direction of that canvas of mine. In he came, and asked about that awful old Buddha; then off-handedly pointed to the canvas. He was old enough to know better; surely he'd have known a dealer would be up to that one? Or was I just an amateur kind of suburban dealer? Anyway, I caught his excitement immediately; discounted the over-casual 'I rather like it—in it's way', brought him sharply to heel by saying I'd done it myself. 'Got any more?' he said too quickly; and laughed as he caught my eye. We were in it together, his laugh said. And so we were.

I took him back to the flat and showed him the other canvases. He liked them. I liked him. He ran a gallery off Bond Street. He'd like to try them out. Within a week we were in business together. The paintings sold—and very well at well-inflated prices. And I was set to painting furiously for a show he was now very keen to arrange. Obviously, all this took my mind off other things. Mark receded. Or rather, he took on a different perspective. I was, in fact, playing his own game. Two could play at it, I began giddily to gloat—and went so far as to paint a picture of him surrounded by *really* umbilical, bleeding tape and with an elongated prehensile nose, entitling it, I'm afraid, *Eine Kleine Fleischmusik* (later, scrubbed out.)

December appeared. Mark wrote that the whole thing was culminating famously, much quicker then he had ever thought possible. Christmas ahead, he said—complaining that I'd never told him what I myself was doing. How thoughtful! He himself would be working . . . except for some sort of celebration with a wandering witch, a wop figure called the Befana, around Epiphany he said. (Very neat, I thought, to have achieved both a private and public witch.) And then, God save us, there was to be a trip on the *Spada* to Greece! Something to do with observation of ancient sculptures on the spot, muscular tensions in their original light, more of his blasted flesh. But I did note, and darkly, that this was the first time he had actually mentioned a place he was travelling to. Why? Greece too far for me? He didn't know what I was earning now. I'd kept the painting game to myself. Besides, it was really early days to be sure how much the show would bring in.

So I concentrated. Not only was the therapy working its wonders, but these fortuitous canvases had put a real weapon in my hands—money, and possible notoriety to match, in its lesser way, with Mark's. A matter of chance? Possibly. But possibly also it was a time when our separation might have 'settled in'. The natural human spirit must be conditioned to retrieve itself just as naturally as a physical wound creates a nice healthy scab. If the art dealer hadn't turned up, something else would have made me my lovely scab. After all, dulled by doubts and frustration, I had very much needed action and affirmation. A general motive, but we are all far too mad about motives—just as if one can go back and redirect them: much more important are results.

One result of my painterly launching—it was scheduled for February—was a need for absolute concentration. Much less was seen of my immediate friends. Curly had stopped coming, frightened off despite his sexual security. Pat Edgworth and my cool young Sally had ceased to be necessary. I ran into the Greens once in a supermarket—they cut me, trolleying past me with distant eyes averted. I did see a lot, naturally, of my dealer friend. I liked him. He was a spur. But also he was armoured with some sort of reserved aesthetic aplomb, a suave man you couldn't ever get at. It was possibly this that impelled me, as the weeks went on, to make first a tentative, then quite a flagrant pass at him. Or was it just propinquity-plus, like the shared work and thereness of secretary and boss? The Mark-Nose syndrome? Anyway, my dearly beloved dealer only twinkled a mite more knowingly, and changed the subject. I was repulsed. Nor did it much matter: though subconsciously it might have sown certain seeds to flower later, Christmas roses, as it was to turn out.

Meanwhile the pressure of painting too much too quickly had its usual results: first, an access of brilliance, a rising momentum of enthusiasm and liberated energy; and then the fall, the fall of facility. I began to lose hold, exceed my limits. And when, the week before Christmas, I had got on to a fantasy of white-overalled house-painters with white pierrot faces climbing about the white bark of a birch-copse, I began to guess I had done, for the time, enough. It had to stop. A holiday was the obvious exit. But the thought of Christmas with sherry-soaked friends and their toy-flushed children panicked me. Cash in hand, I could go anywhere. But settled for something quite unglamorous, above all restful: a small hotel in a Suffolk estuary. I suppose physical exhaustion had something to do with it, too.

But did physical exhaustion have anything to do with the impossible fact that after four nights up there, I found myself in bed with a local farmer? A nasty little man, with hard black eyes in a beetrooty face?

The weather up there was blowy and wet, with cold sea-mists rolling in over the bleak mud-flats to make the outlying, colour-washed cottages of the town come and go like a ghost-huddle of pink, blue, green villas of the south. These, and the wet brown antithesis of their muddy surroundings, brought up again repercussions of the forlorn Tuscan summer — and once again a bedevilled state of mind.

Though my lonesome little yule began fairly well. A crummy hotel — but for me the best front room with blessedly Edwardian furnishing, great faded chintz curtains across a bay window, downy white pillows, two hot water bottles. I had an omelette and tea up there for my supper, and lay back in the electric glow of the fire and watched good English rain from what was once called the German Ocean dribbling down my big, black, wind-thumping windows. It was warm heaven, I was back in dear old childhood; nothing could hurt me here, eyelids drooped and hot water bottles nestled like cats against a warmly winter body.

And a cheerful enough breakfast. But after a wet walk on the quay and a lonely lunch of tired mutton, who came in but the dark non-stranger, accidie? Books I had brought were picked up and soon put down again. If this was a return to childhood, it was to be a petulant, lonely one. I thought of my mother —

she'd be down in the West Country wrapping parcels as she'd always done, fussing with string and even sealing wax, thinking back on her own childhood. There was a spare bed in her flat, why hadn't I gone down? Oh, the journey, her own circle of friends . . . and now I was having a false childhood without her, blaming the world for my self-imposed loneliness, once again the little girl left out. Dark December afternoons, when a long time ago I would have hurried back to yellow windows, fire-light and tea—this was the worst time.

So it went on. I walked about the town and felt noticeably a stranger. I sat alone in the little hotel bar and listened to the loud, sure talk of the locals unaffectedly concerned with small local happenings, a friendly language lost to London—and again felt left out. Otherwise there was little for it but to sit in my bay window and watch the long estuary water, the leaden sea, the mud and its coloured ghost-village on the far bank. And Christmas, I thought, this Christmas I loathe yet long to join in with. So at a cheerlessly prompt one o'clock I ate Christmas dinner alone in the dining-room; thin-sliced turkey, tinned plum pudding, one or two friendly faces and wine glasses raised in my direction. Somebody even asked me to pull a cracker. I lost.

But that evening there was a special dinner put on, a gathering of some local club at a long table for a dozen or so. This time I was not left alone. They kept on sending me over glasses of wine—particularly one man, red-faced against his white collar and blue best suit, a thirty-year-old with sharp black eyes and some sort of presence, or arrogance, which set him apart. His voice was louder than the others when he spoke, he moved with personal authority—determined and at ease. When he came over to my table with a glass of port, he wore a blue and gold paper kepi. He'd won *his* cracker.

'You a lonely Londoner, Miss'? he asked. 'Have a glass with a country bumpkin, it's Christmas, you know.'

It was this kind of inverted snobbery from the very first.

With irritating arrogance he played the lackey, put me in the wrong, and ate at me with his dark acquisitive eyes. He sat down without asking, I could scarcely refuse, and went on ironically to put me through my paces: 'Of course, it's not very grand down here;' and 'Where's that posh boy-friend of yours, off on the Continent no doubt?'

'As a matter of fact,' I said, 'he is. And as a second, he's my husband.'

This seemed to amuse him, his smile was long and knowing — of course, he was well wined and dined, and doubtless beered up before, but nevertheless I didn't that much fancy being leered at like a merry young grass widow, a likely morsel of Christmas crumpet. So, instead of rising to leave, I did the opposite — stayed to parry him, to point out that yuletide was known for its cheer, not its sneer. Looking back, I can see he was doubly welcome as an adversary I could at last hit back at, something at last more solid than the shapeless frustrations of recent months. He must have been surprised, though he never showed it. I suppose I was promoted from idle crumpet to fettlesome filly.

So I gave him a politely telling talking-to. And the port went down. And he was not in the least disturbed by what I said. His eyes simply went on licking me up. Once or twice people at his table called to him, the women there turned and giggled — he just easily waved them quiet. Then he brought out a pipe; and puffing this in my face, grew gaiters and a moleskin coat: I saw that his face was not truly beer-beetroot, but weathered, there was a touch of yellow tan round the strong neck that bulged above his festive white collar.

Finally, we began laughing at ourselves: his sarcasm had drooled on about the 'honour' of sitting with 'a lady' — I told him to stuff it — but I suddenly felt it was not all sarcasm, he meant it not as a gentry joke, but in its kinder, chivalrous, protective sense. And, by God, I found myself preening. Adoration and contempt, they tell me, make a heady mixture.

His fingers were small and white, like little parsnips primping out of muscle-strong hams; he told me about his farm, his roots and cattle and beet, his oyster bed too—I could have a dozen in the morning, if I wished. He looked at his watch: 'Better join the others,' he said. 'See you later?' But it was hardly a question, the way he put it.

Normally I'd have gone up to bed: but I made excuses to myself, sat on. Was it all a kind of compensation for that rejection by my wheeler-dealer man in London, a need to prove myself? Scarcely—his first attentiveness would have been enough to see to that. There'd have been no need to go further, no need to wait while his party took its long farewells, no need to get my coat and walk out on the wintry quay; no need to be found by him, led away from the lamplight, pressed against a dark wall and soundly kissed. Then it was his car, a short and silent drive to his cottage, his whisky. The rest followed. Why? Loneliness? Christmas? The well-known trip-rope of 'being away'? Or something a lot more sinister, something endemically commanding about him . . . and me at the end of my ever-lengthening tether? Or even a kind of Chatterley relapse, a relapse into the sweat and buckskin call of the soil?

It didn't feel like that in the morning. The morning was a very different matter. What had seemed the night before to be a chintzy oil-lamped room turned out to be ordinarily modern, even to a kidney-shaped dressing table. We were awkward. He got me a cup of tea; I dressed very quickly while he made it. He drove me back, not to the hotel, but to a windowless timber yard near it. 'Don't want talk,' he said, 'there's tongues everywhere. See you around lunch,' he said, casually decided. 'I'll bring you the oysters.' Then I suddenly thought of that feminine dressing-table. 'Your wife,' I said, 'you've got a wife, where is she?' For the first time he looked slightly embarrassed. 'Hospital,' he said, then cheered up: 'Nothing serious,' and waved me goodbye, my man of the soil in a scarlet anorak and jeans, the bastard.

Long before midday I was on a train back to London. No question about that, such lapses had to be cut short, very short indeed. What in the hell had happened to me, the mid-morning light asked? I should have felt shame, the tart feeling: but then he had never made me feel like that, and there was no denying a certain rather too-warm feeling of contentment, of surrender, of purely physical satisfaction. Bitch and bastard, I thought. 'Coffee, madam?' said a steward in a soiled white coat. Life, even on Boxing Day, was resuming itself.

And Boxing Day begat January and January begat the run-up to February, whose Kalends begat my official début as a painter.

The show was an immoderate success. The Christmas break, and what had gone with it, had sobered me: I'd plunged back into compensatory paint, retrieved my balance, risen varnished and ready for the worst. But it was the best. Everything sold, reviews carefully raved, enquiries came tumbling in. However, I knew enough about the game to see myself as a very possible flash-in-the-pan, my technique was not all that unusual or special, and the novelty of the subject matter might just have hit a need for a fashionable trend. So in thankful but sanguine mood, I sipped my celebratory martinis and champagne, while preposterous four-syllable words about my painterly endeavour were spoken by emaciated young men and portly older ones, both of whom should have known better.

But sanguine I was not in reaction to thoughts of that Roy, king of the beet-belt—I woke up in the night and felt deeply terrible about it, small and dirty and deceitful. It was like thinking of a sharp accident narrowly missed, my whole body went hollow at the thought—and then filled again with self-disgust at the memory, in muzzed detail, that this was an accident definitely *not* missed. However, I did feel a lesson had been learned—this kind of thing had to stop, Mark or no Mark I didn't want to turn into a tramp. Though Mark came in for much of the blame, it was *his* absence, *his* infidelity, *his* distrust which had left me lost enough to lose myself.

Not quite true. And now dates must be defined. I've since looked in my diary, and found a cross marking February the fifteenth as curse-day. Allowing four days or so, and adding the extra, I could pin-point the so-called safe period. It was definitely after this, in the new days of danger, that one evening the 'phone rang. Roy. He was in London. When could we meet? Tonight? No? Then tomorrow. As if that clinched it. Again, I said my 'No!' But he was at Liverpool Street! (As if that made any difference!) 'I got your address from the hotel book,' the little black voice said proudly. 'I've got something for—'

But I clicked the receiver down. Christ, I thought, no more of that! But what a damn cheek, what a damn thick skin, after me leaving the place so pointedly—yet his voice had sounded as sure of itself as ever. Nasty little man, I thought, with his wife in hospital. Poor little man, I thought pleased, laying a lady and not forgetting her.

About an hour later the front-door bell rang. By then, I'd forgotten about him. But there, of course, he was. As short as before, but now immensely broad—carrying a wooden crate and with his raincoat pockets bulging. He stepped in before I could stop him. 'Carried these blasted things all the way from Suffolk,' he said by way of greeting. 'Your oysters, ma'am.'

'But I don't want—I'm busy—I—'

'Three dozen,' he said. And pulling at his pockets, 'With a bottle of dry white apiece,' banging down Chablis in the hall-chair. 'Lemons, too. Think of everything,' he smiled, throwing these at me to catch. 'How you keeping?'

He was still only a foot inside the door.

There was still time.

But—oysters! Had it been flowers, or chocolates or anything dispensable, I'm pretty certain I'd still have shut the rest of the door in his face. But oysters—wet, living oysters! What on earth could he do with them?

'I—I don't want them—' I began to stammer.

'Come on,' he said easily, 'we can't waste the buggers, can we? A good few quids' worth, not counting the weed . . .'

It was all so absurdly unexpected I let him in. I suppose the mighty question of waste was the point of no return, that and a little estuary water dripping on the hall carpet . . . what the hell could he do with dripping oysters? 'The kitchen's through here,' I said.

And again he took command. He'd brought his opening knife with him. He even had a corkscrew.

And much later, after the oysters, the wine, the recriminations, the persuasion, there I was once again snarled up in his arms. It would never have happened but for those ludicrous oysters: my only possible other excuse was pathetically physical, because it was as near rape as dammit, and not in bed but on the sofa. But note that 'near'; I can't say I struggled all that much, though I tell myself I finally gave in to get him away and out as quickly as possible; but not without a kind of slavish pleasure too? There is, I suppose, this perverse desire to immolate oneself, the bitch in everyone – not quite intended, but all too easily accepted. I fear, too, that awful kind of man might too often have got what he wanted through his absolute lack of fear, a juggernaut effluence, a marvel of E.S.P. Yet would it have happened but for those oysters? How often something as absurdly material affects the best-ordered lives, paint on the hands when the vital telephone rings, a laddered stocking at a critical interview.

He stayed till dawn, curled up peacefully like a great big horrible ba-ba. And ba-ba didn't even snore. I was pretty thin-lipped with him when we got up; but all too well do I remember saying to him just before he left: 'Well – you'll have to pay a pretty useless hotel bill now.'

'Hotel bill?'

'You must have booked in somewhere?'

He winked: 'Not on your life. I thought it was a pretty fair risk . . . .'

So he left, and the pretty fair risk stood in her dead hallway furious and cheap, a shameful pushover and very frightened of herself—looking at it grossly it had just been possible earlier to excuse a 'one-night stand', as the delightful saying goes, but here it had happened twice, it was like having an affair on my hands, however oblique, and 'He'll come again,' I thought, and by all that's wonderful looked up at the door-bolts.

Later I Lady-Macbethed the thing with a good brisk bath: and then began taking it out on the furniture, moving this here and that there, making a change at all costs, putting a full stop to the past. And I locked up Mark's room.

The hell with the shop, I thought, and went out to refresh myself further at the ever-provident hairdresser. Whose *Harper's* now gave me my own *arriviste* face blinking in the party flash-light, the pushover pushing ahead of her celebrated husband. But Mark was quick to follow: like a wishful arrow the evening paper diary column announced his imminent departure for Greece on the Nose's yacht.

Back in the flat, the furniture looked awful and I spent a dreary hour putting it all back where it was before. But vaguely planning at the same time. I was free, I had money, I needed a change—and in view of last night's unsavoury lapse it seemed vital I took another stab at seeing Mark, a real stab this time. I had to save us. Somehow. Anyway, I'd got myself into a fair state by mid-afternoon and was trying to telephone the old signora at Santa Vilga. Finally I got through. Was the *Spada* still in port, did she know?

It was. She'd seen it only that very day, newly painted. It was almost a sign of spring, wasn't it? How was the good signora? Oh, very well thanks. Frightfully well, indeed.

I think that word 'spring' about clinched it—cleansed winter branches, buds on the blossom, the southern spring. Appealing. It weighed my scared scales. And within a hysterical twenty-four hours, I was enplaned for my past, my present, our future.

A risk, and not a pretty fair one at that. The Nose could very easily have ordered the yacht to somewhere on the Adriatic, Bari or Brindisi, on the way to Greece. But scarcely hesitated. The chastened pushover had grown hot feet. And a steely shrug—if they weren't there, what had I got to lose? Just now I needed a change of scene: I might as well be anywhere.

Rome, the train along the coast, the taxi out to the port—and at last, rinsed in early spring sunlight, the warm apricot roofs of our summer idyll.

Cleansed of its tourists, Porto Santa Vilga felt like a ghost town. Common enough these days to return to places of beloved and long-ago holidays, honeymoons, and to be shocked by their tourist development, crowds, pédalos, trinket shops, the redoubtable rash of new villas. With me, it was, of course, the opposite: for the first time (or perhaps the second, counting my last early morning among the langoustes and anchors) I saw the place as a properly Italian small port, slow, easy-going, with empty cafés, an echo of fitful hammering round the boats themselves, and in the main street only a few late afternoon shoppers, the brief-cased step of the local *avvocato*. Not a flowered shirt in sight, not a pair of shorts, never a turquoise postcard. Even the dredger was gone.

There was indeed the foreseen excitement of spring in the air, a sprouting of yellow-green buds, white almond blossom and its blown petals the only litter on cleansed pavements. I easily got a room at that marble Imperiale Hotel of the Greens, inhabited now out of season only by what amounted to my personal posse of waiters. From there it was learned that the Contessa, as far as they knew, was not in town. So that was that. I just unpacked and went for a sobered stroll about the familiar, unfamiliar streets.

In Tonietta's café in the square I was unknown; just so at another, and at the hairdresser's where I called in for some sort of old time's sake. Formal clothes and properly-dressed hair must have disguised me: either that, or the summer's so personal affability had only been part of the tourist trap. However, our old signora-landlady certainly did recognize me – and after the first embraces, went into a long torrent of Italian. My ear was not yet properly tuned in, so I simply nodded and smiled, hoping for the best. One thing, however, was very evident – she wanted me upstairs in our old room, and seemed surprised I was staying alone at the hotel. *Arrivederci*, I finally managed – and oddly this seemed to cheer her up. *Domani*, *domani*, she belled at my retreating wave.

Domani, of course, saw me down at the quay having a good look at the now spick and span *Spada*. No sign of damage, she had been efficiently refitted by the local yard. There was a sailor aboard, fiddling about with something on deck. I nearly hailed him to ask about any sailing instructions. But didn't, as the wild idea came of inviting myself and my luggage aboard as a guest – why, had they not received a telegram? All with my foreign milordess's aplomb to carry the day – and thus finally delivering myself *in toto* to Greece and the peripatetic Nose. But to do this, I'd have to find out the sailing date. From whom? The harbourmaster? The office was shut.

The only thing was to wander about; and wonder, too about the lack of an expected sadness – I'd almost looked forward to a stiff-lipped dry-eyed wallow in pains of the past. But it wouldn't work. Too much water had passed under too many bridges, most of which had been burned. The Mark and me of the summer were like those old photographs again, recognizable but not quite credible. Of course, the springtime aspect of the port plainly had much to do with it – where were the grinning cut-out chef figures offering their pizza outside our old restaurants, where was Geoffrey de, where Rinaldi? Trying then, to be properly sad, I was disappointed – a new hardness had taken its complete and thin-lipped charge. The passage of time was too short for nostalgia, too long in its day-to-day dreariness to be anything but void. And the wide, wide air of the southern sea only invigorated and charmed; one could hardly help enjoying this and its proposition of new life, a future. Not yet the heady hyacinth of the full-blown cruellest month, sapful April: this was early stuff, the breath of a new beginning.

And a beginning there was that very day. I'd decided to take a walk up the hill to that old ex-voto chapel I'd once painted, and indeed once adorned with Mark's errant sock. That at least should bring a fine sentimental pang, I thought — I couldn't be, well, sockproof? . . . and looked up to find myself face to face with Rinaldi.

Now there was instant recognition! Over our clasped hands he even shouted out *Oggi! Oggi!* as if that damned magazine was still held between us. But what he was on about was a much more immediate *oggi* — today, in fact, *today* was the day when the Contessa and my husband were to return to Vilga — but of course I must have come with them? O joyous reunion! What merriment ahead after the long dull winter!

As soon as I could I left him, and hurried down to the shops to buy what previously I had intended, two large lungs from the butcher.

I went back to the hotel and dressed in the best suit I had. This time I was taking no chances. And then, armed with my butcher's lungs, and my own lungs and heart in my mouth, I took a taxi up the hill towards the villa. But not to the gate. I got out a few hundred yards away and walked a long way round to the back. No tempting of providence with a second go at that front door.

Then it was over the wire where yuccas and agaves screened me, and a neat drop down into the garden. Neat? On the drop-down the seat of my trousers caught just at the last moment, so that, lungs in hand, like some absurd prestidigitator, I had very very delicately indeed to swing my hip to and fro to get myself free. Life the old banana-skin — this was the moment for seventeen gardeners to erupt and find the Lady Raffles doing a slow hip-dance with furtive bumps at the blasted bottom of their patch.

But it was a measure of my determination that at the time I felt not at all absurd, I felt plain angry, I was in a cold fury to blow this whole thing up, have it out with her and put Mark exactly back in his place, get on that boat and get to Greece with my pride if not now my trousers intact: all not so abruptly daring as it may seem, for in the long reaches of the night I'd coolly worked out that if their work together was almost finished, as Mark had said, then she was not going to break any contracts, spoil no ships for ha'porths of my kind of tar.

So a final bump free, and then a careful snaking up the garden screened by bushes. But no gardeners, no dogs—and the veranda doors to the terrace were wide open. Then, as I got to the doors themselves, I spotted the two bull-shouldered mastiffs I'd been frightened of—and another miscalculation: it was feeding-time, their sharp-toothed muzzles were buried deep in feeding-bowls. As I passed, they wearily managed to roll their eyes up at me, lugubrious as dedicated clerks disturbed at work, and went on eating. So I was not worth bothering about?

'Pussies,' I breathed at them, 'bloody pussies,' and flung them their infernal lungs.

And in. Nobody about. But not quiet—there was music coming from upstairs. I remembered roughly where the Nose's bedroom lay, and now, cold with success, went quietly up there. But stopped outside the door. From inside there came an unearthly extraordinary sound . . . a voluminous effort of giants wrestling, a muscular writhing as if the very air itself, not sound, was pressing and straining and grunting all around that empty landing; as if inside the room immense pythons coiled and uncoiled, wreathing eiderdowns of pure tegument, octopoid stomachs folding and unfolding; an almost plastic sound indescribable, something like the giant statuary of an ancient world given life and now groaning its hot marble skin in a toil of impossible rut, of essence of body, not sound so much as deafening presence — and of course I knew what it was, I had heard the vestigial beginnings on early tapes ... but now the fury of it overwhelmed and heightened my own small fury as I stood outside that very plain white painted door and felt this excess of straining flesh drumming, expanding, contracting from inside and imagined those two listening, or hardly listening but rather involved, sensuously lost in the enormously sensual pure presence.

So I flung the door open. The sound redoubled. And there was the Nose calmly sitting on one chair and in another that Italian professor-butch. No Mark at all.

The Nose just lifted an eyebrow, switched off a switch, and I stood there then in what felt like a clap of deafening silence.

'Do you like it?' the Nose asked equably.

'Mark?' I seemed to shout against the silence.

'Of course,' she said.

'No — where *is* he?'

'Oh —' she said. 'Back where he started from, in his old room, he insisted on it. Surely you remember where?'

'Why should I? Why in hell should I know my way about your absurd pretentious villa-thing? The only thing I do know is I'm going to see Mark right now. This whole affair of yours is over and done with —'

'Affair?'

'I'm staying with Mark and I'm coming to Greece. If he's still got to go. And —'

'Greece? Affair?' The Nose tilted itself elegantly round to the butch-professor, sniffing for confirmation, raising its eyebrows, then throwing its whole head back in a long oh-so-lightly-amused laugh. The butch heaved her fat bulk into a sympathetic chuckle.

'There's not going to be any Greece,' this one gurgled deep in her fat purple body. 'Renata's had a much better idea. Now

the music's finished — you heard a bit of it, isn't it stupendous?
— they're going to —'

'Sail,' said Renata, 'right up your blessed Thames, bringing
the brilliant young composer and his music to the nation of his
birth —'

'Where *is* he?' I yelled, and I think it must have been then
that the door opened and a figure from *Harper's* walked into
the room, went straight over to Renata, embraced her and
stood waiting — that blonde so often photographed with Mark,
the other woman's woman.

'May I introduce Miss Maria Vitelli, our lovely coloratura,
in the flesh, as it were. Maria, this is Mrs Forster . . .'

The blonde put her arm round Renata's shoulder, caressing
it. Renata pressed a bell.

'Mrs Forster?' this Maria said. 'I'm delighted — but Forster,
Forster? Of course, Mrs Marcus . . .' Her eyes narrowed and
she looked down at Renata with a kind of triumph. I said,
quietly now: 'For the last time, where *is* Mark?'

There was a knock on the door. A manservant showed himself.

'Giovanni,' the Nose said, 'would you please drive Mrs
Marcus to her husband's apartment? You remember where
it is?'

'*Capito*, Contessa.'

'Drive?' I said. 'Where to?'

'Why, your old room,' Renata smiled. 'Where you were in
the summer. I told you he insisted. You're a lucky woman.'

I almost ran for the door. 'Wait a minute,' the butch said.
'Could you drop me off on the way?'

And there were then once again those long Italian goodbyes,
while I stood impatient, overjoyed, now wondering with a
growing apprehension how he'd be, what would we say? . . .

The door closed behind us, the Butch took my arm and
whispered: 'You see how it is? With them?' And she nodded
back at the closed door. 'She's not really one for men —' and

laughed with a confident delight, one of the ladies' *camorra*. Then sighed: 'Nor really much for us either . . . Renata loves — well, Renata.'

Just then one of the dogs came lolloping up the stairs and made straight for me, though friendlily, making a great friendly fuss of the smell of those lungs, I supposed — but it kept us there long enough to hear a sound like sudden tears from behind the door; and Renata's voice crying: 'His principles, his damned *principles* — '

'Don't be stupid darling,' the blonde's voice said. 'You didn't really want him at all, you just failed for once, and you can't bear failing . . . but you've got the music, my dear, and that's what really counts, isn't it?'

The butch winked at me and nodded. 'See?' she said. '*Capito?*' And *capito* it was, my Italian had risen monstrously to the moment; the moment fitted exactly, and after all this time, with an appallingly deceptive simplicity.

On the way back I was too happy, too relieved to ponder on this plain power-woman complex, this lesbian liberation *ad lib* — I was saying over and over again how sweet, how very dear of him, our room, *our* room — and Santa Vilga had never seemed so vast, streets so phenomenally long, would I never get there?

I did. And there he was, stretched on the bed fast asleep.

And a bit fatter, I thought, as I looked down at him, not knowing what to do. Very gently I touched his face, his lips. He only mumbled and turned over.

Somehow I simply couldn't force him awake — after so long it seemed too rough for what should be a deeply tender reunion: and I even enjoyed a kind of purring forbearance as I sat by his half-packed case and waited; me purring, he so very quietly snoring.

But that was not the only anti-climax. When at last he woke, stretched and focused his eyes, and then sharply sat up —

'Ju!' was all he said. And 'Mark!' was all of a million stored words he got from me.

Then I was in his arms and being kissed, kissed and kissed.

We only kissed, spoke our names, stared at each other close. I think both of us felt it to be too un-loving to make love there and then, too animal. Yet I also remember that I was half-fearful that infidelity had made me perversely virginal, it was improper that I should be touched.

So we sat with clasped hands while a further silliness took over—meeting after so long a time has the awkwardness of a long-distance telephone call, so much to say that it seems there is no time to say it, and what of all the thousands of stifled words to speak first?

But gradually, gradually, stopping and starting, interrupting each other, apologizing, we talked . . . and I heard from Mark that indeed the score was finished, and that the Greece idea was just a news trick, they—now we—were sailing for London. 'I wanted to surprise you,' he said, 'but of course it's really far better like this.'

And the Nose? I asked him. Oh, she'd been all right really—though a bit of a nuisance at first. Wasn't really the lecher I'd no doubt imagined her to be . . . her true predilections lay in a different direction, of which less said the better, though the worst was known in the best circles all over.

We rambled on, and at last, quite suddenly, he took me in his arms, stopped me, and quietly, as if it had only happened the day before, began to make love. Afterwards, in the lovely relaxation of afterwards, it seemed physically as if his body had washed all the past away, I was pure again.

Much later, sitting sewing the little tear in my trousers, I suddenly *saw* myself sitting there sewing, with the sound of Mark's shower providing a reassuring obbligato. And warmed with a comfortable contented love of a passive chore which ordinarily bored me to tears. Life, I felt, was really resuming itself.

The next day we walked about the place, retracing our streets of the past summer—the little backstreet where we had made up a quarrel, the place where the dredger had been, the restaurant of the motor bikes, now shut.

Looking back, the summer seemed to have been a fantasy: now Santa Vilga—the streets, the houses, the spring air, my hand on his arm—seemed far more real, clinically *there*, rinsed in a new light, rinsed by the passage of time, rinsed by the harder facts of life, by doubts and suffering. There was a sense of intense sobriety about.

We happened to pass several groups of painters in baggy white overalls. Houses and shops were being touched up for the new season. With relief I saw that these painters wore little hats made of newspaper, real and sensible anti-splash hats, and from their brushes there exuded real coloured paint, none of my over-wrought white paint from white pierrots on to white birches. Life, again, was resuming itself.

But as the day wore on I began to wonder—isn't this all far too sober, far too cool? Shouldn't there be some sort of—I didn't quite know what—wild affirmative movement? And I remember looking carefully at him when I was sure he wasn't looking—I say carefully, but I mean deceitfully—and wondering whether those damned internal beeps hadn't taken over again. Or was it me—was my own guilt not after all so well repressed, was I turning its repression against him, indeed a means of defence?

Come to that, did I really believe in all this lesbian panoply? It fitted in, it might have explained a lot, but 'a lot' hardly inferred a whole? There was bisexuality? But these were mean, destructive thoughts . . . and so I bought Mark some of his favourite old salami and we ate it together in Tonietta's bar, a Tonietta who now indeed remembered us, particularly the much-photographed Dottore Marcus, and Mark took my hand, and again and again said how awful our separation had been, how neglected and lonely I must have felt, but how doubly awful in its way it had been for him, since he had propelled it, and left in such an underhand way, had afterwards had to toe the Contessa's line, having taken the plunge he really had to see it through, in spite of all his feelings against it, and these were bad indeed at times, there had been moments when he'd nearly thrown the whole thing up, taken a plane home, in fact once had even bought a ticket . . . all of which sounded real enough, or at least a reality I longed to hear of and lapped up with all my heart.

I longed to get rid of all doubt—and remember asking him about that blonde coloratura, was she a special protégée of the Nose's? Because it was surely a bit odd to have a human voice in what was an electronic concretion? 'Oh,' he said, 'trouble there indeed. But I got her taped quickly enough.'

'You mean she *did* make a pass at you?'

'Pass?' Then he laughed and said, 'No, I mean I got her technically taped. I wrote in her voice and she mouthed it.'

'Phew!'

'Renata insisted on having her. But you really can't have a *real* voice, far too vulnerable—chance there of this vaunted porn creeping in.'

And my doubts receded beneath a long disquisition on only bad art producing pornography, the real thing rising always above it: and a lot about stochastics and sine-waves and aleatoricisms which lulled me into a beautifully satisfied stupor.

We dined up at the villa that night, and our Contessa, I must say, went out of her way to be charming. She even made a little speech bidding us raise our glasses to the return of 'the prodigal husband'. I could have thrown mine in her face. But she probably meant it well enough: all the more because she must have known I'd heard her final outburst behind that closed door, that butch would never have kept her fat trap shut.

But she had not altogether relented. I realized suddenly I didn't know the date of the film's opening—and asked her.

'We're hurrying all out for March 31st – in London,' she said. 'Before Darmstadt, Amsterdam, San Francisco. . . .' Just avoiding Fool's Day, I thought – but any fool could see Mark was now going to be just as busy as before. So naturally I wanted to get him away while I could. Even a few days seemed important. 'Why do we have to waste time sailing to London?' I asked her. 'Why can't Mark and I fly off home now, to-morrow?'

'You'd be breaking the contract,' the Nose graciously smiled.

'But, just a day or two? Three?'

'We're sailing for several reasons. It all fits in. The arrival in London – can we tie up at Westminster? I must find out – makes a good news story. Something might happen on the way, too – a nice storm in the Biscay Bay? And above all, this is the psychological moment for a short break, a real rest. The sea's the place for that.'

Mark caught my eye, took the message, said to the Nose: 'But Renata, there's nothing really to be done here. If Ju wants to get going – why, for instance, couldn't we fly to Paris, and get picked up on the French Coast?'

'And lose your retainer, Mark?' The Nose laughed very, very lightly. 'You'd still be breaking the contract.' And then she changed the subject, and Mark let her.

Later that night I asked him to book us to France, willy-bloody-nilly. He agreed.

But by late afternoon the next day he'd done nothing. And when I pestered him, looked vague. 'Darling,' he finally said, 'on second thoughts, it would be a bit silly to lose that retainer. It's quite a lot, you know.' Life was most certainly resuming itself.

The Bay of Biscay was as calm as reasonably it could be, a quietly rolling millpond with a heavy undertow.

These days we live in a fine fat Tudory house near Esher, well off and supposedly settled. Herbaceous borders, a belt of firs, a lawn to mow—and I have my young son Richard toddling between the sundial and the rhodies. He is much beloved, and a saving grace.

Three years now since Mark's great recognition—film, book of the film, discs and cassettes, all were given a fine reception; but like many works of a radically original nature, it belonged too much to a fashionable newsworthy moment, became a ninety-nine days wonder. Two years have passed since Mark himself has been largely forgotten. He works on though, and in the proper atonal quarters has an established reputation. Oddly, it is I whose small popular fame has most persisted, I who have profited most from that disastrous separation contrived for his benefit.

So between us we can keep up this moderately affluent establishment. Mark's away a lot. But I'm seldom lonely, with Richard and my painting and a house to run; seldom exactly lonely, more whatever the word is for living in a vacuum, not vacuous, not disorientated, but lacking, lacking . . . for it has never been the same between Mark and me, the disruption of that one year, with its trail of deceits and distrusts, has had a permanent effect. Otherwise the keel is even. On the face of it we rub along: a miracle of modern science, this frictionless rubbing, but not all that radiant a prescription for wedded bliss, having and holding until the dislocation of death, with its memories of the best days, brings us closer together.

Perhaps it's my fault, for the feeling that I've been trustless and untrustworthy erodes, and the more deeply because it is unfairly diverted against him. Perhaps it's Mark's fault, perhaps his natural remoteness grows too much for me to take: his consuming fidelity to his work, my passing infidelity to him—which makes for the deeper rift? Or perhaps it is all far more simple, simply a change in our fortunes, no longer the small struggle of two-together against a hard-looking world?

But how I search into the eyes of that child! Searching not

only with love but also with cunning, looking for the final physical clue, a feature, a gesture to tell me whom he takes after . . . for by a hair's breadth he just could not have been Mark's. That largely forgotten intruder was probably pirate enough to get round any pill. Though oddly, despite these misgivings, he's been put aside so securely that I almost believe he never existed.

And supposing what is far more probable, that the boy is truly ours, Mark's and mine, who would I like him most to be like? Mark? A sort of inward shudder at that. More me? I'm not at all sure about that either, a fair shadow of a shudder there too. But after all, what does it matter, what does it matter whose he is or whom he takes after? The important thing is he's mine, he's Richard.

Someone to live for, to love. Look on the bright side, I say to myself, look on the Bright Side, as I contemplate rhodies and toddler and lawn, the coming crows' feet of middle age, the long even keel, almost like a sign, of a happily unbroken marriage. Am I not a lot luckier than many, many others?